'How do I bring a little excitement into my life?' Tom asked me.

'While Mary's away ... Why don't you have a little fun?'

'Mowing the lawn? Doing the housework?' he quipped.

'Sexy fun,' I breathed huskily.

'Helen, are you saying what I think you're saying?'

'I'll be honest with you, Tom,' I said, leaving my chair and kneeling at his feet. 'Your wife is away, my husband has gone ... I think we're both in need of a little excitement, don't you?'

Tom said nothing as I tugged his shorts down and gazed wide-eyed at the thick shaft of his flaccid penis. Pulling his shorts off his feet, I parted his legs and watched his balls roll and heave. His shaft stiffening, his long cock finally standing to attention, I could see Alan out of the corner of my eye. His face pressed to the window, he watched as I retracted Tom's fleshy foreskin and exposed the glistening bulb of his swollen knob. What the hell was he thinking? I pondered as I leaned forward and sucked Tom's knob into my wet mouth. Was this what he'd wanted to see?

THE ROAD TO DEPRAVITY

Ray Gordon

This book is a work of fiction.
In real life, make sure you practise safe, sane and
consensual sex.

First published in 2007 by
Nexus
Thames Wharf Studios
Rainville Rd
London W6 9HA

www.nexus-books.co.uk

Typeset by TW Typesetting, Plymouth, Devon

Penguin Random House is committed to a sustainable future for
our business, our readers and our planet. This book is made from
Forest Stewardship Council® certified paper.

MIX
Paper | Supporting
responsible forestry
FSC
www.fsc.org
FSC® C018179

Printed and bound in Great Britain by Clays Ltd, Elcograf S.p.A.

ISBN 978 0 352 34092 4

One

Gazing at my reflection in the full-length mirror, I realised what ten years of marriage had done to me. I was thirty years old, attractive, tall and slim with long black hair. But I looked tired, drained. Was this the fifth or sixth time that Alan had informed me that our marriage was over? How many times had he walked out on me? I couldn't remember. I didn't want to remember. And I didn't want to play his mind games anymore.

The pattern never changed. Alan would pack his case and walk out and then ring me a few days later. Although I never knew what I was supposed to have done wrong, he'd offer to give me a second chance. I'd played the game in the past, begged him to come home, said that I was sorry . . . The trouble was that I'd been subservient. Washing and ironing his shirts, cooking nice meals, keeping the house pristine . . . I'd been the perfect little housewife. He only had to click his fingers and I'd jump to attention. Stupidly, I'd made a rod for my own back.

What would I say when he phoned me this time? I pondered. I'm sorry, it was my fault? Come home and I'll cook a nice meal for you? No, not this time. I had to put a stop to the mind games. I'd wake every morning wondering what sort of mood Alan was in.

1

Happy, annoyed . . . I couldn't live like this anymore. Going from day to day not knowing when he'd next walk out on me, not knowing what I was supposed to have done to upset him, I couldn't go on like this.

My hands trembled and my heart raced as the phone rang. I'd rehearsed my lines again and again, prepared myself for this moment. But I felt like a nervous wreck, I was falling to pieces. I had to be strong, I urged myself mentally as I sat on the sofa and lifted the receiver. I couldn't take Alan back yet again. I couldn't endure his psychological games for a moment longer. If he came back, then I'd be waiting for him to walk out on me for the seventh time. And then the eighth and ninth . . . My life, my future, depended on my decision.

'You're no good on your own,' Alan said condescendingly. 'You're hopeless on your own, Helen. I'll have to come home and . . .'

'I'm fine on my own,' I interrupted him. I tried to sound firm rather than angry. 'I'm doing very well without you.'

'Don't be silly, Helen,' he returned mockingly. 'You can't cope without me. I'm prepared to give you another chance. You're no good without me, so I'll come back.'

'No, Alan,' I said with resolve. 'I don't want another chance.'

'What do you mean?'

'I've been thinking about the things you said before you left. And I agree with you.'

'Agree with what?'

'For years you've been saying that our marriage isn't working. And God only knows how many times you've walked out on me. You've finally convinced me that you're right.'

'What are you talking about, Helen?'

'I've lost count of the times you've said that we're finished, the times you've told me that our marriage is over. You've finally convinced me, and I now realise that the marriage has come to an end.'

'Don't be ridiculous, Helen.'

'Alan, I'm agreeing with you. How can my agreeing to what you want be ridiculous?'

'You don't know what you're saying. You need help, and I'm the only one who can help you. I'll be home in an hour.'

'I don't want another chance, I don't need help, and I don't want you to come back.'

Replacing the receiver, I let out a sigh of relief. I'd done it, I thought triumphantly. Despite my trembling hands, my racing heart, my churning stomach, I'd been strong. Alan would be fuming. No, he'd be floundering in confusion. I'd not played my part in his game, I'd torn up the script and not played my role. Round one to me, I reflected. Did I have the strength to win round two? How many rounds were there to be before the final bell?

He turned up an hour later but I'd bolted the front door. Banging, ringing the bell . . . In his desperation, he finally called through the letterbox. I was upstairs in the bedroom, ignoring him. Was I hiding? Yes, I suppose I was. I couldn't face him. He'd only try to grind me down and wheedle his way back into the house, back into my life. I'd come to a decision, and was going to stick to my guns. No longer would I allow Alan to play his psychological games with me. This was day one of my new life, a new beginning.

He finally gave up and lugged his suitcase back to his car. No doubt he was beginning to worry. He'd be pondering on the future, wondering where he was going to live. He'd walked out on me, so he only had

3

himself to blame. But Alan had never accepted it when he'd been in the wrong. I knew that he'd blame me as I watched him drive down the road. In the past, he'd said that I was wrong. But he was definitely wrong this time. He'd pushed me too far, and he'd lost me.

The phone rang a dozen times over the next few days, but I ignored it. I was too busy planning my future to listen to Alan and his whining. Deciding on my new look, I went into town and bought a couple of miniskirts, thongs and skimpy tops. The new me, I thought happily. The old me, before I'd met Alan. Happy, vivacious, free and single ... At last, I was dragging myself out of the doom and gloom of Alan's influence and rediscovering myself.

I bumped into a friend of Alan's in town. He asked me how I was and suggested that we have a chat over coffee. I had the feeling that this wasn't a chance meeting. Alan had set this up, I was sure. But Paul was a nice enough man and I accepted his offer. He was single, in his early thirties, not bad looking, and I'd always got on reasonably well with him. But I knew that he'd be reporting back to Alan, so I had to be careful.

'He misses you,' Paul said as we sat in a coffee shop. 'He was saying that he can't even remember what the argument was about.'

'There was no argument,' I returned. 'As always with Alan, he went off on one of his weird psychological trips and walked out.'

'How long are you going to make him wait before you take him back?'

'Take him back?' I echoed with a giggle. 'Paul, he doesn't want to come back.'

'What?' He frowned at me. There was confusion reflected in his dark eyes. 'Helen, of course he wants to go back to you,' he breathed. 'He was saying that –'

'Paul, I've lost count of the times he's left me. For years he's been saying that we're finished and the marriage is over. Are you trying to tell me that he was joking?'

'No, it's just that –'

'Perhaps he was lying? Is that what you're trying to say?'

'No . . .'

'Paul, if someone continually tells you that your relationship is over, if they walk out on you countless times, what would you gather from that?'

'Alan can be a bit funny at times,' he conceded. 'But he wants to be with you, Helen.'

'So that he can walk out on me, yet again? Do you honestly think that I'd put myself in that position again? Never knowing from one day to the next whether my marriage is over or whether my husband is going to leave me? Get real, Paul.'

'Have you met someone else?' he asked me, watching closely for my reaction.

'As it happens, I've met someone I used to know. Someone who's special, someone who's happy and doesn't play weird mind games or –'

'Is it anyone I know?' he interrupted me. 'What's his name?'

'*Her* name, is Helen.'

'Oh, I . . . I see what you mean.'

'I know that you're only trying to help, Paul. And I know that you'll be telling Alan everything I've said. So, I'll leave you with this thought. All I'm doing is going along with what Alan has wanted for years.'

'Yes, I can see that.'

'I didn't want the marriage to come to an end. But he obviously did.'

'OK. Well, I'd better be going. Er . . . You've got my number, so keep in touch.'

'Yes, yes I will.'

'It's funny how things turn out,' he breathed, rising to his feet and pushing his chair under the table. 'I'd always thought that you and Alan would be together for life.'

'So did I, Paul. So did I.'

As he left, I finished my coffee and turned my thoughts to my new clothes. It was all very well dressing up and feeling good, but it would be a waste of time if I was going to sit at home alone. Leaving the coffee shop, I decided to wander down to the local pub that evening. I'd have to get out and about and make new friends if I was going to move on in life. Alan didn't like pubs, so there was no chance of bumping into him and having my evening ruined. Alan was in my past, and I had my future to look forward to. This was the beginning of a new era, I thought happily as I headed home. This was the beginning of my new life.

I'd changed into my new clothes and was gazing out of the bedroom window when I saw Alan creeping up the drive. Like a thief in the night, he kept looking at the house and slipping behind the bushes. What the hell was he up to? I wondered as I dashed down the stairs and slid the front door bolt. Wandering into the lounge, I was about to peep through the net curtains when I noticed him looking through the window. I thought that he'd want to talk to me and tap on the window, but he stood to one side and watched me. More mind games?

Making out that I hadn't seen him, I sat in the armchair and flicked through a magazine. What with Paul just happening to bump into me in town and now Alan spying on me through the window, the situation was ridiculous. What was Alan hoping to achieve? I wondered as I peered at him over the top of my magazine. Perhaps Paul had phoned him and told him that I'd bought some new clothes. Looking down at my red miniskirt, I wondered what Alan thought of my new look. I wanted him to know that my life was changing for the better. He'd always said that I'd be useless without him, nothing without him, and I wanted to prove him wrong.

As I reclined in the armchair and parted my thighs, I knew that Alan could see my new thong: heart-shaped, scarlet with black lace trim ... My clothes made me feel good, sexy. I'd always worn plain knickers and knee-length skirts, but this was the new me. What was he thinking? I mused, moving forward in the chair with the roundness of my buttocks over the edge of the cushion. Parting my naked thighs further, I felt my stomach somersault, my womb contract. To my amazement, my arousal was heightening. Was it because I knew that my husband was spying on me?

My sex life with Alan had never been particularly exciting. He'd snuggle up behind me in bed and push his hard cock into my vagina and fill me with sperm. He'd then fall asleep, leaving me wanting, wondering. Becoming less and less aware of my body over the years, I'd worn clothes that were comfortable rather than fashionable and sexy. But that was changing. I was now dressing to look sexy, feminine. I felt good in my miniskirt and thong. No longer a chained housewife, I felt like a free woman.

I tossed the magazine aside, pulled my skirt up over my stomach and parted my thighs to the extreme. I don't know what possessed me, but I slipped my hand beneath my thong and ran my finger up and

7

down my wetting sex crack. My juices of arousal flowing freely from my neglected vagina, my clitoris solid beneath my massaging fingertip, I'd not felt so turned on in years. Was it the thought of Alan watching me? I again wondered as I closed my eyes and breathed heavily in the grip of my self-loving.

Through my eyelashes, I could see Alan staring at me through the net curtains as I masturbated. Whether I wanted to shock him or prove something to myself, I had no idea. But I slipped my thong off and exposed my gaping sex crack to my voyeur. It was funny to think that he was my husband. We'd had some good times together, I reflected as my clitoris pulsated. Walks in the countryside, evenings out . . . But, now, we were like strangers.

Stretching the fleshy pads of my sex lips wide apart, exposing my unfurling inner labia, my feminine intimacy, I slipped my hand beneath my thigh and eased a finger deep into my tight vagina. Hot, creamy-wet, yearning in neglect . . . My clitoris painfully solid, my juices of lust squelching with my thrusting finger, I couldn't understand why I felt so sexually alive. Was it my new clothes? Was it because Alan was watching me? Changes around me were bringing changes within me.

My orgasm came quickly. Writhing and whimpering as my body shook violently, I fingered my drenched sex sheath and massaged my pulsating clitoris with a fervency that no doubt shocked Alan. My breasts were hard, my nipples elongated and extremely sensitive, and I felt sexually alive as never before. This was the way I'd been in my teens. Masturbating, revelling in multiple orgasms, enjoying the delights of my young body . . . I could feel my juices of lust running down to my bottom-hole as I sustained my orgasm. And I could see Alan watching me. Was his cock hard? The old me was beginning to surface from the swamp of marriage.

Finally relaxing in the aftermath of my pleasure, I reclined in the chair with my legs wide open, the yawning valley of my wet vagina blatantly displayed to my husband. Perhaps he'd now realise that I didn't need him, I mused dreamily. I had my fingers to fulfil my tight vagina, to appease my yearning clitoris. I didn't need a man. Pondering on buying a vibrator as I watched Alan slip away, I hauled my trembling body out of the chair and covered my glowing pussy with my thong. My orgasm was like a tonic, I felt invigorated, young and sexy. This was the beginning of my new life, I again thought happily as the phone rang.

'Helen, it's Paul.'

'Oh, hi,' I breathed. 'Have you reported back to Alan?'

'What? Er . . . No, no I haven't. I was wondering whether you'd mind if I called round this evening?'

'Round here? What for?'

'Well, for a chat. I thought that you might be feeling lonely.'

'Far from it, Paul,' I returned. 'I'm planning to go out this evening.'

'Oh, fair enough. Perhaps another time, then?'

'Actually, I don't feel like going out,' I said, wondering what he'd planned with Alan. 'Yes, come round. It'll be nice to have some company.'

'That's great. I'll see you about seven.'

'I'll look forward to it, Paul. Oh, and bring some wine with you.'

'Yes, yes I will.'

Reckoning that he'd planned something with Alan, I was determined to discover what was going on. There again, what could they have planned? I should be moving on, I reflected. I should go to the pub and make new friends rather than have Paul round for the evening. Why was Alan still in my thoughts? I knew that it would take time for me to move on but, with Alan spying at me through the window, would I ever be rid of him? Knowing that he'd been spying at me, I shouldn't have masturbated. All I'd done was encourage him, and that wasn't the way to move on in life.

Paul arrived at seven o'clock clutching a bottle of white wine and a bunch of flowers. I didn't want this, I thought agitatedly, unceremoniously dumping the flowers in the kitchen sink. Chrysanthemums. Were the flowers supposed to cheer me up? I didn't like chrysanthemums. And I didn't need cheering up. I should have gone to the pub, I again thought. Meeting people and making new friends was the way forward. Inviting Paul round wasn't going to get me anywhere. Alan had obviously sent him round to work on me, to talk me into taking him back. I'd spend half an hour with Paul and then walk up to the pub, I decided. Half an hour, and no more.

Opening the wine as Paul said how good I looked in my miniskirt, I wondered what he'd think if he knew that I was wearing a thong. Had Alan told him that I'd masturbated? I didn't like the situation. Alan spying, Paul coming round . . . I was beginning to feel hemmed in, and that's exactly what I'd been planning to get away from. Hemmed in, suffocated . . .

'You look great,' Paul again complimented me as we sat in the lounge. 'If only Alan could see your new look.'

'Alan is in my past,' I sighed. 'He's history. I hope you've not come here to try to convince me to take him back?'

'No, not at all.'

'Have you spoken to him today?'

'No, I . . . I've not seen Alan today,' he replied awkwardly.

Why didn't I believe him? 'Here's to the future,' I said, raising my glass.

'Yes, the future.'

'So, there's still no chance of you finding a nice girl and settling down?' I asked him.

'That's not for me, Helen. Marriage, ties, restraints . . . I'm happy with the way I am. Staying single suits some people. Others, such as Alan, can't seem to get along on their own. I remember when . . .'

As Paul related some story or other about his teenage years, I was sure that I saw someone through the window. Not Alan? I thought angrily. What the hell . . . It *was* Alan. Spying through the net curtains again, watching me, checking up on me. What had he planned with Paul? I mused. The two of them had obviously got together and come up with some scheme or other. Seemingly oblivious to Alan, Paul was relaxing on the sofa, sipping his wine and ranting about a girl he once knew. From the armchair, I could clearly see Alan hovering, lurking, spying. Was he going to ring the doorbell? Two against one, was that the plan?

Ignoring Alan, I turned my thoughts to Paul. Wearing a white shirt and dark trousers, he looked pretty good. His black hair swept back, his dark eyes catching mine as he told his story of love lost, I wondered why he'd never married. He was more Alan's friend than mine, and I'd never really taken any interest in him. He'd come to one or two of our barbecues and we'd chatted about this and that, but I was now looking at him in a different light. He had a lovely smile, nice white teeth . . . He wasn't at all bad looking.

Paul's words tailed off as I reclined in the armchair and allowed my thighs to part wide enough to display my red thong. I asked him about the girl he'd been talking about and he stammered his reply. What was he thinking as he gazed at my thong? What was Alan thinking? More to the point, what the hell was I thinking? I felt my clitoris swell and my nipples elongate as Paul stared between my naked thighs. My juices of arousal seeping between my swelling outer labia, I wondered what on earth I was playing at.

Paul would be reading my messages, my body language, and believe that I was offering him sex. Was that what I wanted? I pondered in my rising confusion. Sex with Paul while my husband watched? God, no. Paul was a nice enough man, but I certainly didn't want a sexual relationship with him. He was Alan's friend, and I didn't want *any* kind of relationship with him. I should have gone to the pub. Inviting Paul round had been a stupid mistake. I should have known better. I had to straighten out my thinking, I decided, sitting upright and pressing my thighs together.

'So, what's this all about?' I asked Paul. 'What's the plan?'

'I haven't seen her for years,' he sighed. 'There is no plan.'

'I'm not talking about the girl you once knew, Paul. I'm talking about this evening, you coming here this evening.'

'Oh, I see. I don't have anything planned, apart from chatting with you over a drink.'

'Where does Alan fit into this?'

'Alan?' he echoed. He looked genuinely confused. 'What do you mean?'

'I reckon that the plan is to test my fidelity. No, no . . . I reckon that you've come here to seduce me so

12

that Alan can divorce me on the grounds of adultery. Is that it?' \

'Helen, I have no idea what you're talking about,' he returned with a chuckle. 'Seduce you? Adultery? I haven't come here to try to score with you.'

'Haven't you? I thought that Alan might be taking photographs of us and –'

'Taking photographs? Alan has gone to look at a flat in Newton. He had to be there at seven o'clock.'

'So, you *have* talked to him today?' I said accusingly.

'Well . . . Yes, I spoke to him this afternoon. We talked, but we certainly didn't plan for me to seduce you while he took photographs. He's out of town, looking for a flat to rent.'

'Does he know that you're here?'

'Actually, it was his idea,' he confessed sheepishly. 'He said that he was worried about you. He suggested that I call round to make sure that you're all right.'

'Why does he want a flat in Newton? He'll have a hell of a drive to work and back every day.'

'I don't know, Helen. All he said was that he had to view a flat at seven o'clock.'

Was Paul conning me? I wondered. Or had Alan conned Paul? This was exactly the sort of thing that Alan would have planned, I reflected. This was typical of his weird psychological games. Parting my thighs again, I wondered whether I was trying to seduce Paul. Was it that I wanted to prove something to myself? Or was I trying to prove something to Alan? All I wanted was a divorce. Whether Alan divorced me on the grounds of adultery or not didn't bother me. I didn't give a damn what it said on the divorce papers. And I didn't give a damn about Alan's games. The time had come for me to play games of my own.

'I haven't had sex for over a year,' I blurted out.

'Really?' Paul breathed, his dark eyes frowning. 'Helen, I didn't come here to seduce you. I won't say that I don't fancy you, because I do. You're an extremely attractive woman. But I had no intention of seducing you.'

'I know that,' I said apologetically, keeping an eye on Alan as he peered through the net curtains. 'It's just that I thought Alan might have put you up to it.'

'God, no. And I certainly wouldn't have agreed to it if he had. So, what you're saying is that your marriage has been on the rocks for over a year?'

'Yes, it has. That's why I don't want Alan back. As I said to you in the coffee shop earlier, I've met someone I used to know. I've met someone who's special, someone who's happy and doesn't play weird mind games. I've rediscovered myself, Paul. When I was in my teens –'

'You were as beautiful as you are now?'

'Flattery will get you everywhere, Paul.'

'Helen, this discovery of yours. This new look, the real you . . . What I'm trying to say is, what were you like in your teens? What were you like before you met Alan?'

'What was I like? Young, alive, happy-go-lucky, vivacious, sexy . . .'

'Did you have many boyfriends?'

'Quite a few. I didn't put it about, if that's what you mean. I enjoyed sex, I enjoyed . . . I enjoyed everything. Until Alan got a strangle hold on me and suffocated me, I enjoyed my life to the full.'

'Would you like to enjoy sex again?'

'Yes, of course.'

'With me, I mean.'

Dripping in confusion, I didn't know what I wanted. Ten years with one man, ten years of having

14

a penis shoved into my vagina from behind once a week ... Alan was still lurking, spying. This was my chance to ... to what? To show him that, although I was thirty years old, I could still pull? I felt my clitoris calling for attention as I imagined Paul's wet tongue licking between my swollen pussy lips. This was the beginning of my new life. Should I start by having sex with my husband's friend?

I reclined in the armchair, parted my thighs wide and blatantly displayed my pussy-wet thong to Paul. I was giving out messages of sex. What messages was Alan receiving? I pondered. Licking my lips provocatively as Paul smiled at me, I wondered whether I was being driven by a need for sex, or a thirst for revenge. The very notion of Alan watching another man fucking me sent quivers through my womb. He'd think me a slut and, hopefully, want nothing more to do with me. He wouldn't want me back after I'd been fucked by another man. He wouldn't want to know me after I'd opened my pussy to another man's cock. I was sure that this was the only way to be rid of him, once and for all.

As Paul left the sofa and knelt at my feet, I noticed Alan move closer to the window. I reckoned that he'd do one of two things as Paul leaned forward and kissed my thong. Alan would either hammer on the window to put a halt to the imminent fucking of his wife, or he'd leave and never bother me again. I could feel Paul's dark hair tickling my inner thighs, his hot breath warming me through the wet material of my thong. My nipples becoming erect, my clitoris stirring within my valley of desire, I realised just how much I'd missed sex. Was Alan missing me now?

Alan used to lick and suck my clitoris to orgasm, I used to take his swollen knob into my mouth and swallow his sperm ... Heady days of love and sex.

What had happened to us? I mused dreamily as Paul nibbled and licked the smooth flesh of my inner thighs. Alan had been prone to strange moods from the day I'd met him, and he'd always been incredibly insecure. But I'd never thought that we'd end up like this. And, never in a million years would I have dreamed that another man would be burying his head between my naked thighs.

Parting my legs further, offering my tensed body to Paul, I realised that I was sitting in Alan's favourite armchair. This was the marital home, I thought as Paul sucked on my pussy-wet thong. The bookcase I'd bought Alan for his birthday, the coffee table we'd bought as a mutual Christmas present . . . Why had Alan had to play his ridiculous mind games and destroy our marriage? One thing was for sure, our marriage was in ruins now.

'You're beautiful,' Paul murmured, pulling my thong to one side and running his tongue up and down my drenched sex valley. 'God, you're so wet.'

'And you're good,' I breathed shakily. Although Alan couldn't hear me, I knew that my words were intended to shock him. 'Suck out my juices,' I gasped, arching my back. 'Drink from my pussy.'

'God, you really are beautiful,' he said as he worked his tongue into my vaginal entrance.

Beautiful? I mused, my clitoris responding to his wet tongue as he moved up my gaping sex crack. I was an adulteress. But Alan had walked out on me, I reminded myself. He'd told me time and time again that we were finished, drummed it into my head over the years. He now obviously realised that he'd pushed me too far. Watching another man licking between the engorged lips of my vulva, he'd be in no doubt that we really were finished this time. He'd not wanted this any more than I had. So, why had he done it? He couldn't help it, I reflected. The way his mind worked, his insecurities, his crazy psychological games . . . He couldn't help the way he was. But I no longer wanted to be part of it.

Paul sucked my solid clitoris into his hot mouth and repeatedly swept his tongue over the sensitive tip, and I quivered and writhed in the armchair, in Alan's armchair. The wonderful sensations of sex rippling throughout my sweat-soaked body, I knew that Paul would be calling round to see me again. But I didn't want a relationship with him. I was free, after ten years of marriage. The last thing I wanted were ties and commitments. All I wanted was hard, cold, gratifying sex. What the hell was happening to me?

To my surprise, Alan didn't leave. Was he deriving some sort of weird sexual pleasure from watching another man licking my clitoris? Unbuttoning my blouse and lifting my bra clear of my firm breasts, I placed my legs over the arms of the chair and toyed with my sensitive nipples as Paul drove his wet tongue deep into my hot vagina. I felt like a whore, a common slut. I was going to come, I knew as I watched Alan through my eyelashes. I was going to come in another man's mouth while my husband watched.

Paul's timing was perfect. He sucked my clitoris into his mouth and drove two fingers deep into my contracting vagina as my orgasm exploded. Shaking wildly, I let out a cry of satisfaction as my clitoris pulsated and my orgasmic juices deluged from my fingered vaginal sheath. My head lolling from side to side, my stomach rising and falling, my thighs twitching, I wallowed in the incredible pleasure Paul was bringing me. I was committing adultery in front of my husband. And loving it.

I'd barely recovered from my climax when I felt Paul's solid knob slip between the engorged inner lips

17

of my vulva. He was about to impale me on his manhood, he was about to fuck me. His silky-smooth glans pressing against the wet cone of flesh surrounding my vaginal entrance, he paused. Was he waiting for my consent? Confused thoughts careering around the wreckage of my mind, I knew that I only had a second to halt the imminent act of adultery. Should I leap out of the chair and order Paul to leave? Should I allow him to push the solid length of his penis deep into my yearning vagina? Alan was watching me, I didn't know what to do, what to say to Paul . . .

Paul's knob journeying along the wet sheath of my vagina and pressing hard against my ripe cervix, I let out a rush of breath. He'd done it, I'd done it . . . Impaled on another man's solid penis, I'd finally committed full-blown adultery. As Paul rocked his hips, his beautiful cock gliding in and out of my tightening vagina, I peered at Alan through my half-closed eyes. His face pressed against the window, he was watching my adulterous act. What the hell were his thoughts now? I wondered anxiously. The marriage really was over this time. There was no turning back now that my marriage vows had been shattered, torn asunder. This was the end of an era.

My solid clitoris massaged by Paul's wet shaft as he fucked me, I knew that I wasn't far off coming. Pinching and pulling on my nipples, I tossed my head from side to side as my juices of arousal spurted from my bloated vagina and my illicit pleasure heightened. I could feel Paul's knob pummelling my cervix, his swinging balls battering the firmness of my naked buttocks. Gasping, writhing in my new-found adulterous pleasure, I arched my back and cried out in my sexual ecstasy as my orgasm erupted.

Oblivious to my voyeur as Paul pumped his creamy sperm into my contracting vagina, I again let out a cry of pleasure. My half-naked body rocking back and forth, the squelching sounds of sex resounding around the lounge, I'd broken the monotony of ten years of marriage. The mind games, the day to day uncertainty . . . I'd broken free from my chains. My pioneering orgasm shaking me to the core, I instinctively knew that this was only the beginning of a fulfilling life of sexual gratification.

Adultery. Somehow, the word thrilled me. I felt like a naughty little girl, bad, wicked. Another man's cock shafting my tight pussy, another man's sperm filling me . . . And, heightening my wickedness, my husband was watching me. Was his heart breaking? Was he wallowing in self-pity? Revenge is sweet. Revenge is blatant adultery. Alan's comeuppance must have hit him hard. To watch his wife, his vagina of ten years, being crudely fucked by another man . . . How did he feel? What were his thoughts? He'd played his mind games – and lost. Had I won? I'd not set out to play games, to win games. There could be no winner.

'You really are amazing,' Paul gasped, finally withdrawing his deflating penis from my sperm-laden vaginal sheath. 'I'll have to call round again.'

'Yes,' I murmured nonchalantly, closing my thighs as Alan slipped away.

'How about going out for a drink one evening?'

'No thanks, Paul,' I replied coldly. 'I don't want a relationship.'

'But, I thought –'

'You thought what?'

'Well, I don't know. After making love . . .'

'We didn't make love, Paul,' I corrected him. 'We fucked. And there's a huge difference.'

'Yes, yes of course.'

'I think you'd better go. I'll be in touch, OK?'

'You want to see me again, then?' he asked me hopefully.

'Of course I do.'

'Oh, right.'

'I'll ring you, Paul.'

Wicked, naughty, revengeful ... As Paul left the house, my feelings changed. I felt remorseful, guilty and ashamed. What had I done? I'd behaved like a common slut. But I'd only done it to be rid of Alan, I tried to console myself. Hopefully, he'd now got the message. The marriage was over. There was no point in him phoning me or coming round to the house. After ten years, we were finished, the marriage had come to an end. Watching another man fucking me, Alan must have realised that the marriage had finally died. Pulling my skirt down to conceal my sperm-oozing sex crack, I pondered on the days to come. I was alone now, facing an uncertain future.

Two

The phone woke me at eight o'clock the following morning. The sun was shining through the window, birds were singing in the garden . . . It was going to be a nice day. Clambering out of my bed, I ignored the phone and went into the bathroom. I instinctively knew that it was Alan as I stepped into the shower. Did he want to accuse me of committing adultery? Had he taken photographs of my adulterous act? Was he triumphant or devastated? He probably wanted to talk about solicitors and divorce. I really didn't care what he wanted, what he had to say. As long as he now realised that the marriage was over and he'd leave me in peace, I'd be happy.

Washing away the dried sperm from my vaginal crack and my inner thighs, I wondered what the day would bring. Would Paul turn up wanting sex with me? Would Alan hammer on the front door demanding that I talk to him? The phone rang again as I returned to the bedroom. Dressing in my miniskirt and thong, I dried and brushed my hair before going downstairs to the kitchen and filling the kettle. Perhaps I should have answered the phone, I mused as the front doorbell rang. Perhaps I should have gone to the pub the previous evening.

'Yes?' I said coldly, opening the door to find Alan standing on the step.

'Helen, we need to talk,' he breathed, walking past me into the hall.

I closed the door and followed him into the lounge. 'What about?' I asked him.

'Us, the future and –'

'There is no future for us,' I cut in. 'You wanted to end the marriage, and that's what we've done.'

'That skirt's rather short, isn't it? What did you get up to last night?'

'Yes, my skirt is short,' I snapped. 'And I didn't get up to anything last night. What did you do last night?'

'I had a great evening,' he replied, grinning at me like a silly schoolboy.

'Oh, er . . . Good,' I stammered, wondering why he wasn't having a go at me. 'I'm pleased for you.'

'I really enjoyed myself, Helen.'

'Are you going to tell me what you did?'

'No, no I don't think I'd better. Suffice to say that I had a brilliant evening.'

'Oh, right.' His peculiar reaction to my adultery had really thrown me and I wasn't sure what to say. 'So, what do you want?' I finally asked him.

'Helen, about the future –'

'Alan, there is no future for us. I've already told you that.'

'OK,' he said, much to my surprise. 'Have you anything planned for this evening?'

'No, no I haven't. Why do you ask?'

'I just wondered. Right, I'd better be going.'

'Is that it?' I asked him. 'You came here to ask me what I'm doing this evening?'

'As I said, I just wondered whether you had anything planned.'

'It wouldn't affect you if I did have plans,' I returned. 'What I do is my business.'

'Yes, of course. Well, I'd better get to work.'

As he left the house, I wondered whether I'd imagined seeing him at the lounge window the previous evening. No, I hadn't imagined it. He'd definitely been there, watching Paul fucking me. So, why hadn't he ranted and raved about my committing adultery? I'd thought, I'd hoped, that he'd demand a divorce. He hadn't got some sort of kick from watching his wife get fucked, surely? I pondered. I'd heard about voyeurs, husbands watching their wives having sex with other men. But Alan wasn't like that. Or was he? Totally confused, I didn't know what to think. I'd imagined that he'd be disgusted by my lewd behaviour and want nothing more to do with me. Why had he asked me whether I had anything planned for the evening? Was he hoping to watch me get fucked again?

Although I spent the morning busying myself with housework, I couldn't stop thinking about Alan. I finally came to the conclusion that he'd not only enjoyed watching me have sex with another man, but he was hoping to spy on me again. This wasn't at all like Alan, I mused. He'd always been horrendously possessive and deadly jealous. To derive pleasure from watching me ... Had he set it up with Paul? Again wondering who was conning whom, I decided that he had set it up with Paul. They'd been in it together, planned my seduction, used me and ... I'd have nothing more to do with Paul, I thought angrily. Reckoning that they'd met for a drink after I'd been fucked, I imagined them talking about my body. They'd have laughed and joked and no doubt planned another evening of seduction and voyeurism.

I'd been duped, and I was extremely angry. But I couldn't deny that I'd derived immense sexual pleasure from the adulterous coupling. Knowing that Alan had been watching me had heightened my arousal beyond belief. If this was Alan's latest game, then I was enjoying it. Unlike his usual mind games, this one was exciting, and sexually gratifying. But I didn't want Paul involved. I didn't want scheming and dirty talk going on behind my back. If Alan was hoping to spy on me and watch me getting fucked again, he wasn't going to see me with Paul.

Paul rang me, as I thought he would. He wanted to come round at seven o'clock, the very time he'd called the previous evening when Alan was supposed to have been viewing a flat. I still couldn't believe that Alan had enjoyed watching me have sex with another man, but that's the way it seemed. Sure that Paul had planned this with Alan, I finally agreed and told him to bring a bottle of wine. Little did he know that a wicked plan was growing in my mind.

Dressed in my miniskirt and a skimpy top, I wandered out into the garden. The lawn needed cutting, the weeds were beginning to sprout . . . Alan had always kept the garden so nice, but he was no longer around. Wondering where he was living, I realised that my life was going to change in many ways. The house and garden were now down to me, and I'd need some money coming in if I was going to survive. Fortunately, the house belonged to my grandmother. The idea was that I pay her rent until she passed away and then the property would come to me. Alan wouldn't have a look in.

'Nice day,' my neighbour, Tom, called over the fence.

'It is,' I agreed. 'How's Mary?'

'She's fine. She's staying at her mother's for a couple of days. How's Alan? I've not seen him lately.'

'We've split up,' I enlightened him. 'He's gone.'

'God, I had no idea. I am sorry, Helen.'

'It's all right, it was a mutual decision.'

'I thought you two were . . . I don't know what I thought. Are you coping OK on your own?'

'Yes, no problem. But it does seem strange spending the evenings alone after ten years of marriage. Sometimes I wake up at night not thinking that he's gone and . . . We've done the right thing, I'm sure of that.'

'Come round any time,' he invited me. 'Mary's away at the moment, but she'd be delighted to see you when she's back. You're welcome to come round any time.'

'That's very nice of you, Tom,' I said, smiling at him as my plan formulated. 'Look, as Mary's away, why don't you come to my place this evening? We might as well sit together rather than alone.'

'OK, that's a great idea. I've got some beers in the fridge, and some wine.'

'Say, seven o'clock? I'll leave the back door open.'

'Seven, it is.'

Returning to the house, I felt butterflies fluttering in my stomach, my womb contracting. Tom was about twenty-five, handsome, good looking and rugged . . . And his wife was away. Things couldn't have turned out better, I reflected. Wicked images forming in my mind, I grinned: my legs spread wide, Tom lapping up my pussy milk as my husband watched . . . But I was beginning to wonder what my ultimate goal was. My original plan had been to shock and disgust Alan with my decadence. But, far from wanting nothing to do with me and leaving me in peace, he seemed to be enjoying my adultery as much as I was.

Writing a note, I checked my watch. One hour to go, I mused, pinning the piece of paper to the front door.

In my note, I'd instructed Paul to go to the local pub and wait for me. I'd said that my mother was coming to see me but I'd meet him in the pub for a drink. Hopefully, he'd arrive at the house on time and be gone before Alan turned up. Alan was in for a shock, I thought in my rising wickedness. Expecting to see his partner in crime screwing me, he'd witness young Tom shafting my tight vagina. Of course, I was assuming that Tom would succumb to my offer of sex. If he didn't, then my plan would be in ruins. Feeling the firmness of my breasts through the thin material of my top, I was confident that Tom would fall prey to my willing body.

From my bedroom window, just before seven o'clock, I saw Paul walk up the drive. He was clutching another bunch of flowers and a bottle of wine. He was out of luck, I thought as he read the note. He wouldn't have the pleasure of my tight pussy again. He'd conned me once, but never again. Once he'd left, I dashed down the stairs and removed the note from the front door. So far so good, I thought as Tom knocked on the back door. Making my way to the kitchen, I realised that this was a risky business. I'd seduced Paul, and was now hoping to seduce Tom. What the hell was I playing at? I wondered, inviting Tom into the kitchen. What was I becoming?

'Hi,' he said, dumping several cans of lager on the work top and passing me a bottle of chilled white wine. 'Not too early, am I?'

Thankfully, there were no flowers. 'Not at all,' I replied, eyeing his shorts. 'You look very summery.'

'It's a warm evening. Had Mary been here, we'd have fired up the barbecue.'

'Had Alan been here . . .' I began, recalling our barbecues. 'So, here we are. Two lost souls.'

'Helen, I don't want to pry . . .' he began, frowning at me. 'Are you sure that you're all right? It must be quite a shock to find yourself on your own.'

'Alan and I had been talking about splitting up for ages,' I replied, opening the wine. 'We just drifted apart and finally realised that we were wasting our lives. Yes, I'm fine, Tom. To be honest, I'm rediscovering myself. I'm actually having some fun after ten years of . . . No, I can't say that the marriage was bad from the start. We drifted apart, and now we've gone our own ways.'

Pouring myself a glass of wine as he popped a can of lager, I felt my hands trembling. Had Alan seen Paul walking away from the house? Paul might phone Alan to tell him that the evening of sex was off. Would Tom notice Alan spying through the lounge window? Would Alan hammer on the window and . . . I began to think that this was a mess, but quickly realised that I was in control. This was my life, and I was beginning to enjoy it. If I wanted sex with Tom, that was up to me. This had nothing to do with Alan, Paul, or anyone else. I'd had too many years of suffocation, I reflected. I was now free to do what I liked, when I liked.

Again looking at the slight bulge in Tom's shorts, I became aware of my nipples brushing against the thin material of my top. The day had been hot, and I'd not bothered wearing a bra. Apart from the heat, I'd hoped that the sight of my milk teats pressing through my blouse would stir Tom's libido and rouse his cock. Would he make a move? I pondered. Would he succumb to his male desires? Or was he faithful to his sweet little wife?

'Shall we sit in the garden?' he asked me.

'Er . . . Maybe later. It's pretty hot out there so let's sit in the lounge until the sun goes down a bit.'

'OK, fine. Where's Alan staying?'

'I'm not sure,' I replied, leading him into the lounge and indicating for him to sit on the sofa. 'He's probably staying with his parents while he looks for a flat.'

'Hasn't he told you where he is?'

'No, he ... Let's not talk about Alan,' I said, settling in the armchair.

'No, no of course. You look great, Helen. I've never seen you in a short skirt.'

'It's my new look,' I replied with a giggle. 'I was a housewife, and I'm now free and single and ...'

'And stunning, if you don't mind my saying so?'

'Thank you, Tom. Apart from my new look, I plan to get out and about and make new friends. After ten years ... Well, I suppose I've stagnated.'

'Mary and I have only been married for five years. But I do know what you mean. Marriage seems to become a rut after a while. The same old things day in day out ...'

'Are you two OK?' I cut in.

'Oh, yes. It's just that ... Oh, I don't know. Maybe I'm beginning to stagnate.'

'Well, I hope you don't end up the way Alan and I have. You need to spice things up a bit, Tom. Bring a little excitement into your life.'

I caught sight of Alan through the window, and felt my stomach somersault. I now knew the answer to a nagging question. It was the thought of Alan watching me that was sending my arousal through the roof. With my voyeur in position, I was desperate for Tom to make a move and seduce me. Not so much for sexual gratification, but to perform in front of my husband. Gazing at Tom's shorts, I found myself wondering how big his cock was. Had he been wanking while Mary was away? I mused. Did Mary suck his swollen knob and swallow his spunk?

28

'How do I bring a little excitement into my life?' Tom asked me.

'While Mary's away ... Why don't you have a little fun?'

'Mowing the lawn? Doing the housework?' he quipped.

'Sexy fun,' I breathed huskily.

'Helen, are you saying what I think you're saying?'

'I'll be honest with you, Tom,' I said, leaving my chair and kneeling at his feet. 'Your wife is away, my husband has gone ... I think we're both in need of a little excitement, don't you?'

Tom said nothing as I tugged his shorts down and gazed wide-eyed at the thick shaft of his flaccid penis. Pulling his shorts off his feet, I parted his legs and watched his balls roll and heave. His shaft stiffening, his long cock finally standing to attention, I could see Alan out of the corner of my eye. His face pressed to the window, he watched as I retracted Tom's fleshy foreskin and exposed the glistening bulb of his swollen knob. What the hell was he thinking? I pondered as I leaned forward and sucked Tom's knob into my wet mouth. Was this what he'd wanted to see?

'God,' Tom breathed as I took his purple plum to the back of my throat and sank my teeth gently into his hard shaft. 'God, you're amazing.'

'Mmm,' I moaned through my nose as I fondled his full balls.

'Helen, I had no idea that you felt this way about me.'

Felt what way? I mused, savouring the salty taste of his cock-head. Did he think that I'd fallen in love with him? All I wanted from Tom was his hard cock, his creamy spunk. His twee little wife could cook for him and iron his shirts. She could do the mundane

29

jobs while I used his cock for my pleasure. Rolling my tongue over his sperm-slit, I again wondered whether Mary sucked his knob and drank his spunk. When had Tom last fucked his wife? She was a pretty little thing with long blonde hair, and she was quite a bit younger than Tom. But, even if they did have a good sex life, Tom obviously wasn't averse to a little sexual pleasure outside the marriage.

Wanking his hard shaft, fondling and kneading his heavy balls, I bobbed my head up and down and repeatedly took his purple globe to the back of my throat. I could feel my juices of desire seeping between the engorged petals of my inner lips and soaking into my thong. My clitoris erect, my nipples hard and acutely sensitive, I again pondered on the frightening height of my arousal. Totally out of control, I was behaving like a nymphomaniac. This was my next door neighbour, I reminded myself as I glanced at Alan out of the corner of my eye. He was a married man. What the hell?

I'd changed beyond belief since Alan had walked out on me, and I began to wonder whether further changes lay ahead. Paul, and now Tom ... How many more men would I lure into my house and seduce? How many times would my husband witness my debauched sexual acts? The transformation from twee housewife to whore was incomprehensible. Within a week, I'd plunged head first into a pit of depravity. What the hell had happened to me?

Tom announced his coming all too soon. Gasping and shaking as he pumped my gobbling mouth full of sperm, he ordered me to swallow every drop. I couldn't remember when I'd last tasted sperm. Five years? Eight? Savouring the salty liquid, I wanked Tom's solid shaft and allowed my mouth to fill before swallowing his creamy offering. Clutching my head, he rocked his hips and repeatedly drove his orgasming knob to the back of my throat. I gobbled and sucked and swallowed until I'd drained his balls and he finally slipped his spent cock out of my spermed mouth. Another conquest, I mused, licking my sperm-glossed lips. It was a shame that it was over all too soon.

'You're fantastic,' he gasped, his eyes rolling, his body trembling uncontrollably. 'God, that was amazing.'

'I don't think Mary would agree,' I returned coldly. Why was I feeling angry? 'Do you often cheat on her?'

'Er . . . No, I've never cheated on her. Until now, I mean. Helen, are you all right?'

'When's Mary back?'

'Tomorrow morning,' he sighed, grabbing his shorts and pulling them on. 'You're not going to say anything to her, are you?'

'Why would I do that?'

Feeling sorry for Mary, I wondered whether Alan had ever cheated on me. Had he gone sneaking off to some girl's house and pushed his cock deep into her mouth? Whatever Alan was, I knew that he'd not been unfaithful. And neither had I. During our marriage, I'd put up with him, somehow managed to cope with his peculiar ways. But I'd never betrayed him. Perhaps I should have found a little excitement with another man, I pondered. It might have helped me to survive.

'Mary's a lovely girl, Tom,' I said, again feeling sorry for her. 'It's a shame that you don't value your relationship.'

'I do, Helen,' he returned. 'I love Mary to bits. I'd never want to hurt her or –'

'But, you're quite happy to betray her? You're quite happy to commit adultery?'

'No, I . . . Look, I don't want you telling her about us.'

'I won't say anything to her, Tom. I wouldn't spoil our arrangement. You have a lovely cock, and I want more of it.'

'It's all yours,' he said with a chuckle. 'I'm stiffening up already.'

Noticing that Alan was still at the window, I grinned. 'In that case, you'd better give it to me,' I breathed huskily.

Kneeling on the floor with my head resting on the sofa cushion, I yanked my skirt up and pulled my thong to one side. Tom knelt behind me and, in full view of Alan, stabbed at my open sex crack with his bulbous knob. I was enjoying my new-found life, and felt no guilt as far as Alan was concerned. But I was worrying about Mary. She'd be home in the morning. Thinking that her husband had been missing her, she'd kiss him and . . . What Mary didn't know wouldn't hurt her, I decided.

Revelling in my wickedness, my blatant debauchery, I watched my husband out of the corner of my eye. His face pressed against the window, he watched as Tom drove the entire length of his rock-hard cock deep into my tightening vagina. My husband of ten years witnessing another man shafting me? What were his thoughts? What were my thoughts? Revenge, spite . . . I didn't know what I was feeling as Tom impaled me fully on his beautiful cock. This was the second penis to penetrate my vagina in as many days, I reflected as Tom grabbed my hips. Would I be impaled on a third cock the following day?

As Tom rocked his hips, shafting my tightening sex sheath with his rock-hard penis, I could feel his swinging balls battering my mons, hear my juices of lust squelching. His lower belly slapping the rounded cheeks of my bared bottom, he repeatedly rammed the full length of his huge cock deep into my quivering body. When had Alan and I last made love in the lounge? I wondered. When had we last enjoyed varied and gratifying sex? Tom and I weren't making love. We were fucking.

'You tell Mary about this, and you won't have my cock again,' Tom breathed.

'It'll be your loss,' I returned with a giggle. 'OK, and mine.'

'I've often thought about fucking you, Helen,' he confessed. 'I've often imagined fucking your tight little arsehole.'

I'd had no idea that Tom had thought about me like that. Fucking my tight little arsehole? I mused, his crude words sending my libido soaring. Did he push his cock into Mary's bottom-hole? There was far more to my neighbour than met the eye. Intrigued, I wondered how many other men had looked at me and thought about fucking me. There was Alan's younger brother, Bob. Did he think about fucking me? My friend's husband, Terry ... He'd often grinned and winked at me. Had he been imagining his cock embedded deep within my tight pussy?

Realising how naïve I'd been during my marriage, I decided that I didn't need to meet people and make new friends. I already knew several men. Friends' husbands, Alan's brother, neighbours ... Had they all looked at my unavailable body and imagined fucking me? Were all men the same? Lecherous, adulterous. Did they all image their cocks driving into my tight pussy as they fucked their wives or wanked? I'd have to put my new clothes to the test, I decided. Wear my short skirt and skimpy top and discover how many husbands I could seduce.

'Here it comes,' Tom breathed, increasing his fucking rhythm. 'God, you're a tight-cunted little whore. I'm going to fuck you senseless and fill you with spunk.'

His crude words again sending my arousal through the roof, I wondered why Alan had never talked dirty to me. Perhaps he'd thought me too prudish. Perhaps I *had* been too prudish during my married years. Not any more, I thought wickedly as Tom's spunk jetted from his orgasming knob and flooded my vaginal cavern. Again and again, he rammed his bulbous glans deep into my inflamed pussy. His gushing sperm splattering my ripe cervix, his swinging balls battering my mons, he grunted and gasped and fucked me with a vengeance. If I *had* been a prude, things were certainly different now.

My solid clitoris massaged by Tom's wet shaft, I finally reached my mind-blowing orgasm. A creamy blend of sperm and girl-juice oozing from my bloated vagina and running in rivers of milk down my inner thighs, I shuddered uncontrollably in my adulterous coming. I could see Alan peering through the window as Tom pumped me full of spunk. What was he thinking now? Witnessing his wife fucked senseless by another man . . . After all our years together as man and wife, was this really what he wanted to see?

As my orgasm peaked, shaking my body to the core, my vaginal muscles spasmed and a cocktail of male and female orgasmic cream flooded my inner thighs. Tom's wet balls slapping my vulval flesh as he fucked me, my body rocking back and forth, I thought I'd never come down from my sexual heaven. On and on, waves of pure orgasmic bliss crashed through my straining body. Never had I been fucked like this, I reflected happily. Mary was a lucky girl. Having a husband with a huge cock and amazing staying power, she was extremely lucky. But, her husband was an adulterous bastard.

'You're good,' Tom praised me as he finally slipped his dripping cock out of my drenched vagina. 'We'll have to do this again.'

'We will,' I breathed shakily, hauling myself off the sofa. 'You're bloody big, Tom. I've never known such a big cock.'

'I've never had any complaints,' he said proudly.

'Does Mary . . . Does she appreciate you?'

'She's not really into sex,' he sighed, grabbing his shorts. 'We have sex, but it only happens once a week.'

'God, I would have thought that you two . . .'

'People think that we're a perfect couple,' he breathed, running his fingers through his hair. 'Appearances can be deceptive.'

Adjusting my skirt and thong as he pulled his shorts up, I wondered why Mary wasn't into sex. Maybe she had someone on the side, I pondered. She was extremely pretty and could no doubt have any man she wanted. Tom was right, I mused. Appearances can be deceptive. I'd always thought them to be a perfect couple enjoying sex to the full and . . . No doubt that's what people had thought about Alan and me.

'I've never told anyone this before,' Tom said softly.

'Told anyone what?'

Adjusting his shorts, he smiled at me. 'Mary used to be into lesbian sex.'

'Lesbian sex?' I gasped, sitting on the sofa.

'When we met, she was going out with a girl. She was torn, couldn't decide what she wanted. We ended up together and got married, but . . . I sometimes wonder whether it's a male or a female she wants.'

'God, I had no idea. Appearances *can* be deceptive. So, she was having lesbian sex?'

'Very much so. I have a feeling that she only went with me to keep her parents happy. They were becoming suspicious, especially her mother. Mary was always with this other girl and her parents were beginning to suspect that there was something unhealthy about the relationship.'

'God,' I breathed again, in disbelief. 'Did she tell you about it?'

'How do you mean?'

'Well, did she tell you what she got up to with this other girl?'

'She didn't want to talk about it, Helen. It's not the sort of thing you'd want to talk about, is it?'

'No, I suppose not. I can't imagine Mary licking . . . Well, licking another girl's pussy.'

'You seem to be fascinated by the subject.'

'I am. Well, not fascinated. I suppose I'm intrigued.'

'Look, I'd better be getting back. Mary said that she'd phone me this evening.'

'OK, Tom. Thanks for a lovely time. I really enjoyed it.'

'So did I. It's nice to meet a one hundred percent heterosexual girl. I suppose you are heterosexual? I mean, have you ever thought about having sex with another girl?'

'Never,' I returned firmly. 'There was a girl at school that I . . . No, I'm not a lesbian.'

'We will do this again, won't we?' he asked me hopefully.

'Yes, of course.'

'It's funny how things turn out, isn't it? Your husband has gone and my wife is . . . Anyway, I'll see you soon.'

36

'Very soon, I hope,' I said, seeing him to the back door.

Still unable to believe what he'd told me about Mary, I poured myself another glass of wine and sat on the sofa. Fortunately, Alan wasn't at the window. Hoping that he hadn't gone to see Tom, I tried to picture Mary licking another girl's wet pussy. I'd never even dreamed of having sex with another girl. I'd known of a couple of girls at school who'd played about with each other, and I'd been invited to join in. But it was something that I'd never have got involved in. The phone rang. I prayed that it wasn't Alan as I pressed the receiver to my ear. Would my husband like to see me with another girl? Would he enjoy watching me sucking another girl's clitoris to orgasm?

'Helen, it's Paul.'

'Oh, hi. Look, I'm sorry I couldn't make it to the pub. Something cropped up and –'

'That doesn't matter,' he cut in agitatedly. 'I'm phoning because I thought you ought to know about Alan.'

'What about him? What the hell has he done now?'

'After I'd waited for you in the pub for a while, I walked back to your place. Alan was there, looking through the window.'

'Looking through the window?' I echoed, wondering why Paul was telling me this.

'I was about to walk up your drive when I noticed him looking through your lounge window.'

'So, you didn't know that he'd be there?'

'Helen . . . Of course I didn't know that he'd be there. Had I known, I wouldn't have come round.'

'Last night, when you were here . . . Did you notice him then?'

'God, no. Had I seen him looking through the window, watching us . . . Helen, what's this all about?'

37

'I got things very wrong,' I sighed.

'What things?'

'I thought that you and Alan . . . It doesn't matter. Thanks for letting me know, Paul.'

'Where were you when he was looking through the window? Were you in the lounge?'

'No, no. My mother and I sat in the back garden, so Alan wouldn't have seen us. You'll have to come round another time, Paul. It would be great to see you.'

'I could come round now.'

'Er . . . No, not now,' I replied, aware of sperm oozing into my thong. 'Tomorrow, maybe.'

'OK, I'll look forward to it.'

Replacing the receiver, I couldn't believe how wrong I'd been about Paul. Alan had conned both of us, used us for his own sexual . . . But I had Alan to thank for my new-found life, I reminded myself. Had he not spied through the window, I wouldn't have had the opportunity to enjoy sex with Paul and Tom. If it wasn't for Alan, Tom and I would have chatted over a glass of wine, simply spent the evening together. There was no way we'd have ended up fucking.

Enjoying another glass of wine, I pondered on my life, where it was taking me. Where did I want it to take me? Did I want casual sex with several men on a regular basis? Did I want to continue having sex with men knowing that Alan was watching me? I didn't know what I wanted. Peace and quiet, freedom, fun . . . At least Alan was out of my life. Spying through the window at me, but out of my life.

'Hello,' I breathed, answering the phone.

'It's me,' Alan said.

'Hi, how are you?' I asked him cheerily.

'I'm all right. It's you I'm worried about.'

'Me? I'm fine, Alan. Couldn't be better, in fact.'

'Helen, I'm concerned about the house.'

'My grandmother's house? What about it?'

'When it eventually goes to you, I suppose we'll sell it and split the money.'

'Sell it? I can't sell it, Alan. It's been in the family for decades.'

'But, it was our home.'

'Yes, it was. It's now my home, and I intend to keep it that way.'

'How are you managing to pay the rent? You have no income, Helen. Unless you're intending to go on the game, I can't see how you'll manage to pay –'

'On the game?' I cut in angrily. 'What the hell are you implying?'

'I've heard that you've been seeing a couple of men. I've heard that you've been putting it about.'

'I have one or two male friends,' I replied, loving every minute of the game. 'But I'm not putting it about, and I'm certainly not charging men for sex. Now you come to mention it, it's not a bad idea.'

'For God's sake, Helen.'

'What's the matter? If you're accusing me of charging men for sex, I might as well do it. Twenty pounds for a hand job would be –'

As he hung up, I pondered his words. *I suppose we'll sell it and split the money*. There was no way he was getting his hands on the house. Besides, it belonged to my grandmother and would hopefully stay that way for many years. As for his accusation about my taking money in return for sex . . . It wasn't a bad idea. Prostitution? I mused. Easy money, and a good life with plenty of hard sex. Perhaps I should charge Alan for allowing him to watch me fucking other men? I reflected.

Feeling tired, I climbed the stairs. What tomorrow would bring, I had no idea. More cocks, more fucking, more spunk . . . The house was safe enough, I thought happily as I slipped out of my clothes. Apart from a shortage of cash, my life was safe and secure. Catching my reflection in the full-length mirror, I grinned. I had a damned good body. Should I charge men for sex?

Three

After a shower and a light breakfast, I rang my mother to tell her that Alan had gone. Gone for good, this time. I hadn't called her earlier as I'd wanted to make sure that I wouldn't weaken and take him back. I'd not wanted to give her the good news, and then call her back with bad news. She'd known about his peculiar ways, his continual threats to leave me, and she was pleased that I wasn't going to take him back yet again. Although I knew that she didn't mean it, she said that she'd disown me if I allowed him back into my life. That's how strongly she felt about him. She did the usual motherly thing and asked me whether there was anything I needed, anything she could do to help. But I told her that I was fine.

Within minutes of my phone call, my grandmother rang me. She'd heard the good news and cut my rent by half, which was a great relief. But I'd still need to earn some money to survive. Again pondering on Alan's incredible accusation, I couldn't believe that I was even considering taking money in return for sexual favours. The notion was ludicrous. How the hell could I charge Paul or Tom for sex? I'd need to advertise my services and . . . No, the idea was crazy.

Gazing out of the window as the front doorbell rang, I was horrified to see Mary standing on the step. I'd sucked sperm out of her husband's knob, opened my legs and taken the full length of his massive cock deep into my wet pussy . . . How was I going to face his wife? Wandering into the hall, I took a deep breath and tried to compose myself. Tom wouldn't have said anything to Mary about our time together, I reflected. He wouldn't have even hinted about our having sex. All I had to do was come across as normal.

'Hi, Mary,' I said, smiling as I opened the front door. 'It's lovely to see you.'

'I've heard the terrible news about you and Alan,' she sighed as I led her into the lounge. 'I'm so sorry, Helen. I'd always thought that you were such a lovely couple and –'

'No, no,' I cut in. 'It's good news, Mary. Alan and I . . . It was a mutual decision.'

'But, you must feel some sadness?'

'Not at all. In fact, I feel relieved now that it's over. Would you like coffee or tea?'

'No, thanks, I can't stay long. Tom said that he'd been to see you. He told me the news and I just thought I'd come and make sure that you're OK.'

'I'm fine, honestly. I get a little lonely in the evenings, but I'll soon get used to it. It was nice of Tom to come round and keep me company while you were away. We kept each other company.'

'He said that he'd enjoyed talking to you. Tom's always been good with women. When we first met, he used to talk to my sister about her problems and . . .'

Always been good with women? I mused as Mary sat on the sofa and rambled on about her sister. If only she knew just *how* good he was with other women. Had Tom fucked Mary's sister? I wondered. Had he slipped his cock into his sister-in-law's tight little pussy and fucked her? Gazing at Mary's full red

42

lips, I couldn't help but imagine her kissing and licking another girl's pussy. What did lesbians do in bed? I pondered, making myself comfortable in the armchair. Licking, sucking, fingering . . . Mary was so young and attractive. Her long blonde hair framing her fresh face, her small breasts clearly outlined by her white blouse, she didn't look like a lesbian. What did lesbians look like?

Lowering my eyes to her short skirt, her slender thighs, I tried to picture a girl licking her sex crack, sucking on her clitoris and taking her to a massive orgasm. Lesbian sex wasn't my thing, I concluded. A pussy was no substitute for a solid cock. But I was intrigued. I wanted Mary to tell me about her lesbian relationship. I'd never met a lesbian before and I wanted to know why she'd been with another girl, what they'd done together. I couldn't let her know that Tom had revealed her little secret, but I reckoned that I could get her to talk about lesbian sex.

'You're lucky to have Tom,' I said, steering her away from her boring story about her sister. 'You're obviously a very happy couple.'

'We are, Helen,' she replied softly. 'I'm sure that you'll soon find someone and –'

'No, I don't want another relationship,' I cut in. 'After ten years of marriage, I want to enjoy my freedom.' This was my cue to change the subject. 'A friend of mine divorced recently, and she's ended up with another girl.'

'Another girl?' Mary echoed, her blue eyes widening. 'You mean, she's in a lesbian relationship?'

'Yes, and she reckons that she's never been happier.'

'I can understand that,' she breathed pensively. 'Men are so . . . Oh, I don't know.'

'What were you going to say? Tell me, Mary.'

'Before I met Tom, I became very good friends with a girl.' Lowering her head, she twisted her long blonde hair nervously around her slender fingers. 'We – we had a relationship,' she finally confessed.

'Why did it end?' I asked, hoping that she'd tell me the explicit sexual details.

'My parents, mainly. They didn't know about it, but they had their suspicions. Still, that's all in the past.'

'Did you marry Tom to keep your parents happy?'

'Yes, I suppose I did. Don't get me wrong, I love Tom very much. I certainly wouldn't want to be without him. It's just that . . . I miss Lydia terribly.'

'Mary, I'm so sorry. I had no idea. How long were you with Lydia?'

'A couple of years. We did everything together, went everywhere together. I met Tom through Lydia. He was going out with one of her friends, and we ended up together.'

'Just to please your parents? That's really sad.'

'Lydia was devastated when I left her, but what could I do? Looking back, I should have stayed with her. Getting married to please my parents was a big mistake. As I said, I love Tom and I wouldn't want to be without him. But I still want to be with Lydia.'

Feeling sorry for Mary, I didn't know what to say. She obviously wasn't going to reveal the intimate details of her sexual relationship with another girl, and I thought it best not to push her. But, it seemed that she'd had more than a sexual relationship. She seemed to have been genuinely in love with Lydia. How awful to split up with the one you love and marry someone else because it seemed like the right thing to do, I mused. She must have been desperately unhappy.

'Are you still in touch with Lydia?' I asked. 'Do you ever see her?'

'No,' she sighed, again lowering her head. 'I know where she lives. But it would be pointless contacting her.'

'You've made me feel quite sad,' I breathed. 'I was happy when Alan and I split up. But it must be awful to split up with someone you love. So, are you still a lesbian? That sounds dreadful, I'm sorry.'

'Yes, I am a lesbian,' she admitted. 'It's not something that goes away, Helen. I've tried to deny it, but I can't. I sometimes look at other girls and wonder what I should do. I love Tom, but in a different way. It's not like being in love. Tom and I have more of a brother-sister relationship.'

Again focusing on her naked thighs, I knew that curiosity was beginning to get the better of me. There was no way that I wanted lesbian sex, not even as an experiment. But something deep inside me was stirring, something was rousing. What did another girl taste like? I pondered. What was it like to have another girl's tongue between the puffy lips of my vagina? Entwined in the sixty-nine position, writhing naked in orgasm . . . Trying to rid my mind of such illicit thoughts, I wondered how long Mary and Tom's marriage would last. He was screwing me, she wanted another girl . . . That was a recipe for disaster.

'Helen, I have to say this,' Mary began. 'If I don't, then I'll forever be wondering.'

'Say what?' I asked her.

'I've always liked you.'

'And I've always liked you, Mary. You've been to our barbecues and . . . We could have a barbecue this evening. Without Alan, I'll probably make a mess of the fire but . . .'

'Helen, you know what I'm saying.'

'I'm not with you,' I said, knowing full well what she was talking about.

'Now that you're alone, without Alan . . . Perhaps we could get together now and then? What do you think?'

My stomach somersaulting, I forced a smile. 'Yes, of course. You're welcome to come round whenever you like.'

'You look lovely in your skirt. I've never seen you wearing a short skirt.'

'It's my new look,' I said, wondering what she'd think if she knew that I was wearing a thong. 'Now that I'm as good as single again, I aim to enjoy my life to the full.'

'Sexually?' she asked me, cocking her head to one side.

'Well, yes.'

'Helen, I – I'm just looking for some comfort, and a little closeness.'

In a way, I felt quite flattered by Mary's tentatively worded suggestion. She was young and beautiful, feminine and sensuous. She was also Tom's wife. And I wasn't a lesbian. Although I felt sorry for her, I knew that I couldn't give her the comfort and closeness she craved. Men with their hard cocks and heaving balls, their ruggedness, their muscular bodies . . . Mary was soft and gentle. I needed men.

'I shouldn't have said anything,' she sighed. 'But I had to ask you.'

'Yes, I understand.'

'I'm not very good with Tom. We have sex, but I'm not very good.'

'You can't live a lie, Mary. For years, I knew that I didn't want to be with Alan. For years, I lived a lie. And now I regret the time I wasted.'

'I'm happy with Tom. It's just that . . . I've rambled on for long enough. I'd better get back.'

'Come round this evening, Mary,' I invited her. 'We'll have a couple of drinks and a chat.'

'We won't be able to chat with Tom here.'

'Tom won't be here. You come on your own and we'll have a girl to girl chat, OK?'

'Thanks, Helen. I'd like that.'

'Seven o'clock?'

'Yes, seven.'

Seeing her to the door, I knew that I was going to have to control myself. Alone with an attractive young lesbian who'd as good as asked me to have sex with her? I wasn't a lesbian, I again reminded myself. I'd never dreamed of having any physical contact with another girl. After closing the door, I returned to the lounge and flopped onto the sofa. Where the hell was my life taking me now? I mused. I'd had sex with Paul, and then Mary's husband . . . What would Alan think if he saw me having sex with Mary? It didn't matter what Alan thought. He was no longer part of my life.

I spent the morning drinking coffee and pacing the lounge floor. Images of Mary's sex crack continually loomed in my mind, and I knew that I was weakening. She was younger than Tom, about twenty-three, and I knew that her breasts would be firm, her nipples ripe. What on earth was I thinking? I reflected anxiously. Imaging her slender body, her feminine curves and mounds, I wondered what it would be like to lock my lips to hers and kiss her pretty mouth. I had to straighten out my weird thoughts.

I was pleased to hear a male voice when Paul rang me at lunchtime. He wanted to know whether it was all right to come round that evening. He'd want sex, I mused, my clitoris stirring within my moistening valley of desire. He'd want to push the entire length of his solid cock deep into my wet pussy and fuck me senseless. I was in two minds, torn between male and female. Shit, I thought, wondering what to say to him. I either put Mary off, or Paul. Which one? Did I want a cock or a pussy? Confused as never before, I tried to come out with the right answer.

'Not this evening, Paul,' I finally breathed, losing the battle raging in my tormented mind. 'My mother's coming to see me again.'

'Oh, right.'

'Maybe tomorrow.'

'That's what you said yesterday,' he whined. 'Your mother turned up yesterday and ruined things for us.'

'I know, and I'm sorry. I'll make it up to you, I promise.'

'That sounds interesting,' he said with a chuckle. 'OK, I'll ring you tomorrow.'

Why the hell had I said that I'd make it up to him? I wondered as I replaced the receiver. Reminiscent of my time with Alan, I thought. *I'm sorry, Alan, it was all my fault. I'm sorry, I want you to come back ...* The way I'd played along with Alan and his crazy mind games, I must have been mad. I didn't want Paul to think that we were an item, that I somehow belonged to him simply because he'd fucked me. I didn't want him ruling my life the way Alan had. Paul had a lovely cock and he fucked long and hard. And that was as far as it went. If he was going to start coming on strong and complaining, then he'd lose me. Paul was nothing more to me than a good fuck. What was Mary going to turn out to be? A good lick?

The afternoon dragged by and, at six o'clock, I started on the white wine. Six o'clock, the time Alan used to get home from work. I'd have a nice meal ready for him, offer him a drink, ask him how his day had been, pamper him ... All day, my thoughts had centred on Mary, and I'd not been able to eat anything. At least I'd had a routine with Alan.

Regular meals, shopping trips, housework, and a weekly fuck. Regular, boring, mundane, and extremely monotonous.

Mary tapped on the back door at seven o'clock. She was wearing a white blouse and a turquoise miniskirt, and she looked beautiful. Was she wearing any panties? I found myself wondering as I poured her a glass of wine. Her long blonde hair framing her pretty face, I reckoned that her pubes were also blonde. Did she trim her pubic hair? I could see that she wasn't wearing a bra beneath her blouse. Her breasts were naked, small, and no doubt hard. Did I want to suck on her ripe milk teats? Shit, I didn't know what I wanted.

'Come through to the lounge,' I invited her, grabbing the wine bottle. 'We'll have a few drinks and a good old girl to girl chat.'

'I've been thinking about you all day,' she breathed, settling on the sofa. 'I can't stop thinking about you.'

'There's no need to worry about me, Mary. As I said earlier, I'm happy now that Alan and I have split up.'

'No, I meant . . . I've been thinking about you, Helen.'

'I've been too busy to think about anything,' I lied. Should I sit next to her? 'Housework, phone calls . . . God, it's been a hectic day. Hopefully, there'll be no more phone calls and I'll be able to relax now. So, how's Tom?'

'He's fine. He's walked up to the pub. Actually, I think there's something on his mind. I don't know what's bothering him, but he seems to be distracted.'

'What did he say when you told him that you were coming here?'

'Not much. He just said that he'd go to the pub and see me later. Aren't you going to sit down?'

'Oh, yes,' I replied, sitting next to her on the sofa.

I gazed at her naked thighs as she talked about Tom and their relationship. Her skin was smooth, unblemished in youth, suntanned, contrasting beautifully with her turquoise skirt. As she moved about on the sofa, her skirt rode up her slender thighs. She was bound to be wearing panties, I thought. Or was she wearing a thong? Perhaps she was naked beneath her skirt? Was she wet? Was her clitoris stirring at the thought of having lesbian sex with me? What the hell was I thinking? I had to take control of my uncharacteristic desires.

'Helen?' she said, breaking my reverie. 'Did you hear what I said?'

'Sorry, I was miles away,' I replied, dragging my eyes and thoughts away from her young body.

'What were you thinking about?' she asked.

'Nothing in particular. So, what were you saying?'

'I was talking about relationships. When Tom licks me, I try to imagine that there's a girl between my legs.'

'When he licks you?' I breathed, shocked by her openness.

'A tongue is a tongue, right?'

'Er . . . Yes, I suppose so.'

'Male or female, a tongue is a tongue. When I first made love with Lydia, I tried to imagine that there was a boy licking me. I was trying to sort out my emotions, trying to decide what it was that I wanted. Helen . . . Do you like oral sex?'

'Well, yes, I do,' I answered her. I could feel my clitoris swelling, my juices of lust flowing into my thong. 'Mary, the thing is –'

'Only a girl knows how to pleasure another girl,' she interrupted me.

Floundering in my confusion, I knew that I had a chance to experience lesbian sex if I wanted to. It would certainly be a first, I thought nervously. *Male or female, a tongue is a tongue.* Pondering on her words, I imagined her licking between my swollen pussy lips, sucking my erect clitoris to orgasm. Alan wasn't spying through the window. No one would know what I'd done, I mused. If I allowed her to lick and suck me to orgasm, it would be our dirty secret. The notion of coming in her pretty mouth exciting me, I felt my stomach somersault. If I opened my legs and allowed her to ... But she'd want me to reciprocate, she'd expect me to return the pleasure. And I knew that I couldn't bring myself to do that.

'Now that Alan's gone, do you miss sex?' she asked me. 'When did you last come?'

'Mary, I – I haven't thought about sex. Since Alan and I split up, I've been pretty busy.'

'Don't you masturbate?' she persisted.

'Well, I used to. But I've not done it recently.'

'Orgasms relieve tension, Helen. You need orgasms to bring you relief and ...'

'Mary, I know what you're getting at. I know what you have in mind.'

'And?'

'Well ... I've never done anything with another girl. And I don't think I want to.'

'Allow me to pleasure you, Helen. Just this once, allow me to bring you the most beautiful orgasm you've ever experienced.'

'Mary, I can't just open my legs to another girl and –'

'Of course you can,' she said huskily, slipping off the sofa and settling at my feet. 'Please, allow me to love you just this once. If you don't, you'll be left wondering for the rest of your life.'

I closed my eyes as she parted my feet and lifted my short skirt up over my stomach. I tried to pretend that I wasn't there, she wasn't there, this wasn't happening. Running her fingertips up my inner thighs, she kissed the wet material of my thong. I felt dizzy in my confusion. How could I imagine that she wasn't there? The fragrance of her perfume filling my nostrils, her blonde hair tickling my thighs, the feel of her hot breath against my skin . . . There was no way that I could deny the pleasure a young lesbian was bringing me. And there was no way that I could imagine that she was a man.

Moving forward on the sofa until my buttocks were over the edge of the cushion, I reclined and offered her the sexual centre of my quivering body. Pushing my thighs wide apart, she licked and nibbled my thong. She was beautiful, angelic, sensuous in the softness of her femininity. I knew that she'd visit me again, love me again. Was this what I wanted? I wondered anxiously. Breathing heavily through my nose, I trembled as ripples of pleasure coursed throughout my young body. She might call round every evening and settle at my feet and love me. What the hell did I think I was doing? I mused uneasily. This was Tom's wife, this was lesbian sex . . .

Kissing my inner thighs, licking the creases at the top of my legs, she told me to relax. I could feel her blonde hair tickling my thighs, her hot breath, her wet tongue, the softness of her feminine touch . . . Drunk in my arousal, lost in my sexual delirium, I was oblivious to the world about me. Thoughts of my husband, whether or not he was at the window, faded into oblivion as my pleasure heightened. My thoughts, my very being, centred on my solid clitoris, my yearning pussy. My heart racing, my breathing fast and shallow, I knew that I had to relax and give myself completely to Mary. Or be left forever wondering.

No one would know, I again mused dreamily as she slipped my thong off and exposed the swollen lips of my vulva. No one would ever discover that I'd enjoyed lesbian sex with a young girl. The feel of her tongue running up and down my opening sex crack was sending my arousal sky high. I arched my back and opened my legs to the extreme. We were alone, away from the prying eyes of the world. I felt warm and safe as she licked the pink flesh around my vaginal entrance, lapped up my flowing sex milk and drank from my surrendered body. Never had I known such softness, gentleness, warmth ... *Only a girl knows how to pleasure another girl.*

As her tongue entered me, delving deep into the wet sheath of my tight vagina, I let out a rush of breath. Our lesbian coupling felt so natural. A female tongue pleasuring a female, a female mouth drinking female juices ... Mary was soft in her feminine softness, loving in her girl love. And I was lost in a world of ecstasy, drifting on clouds of pure lesbian bliss. Had I found my sexual heaven? Or was this simply another conquest? Paul and Tom had fucked me, used me for their sexual satisfaction. And I'd used them. Was I using Mary? She was looking for love, she was looking for a girl who was desperate to fall in love. Was she in love with me?

Moving up my valley of desire, she swept her wet tongue over the sensitive tip of my erect clitoris. My body rigid, I held my breath as she sucked my ripe sex bud into her hot mouth. She was right, I mused in my sexual elation. Only a girl knew how to pleasure another girl. Men were rough and hurried in their lovemaking. Again slipping her tongue into my hot vagina, she stretched my puffy outer lips wide apart. Opening my sex hole to the extreme, driving her tongue deep into the wet heat of my trembling body, she moaned softly through her nose. I should be with a man, I reflected. This was wrong.

Through my eyelashes, I noticed Alan's silhouette at the window. He was watching, voyeuring, witnessing my illicit lesbian act with Mary. Would he tell Tom? I wondered. Would he try to cause trouble? He obviously hadn't told Mary that Tom had fucked me, so why should he tell Tom that Mary had tongued my wet vagina? It was strange to think that a husband and wife both wanted me for sex. Would Mary enjoy sucking her husband's sperm out of my vaginal duct? Perhaps I should have Tom fuck me and then invite Mary round to drink his spunk from my pussy. It was also strange to think that my husband was watching another girl pleasuring me. Where would this path of decadence take me?

As Mary again sucked my solid clitoris into her hot mouth, I really didn't care what Alan thought or said to anyone. I was living my life the way I wanted to live it, and he had no say in the matter. Ten years of mind games, ten years of suffocation. But, now, I was as free as a bird. Alan might be enjoying his new role of voyeur, I mused. But he'd lost me. What were his thoughts? His mind games had backfired on him. What was he thinking now that he was alone in life and I was enjoying sex with men and women? Was he jealous? I had a house, a home, friends, partners in sex ... He had nothing. Did he never think that he'd go too far with his dramatic walk-outs? Did he never think that the day would come when I'd not beg him to come back to me? Obviously not.

'Are you all right?' Mary asked me, her blue eyes wide as she gazed up at me.

'Yes,' I breathed softly, eyeing her pussy-wet lips.

'Are you ready to come now?'

I was more than ready to come, but I didn't know what to say. How could I tell another girl that I wanted to come in her mouth? How could I bring myself to admit that I was desperate for her to suck a massive orgasm from my solid clitoris? Sliding at least three fingers into the tightening sheath of my vagina, she sucked my swollen clitoris into her hot mouth and repeatedly swept her tongue over its sensitive tip. I didn't have to say anything to Mary. She knew that I was ready to come.

Teetering precariously on the verge of my lesbian-induced orgasm, I tried to relax and let myself go. I'd never allowed another girl to see my most private place. I'd never been touched by another girl. Was this what I wanted? I again wondered in my confusion as Mary massaged the wet inner flesh of my vagina. I felt serene as she sucked and mouthed between the puffy lips of my vulva. Again, I thought how natural our lesbian coupling was. Female with female, girl on girl . . . What did her pussy milk taste like? Would I reciprocate?

'Coming,' I gasped as my clitoris exploded in orgasm within the heat of her pretty mouth. Shaking wildly, breathing deeply, I arched my back and clutched tufts of her long blonde hair as she pressed her full lips hard against the wet flesh surrounding my sex bud. Wave after wave of pure ecstasy crashed through my taut body, shaking me to the very core as I rode the crest of my incredible climax. My head lolling from side to side, my thighs twitching, my heart racing, I knew that Mary would come to see me again. Was this the beginning of a lesbian relationship?

Her fingers slipped out of my spasming vagina and moved up to my pulsating clitoris as she pushed her tongue deep into my sex sheath and lapped up my flowing milk. Massaging the orgasming bulb of my sex bud, sustaining my incredible climax, she sucked out my hot pussy milk and repeatedly swallowed. I glimpsed Alan at the window, his face pressed against the glass as he watched the amazing lesbian coupling. My orgasm peaking, I let out a cry of pleasure and again wondered what he was thinking. Was his cock stiff? Was the sight of a girl drinking from my pussy turning him on? Was he wanking?

'No,' I finally breathed as my orgasm began to wane. 'Mary, please ... No more.'

'Mmm,' she moaned through her nose, sucking out the last of my pussy milk. 'You taste heavenly.'

'God, what have I done?' I murmured as her tongue left the inflamed sheath of my vagina. 'What the hell have I ...'

'You've come,' she said with a giggle. 'You came in my mouth. Did you like it?'

'Yes, no, I mean ... Christ, Mary. I'm not a bloody lesbian.'

'No one is accusing you of being a lesbian. You enjoyed an orgasm, that's all. As I said, a tongue is a tongue.'

'I know, but ...'

'You have a beautiful pussy, Helen. And a beautiful clitoris. You're a beautiful girl.'

'I'm a married woman, Mary. I mean, I was ... I don't know what I'm saying.'

'Just relax and give yourself time to recover. Alan's gone, hasn't he? Now that you're free, you can enjoy my love.'

'Love?'

'I think I've been in love with you since the day we met. At your barbecues, when you've been round to us for drinks ... I've looked at you, admired your beauty. I've always wanted you, Helen.'

'Mary, I . . . God, I must cover myself,' I breathed, looking down at the gaping crack of my sex-dripping pussy. 'Mary, this isn't what I want.'

'You don't want beautiful orgasms?'

'Yes, no . . . Not with another girl. You must understand that I'm not a lesbian.'

'Helen, I know that you're not a lesbian. Just because I've sucked you and made you come, it doesn't mean to say that you're anything other than a normal woman.'

'Normal?' I echoed, standing and pulling my skirt down to conceal my pubes. 'Mary, normal women don't do this.'

'I mean, normal in your sexual craving,' she said, rising to her feet. 'You were desperate for the relief of orgasm, and I brought you an orgasm. There's nothing wrong with that, is there?'

Watching Mary refill our wine glasses, I pondered on her words. *I brought you an orgasm, there's nothing wrong with that* . . . Physically pleasuring me, taking me to orgasm, was one thing. But she was talking about love. I could accept sex for the sake of gratifying sex. Even though another girl had licked and sucked me to orgasm, I could accept that it was purely a sexual thing. She'd brought me one of the most powerful orgasms I'd experienced, and I couldn't deny that I'd enjoyed her intimate attention. And I knew that I'd offer her my open pussy again. But I didn't want love. Sipping my wine, I noticed that Alan had gone. Would he go running to Tom? I pondered anxiously. I was in a mess. I'd lost control, I was no longer in charge . . .

'I need to come now,' Mary said softly.

'Yes, I know,' I murmured. 'But, I can't. Mary, I can't . . .'

'I'm used to doing it myself,' she cut in with a

laugh. 'I'll go home now and enjoy a little self-loving. Tom won't be back for a while so . . .'

'Mary, I'm sorry that I can't do it. I have no inclination, no desire whatsoever to – to lick you. I'm heterosexual, and I can't change that.'

'Time will tell, Helen. Time will tell. I'll see you tomorrow.' Finishing her wine, she smiled at me. 'I'll come round in the morning, if that's OK?'

'Er . . . Maybe,' I said, following her to the back door. 'I'm not sure what I'm doing tomorrow.'

'I know what I'd like to be doing all day tomorrow.'

'Yes, well. It's been nice . . . I mean . . .'

'I know what you mean, Helen.'

After kissing my cheek, she flashed me a smile and left by the back door. That was it, I reflected guiltily, knocking back my wine. Returning to the lounge, I refilled my glass and flopped onto the sofa. I'd experienced lesbian sex. I'd taken another step further away from Alan, another step closer to . . . I had no idea where I was going, where my life was leading me. Lesbian sex, I reflected. Girl on girl, pussy licking, clitoral sucking.

What the hell was I going to do when Mary turned up in the morning? I wouldn't answer the doorbell, I decided. I'd go out and . . . But, she'd only come back, she'd persist. Now that she'd tasted lesbian sex with me, she'd not give up. I should never have invited Tom round, I thought dolefully. These people, this man and wife, were my neighbours. I should never have become intimately involved with them. There was no point in looking back. What was done was done, and I couldn't change that.

However, I couldn't allow changes to rule my life. I had to take control and return to normality. Normality? I reflected. Alan was far from normal, our marriage had been far from normal. And what I was doing now was completely abnormal. I'd had sex with another girl, I mused for the umpteenth time. I'd been licked and sucked and fingered to a beautiful orgasm by another girl. More to the point, I'd enjoyed it. What the hell had I done?

Never again, I vowed, knocking back my wine. Taking another bottle from the fridge, I knew that I was drinking too much. But the alcohol helped, I thought as I pulled the cork and filled my glass. I needed something to get me through my confusion, and all I had was alcohol. Again returning to the lounge, I sat on the sofa. Clutching my glass in one hand and the bottle in the other, I knew that I was treading dangerous ground. I'd take control, I mused as my head began to spin. I wouldn't see Mary again, or Tom. And I'd not turn to drink. Taking control would be easy enough, wouldn't it?

Four

Collecting the post from the doormat, I was pleased to find a letter from Alan's solicitor. Divorce, I mused happily, reading through the legal jargon. Alan had got the message, the end of the marriage was in sight. Ten years of marriage, ten years of Alan's crazy mind games, were going to end in divorce. I felt a mixture of sadness, bitterness and elation. I tossed the letter onto the hall table, and wandered into the kitchen to fill the kettle. Would I ever marry again? I pondered as I opened the back door and gazed at the garden.

I'd not slept very well, and decided to have a relaxing day. Tossing and turning all night, I'd dreamed my dreams of penises and vaginas and sperm and girl-juice and love and lust . . . When Alan had walked out on me and I'd decided never to take him back, my dreams had been so very different. I'd dreamed of meeting new people and making friends, socialising and enjoying life without a psychologically disturbed husband. Would I ever marry again?

I knew that I was going to have to make some definite plans for the future, and that didn't include marriage. I'd done nothing about finding a job and earning some money, the garden was becoming overgrown . . . And I'd had lesbian sex with a young girl. I was going to have to take control of my life. I needed a definite direction. Wandering from one crude sexual encounter to another was fun, but it wouldn't pay the bills. Prostitution?

'Oh, Mary,' I breathed as she appeared as if from nowhere. Recalling her tongue delving deep into my vagina, I felt embarrassed, ashamed of my illicit act. 'Er . . . It's rather early. I've not had breakfast yet.'

'Sorry,' she said, stepping into the kitchen. 'I always get up early in the summer. The birds singing, the fresh air and the temperature beginning to rise . . . I love it. By the way, Alan rang last night.'

'Alan?' I murmured, frowning at her. 'What did he want?' My stomach churning, I feared the worst. 'What did he say?'

'I don't know, Tom spoke to him. They were chatting for about half an hour, but I don't know what they were talking about.'

'Didn't Tom say anything to you?'

'He just said that he'd arranged to meet Alan in the pub.'

'Alan doesn't like pubs. I wonder what they want to talk about?'

'Just a man to man chat over a beer, I would imagine. They're meeting in the pub this evening at seven. You look lovely in your short skirt, Helen. Really sexy.'

'Alan can't stand pubs,' I breathed pensively. 'Why on earth would he . . .'

'You seem worried,' she interrupted me. 'Is everything all right?'

'I'm going through a divorce, Mary,' I snapped. 'Of course I'm worried. Alan moves in mysterious ways, to put it mildly. God only knows what he's up to. If he starts ranting to Tom about . . .'

'Ranting about what?' she cut in. 'Our secret's safe, isn't it?'

'Why I allowed you to – to do what you did, I'll never know. Christ, I've had lesbian sex.'

'So?'

'I'm going through a divorce, I've had lesbian sex, I've had sex with Paul –'

'Who's Paul?'

'No one, it doesn't matter.'

'Is that why you and Alan split up?' she persisted. 'Is it because you had an affair?'

'No, no. I've made a mess of things, Mary. When Alan left, I was fine. I had plans and dreams and I was beginning to look forward to the future. And then I had sex with a friend of his.'

'God. Does Alan know?'

'Does he know? He knows, all right. He was watching us.'

'Watching you have sex with his friend?' she gasped, holding her hand to her mouth.

'I don't want to go into the details, Mary. In fact, I don't want to talk about it.'

'So, you think that Alan might tell Tom about it? I don't see that it matters. I don't suppose Tom's interested.'

'There's more to it than that, Mary. It's a long story.'

'Why did you allow Alan to watch you having sex with his friend?'

'I didn't allow him,' I snapped. 'He happened to . . . Look, I don't want to talk about it.'

'OK, I'm sorry,' she sighed. 'I just thought that, as a close friend, I may be able to help.'

'I didn't mean to snap at you, Mary. It's just that there's so much going on in my life at the moment. And, after what we did last night . . .'

'Do you have a problem with that?'

'Of course I have a bloody problem with it. For

God's sake, I had lesbian bloody sex. I'm not a lesbian, Mary.'

'We went through all this last night,' she sighed, cocking her head to one side and smiling at me. 'I made you come, Helen. It's as simple as that.'

'I love your black and white outlook,' I said with a chuckle. ' "You made me come, it's as simple as that." Forget the fact that we're both female, forget the fact that you're a married woman, forget the fact that I'm going through a divorce and –'

'You're creating problems, Helen. Aren't you going to make some coffee? The kettle boiled ages ago.'

'Yes, I suppose so. Would you like a cup?'

'Please.'

Perhaps I should take on a simplistic attitude, I thought as I poured the coffee. Mary was right. She'd licked and sucked me and brought me off, so what was the big deal? The big deal was that Alan had been watching us. It was *our secret*, as Mary had put it. If she discovered that it was far from secret, that my husband had been watching our illicit lesbian act and he might well tell her husband, she'd understand why I was worried. There again, even if Alan did tell Tom, nothing would come of it. Tom wouldn't believe that I'd had lesbian sex with his wife. He'd think that Alan was trying to cause trouble. I had to calm down and relax, I decided, following Mary out onto the patio with the coffees. I had to relax and take control.

'It's hot again,' Mary said, looking up at the clear blue sky. 'I might do some sunbathing.'

'I might put some old shorts on and have a go at tidying up the garden,' I sighed. 'If I leave it for much longer, it'll become a jungle.'

'I'm pleased that we've got to know each other, Helen. I know that we've been to your barbecues and

63

you've been round to us for drinks. But I'm pleased that you and I have become close friends.'

'Rather too close, I reckon,' I returned. 'It's good having you next door, Mary. It's good to have you as a friend. But that's as far as it goes. I made a big mistake last night, and I don't want to repeat it.'

'OK,' she said, grinning at me. 'Just let me know when you need another beautiful orgasm.'

'Mary, I ...' Hearing a noise in the house, I frowned. 'Did you hear that?' I asked.

'Hear what?'

'I thought I heard something. Wait there, I'll take a look.'

I crept through the kitchen into the hall and listened. Noticing that the letters were in a neat pile, I knew that Alan was in the house. I'd definitely tossed the letters onto the table, so he must have looked through them and then stacked them in a pile. What the hell was he up to now? I wondered anxiously. More to the point, where was he? I couldn't have him wandering into the house whenever he felt like it. I loved the idea of him watching me have sex with other men, but I didn't want him in the house. Deciding to have the front door lock changed as soon as possible, I returned to the patio and sat opposite Mary at the table.

'What was it?' she asked me.

'Nothing,' I replied, sure that Alan was not only watching us, but listening. 'I must have imagined it.'

Eyeing the tight patch of white material between her parted thighs as she moved about on the chair, I wondered whether she'd deliberately worn her short skirt to try to lure me into lesbian sex. Noticing a damp patch adorning the crotch of her panties, I knew that she was feeling horny. Did she really love me? I mused fancifully. One thing was for certain, she wanted my tongue between the lips of her young vagina, her orgasming clitoris pulsating within my mouth. But I could never bring myself to lick another girl's pussy.

'Are you going to put your bikini on?' I asked her in the hope of seeing more of her young body.

'My bikini?'

'You said that you might sunbathe.'

'Oh, I see. No, no I never wear a bikini. I like the feel of the sun on my body, so I always sunbathe naked. Are you going to join me, then?'

'What, naked?' I breathed, frowning at her.

'Yes, why not? Your garden is secluded, so no one will see us.'

'I don't know,' I said, wondering whether Alan was still in the house.

Imagining Mary's naked body, I became intrigued. Her young breasts, her ripe nipples, her moist pussy crack . . . It would certainly give Alan something to look at, I thought as my clitoris swelled. With the sun rising in the sky, it was getting hotter by the minute. Where was the harm in sunbathing naked? I pondered. Where was the harm in gazing at Mary's beautiful body? Noticing the dining-room curtains move, I knew that Alan was there. What the hell was the bastard doing in my house? I thought angrily. I'd always known that he wasn't right in his head, but I'd never thought that he'd go creeping around my house and spying on me and . . . I didn't know what to make of him.

'OK,' I said, unbuttoning my blouse and smiling at Mary. I'd give Alan something to think about, I mused. 'Let's go for it. Let's sunbathe naked.'

'Great,' she trilled excitedly, leaping to her feet.

Slipping my blouse off my shoulders, I watched Mary pull her T-shirt over her head and unhook her bra. The cups falling away from her firm breasts, the teats of her brown nipples rising in the relatively cool air of the garden, she lowered her skirt and kicked it aside. She was slim and yet curvaceous, young and fresh and beautiful . . . But I couldn't imagine myself making love with her. To lick and suck another girl's pussy just wasn't in me. As beautiful and sensuous as she was, I wasn't a lesbian. I couldn't love her the way she'd loved me.

Slipping my skirt off, I felt my stomach somersault as she began to pull her white panties down. This had nothing to do with getting a suntan, I mused, feeling the heat of the sun on my back as I removed my thong. My pussy lips swelling, my clitoris calling for attention, this was to do with sex. Maybe I should allow her to love me again, I pondered, imagining her wet tongue working around my solid clitoris, delving deep into my wetting vaginal sheath. What the hell would Alan think if I was to tongue Mary's young vagina?

'God,' I breathed, gazing in awe at the hairless lips of her young pussy. 'You've shaved.'

'I've always shaved,' she returned as a matter of fact as she settled on the lawn. 'I prefer it that way.'

'You look so young,' I said, eyeing the inner lips of her pussy emerging alluringly from her tight sex crack. 'You look like . . .'

'Why don't you shave, Helen? I'm sure you'd like it.'

'I don't think so,' I replied, joining her on the lawn.

'You're reluctant to try anything, aren't you? You should experiment, Helen. Let yourself go and have some fun.'

'Maybe you're right. But I'm still finding my feet after . . .'

'You have beautiful tits,' she said softly, eyeing my ripe nipples. 'You have a beautiful body.'

66

'It's a shame Alan didn't appreciate me,' I sighed, spying at him out of the corner of my eye. He was hiding behind the curtains, watching me. 'Alan didn't want me, sexually or otherwise.'

'He must have been mad. You're beautiful, absolutely beautiful.'

'And I'm a married woman,' I reminded her. 'In fact, we're both married women.'

'Two married women having sexy fun together behind their husbands' backs.'

As she reclined on the soft grass and spread her naked body out beneath the sun, I felt my clitoris stir. With Alan watching, I felt wicked, revengeful. To walk into my house and look through my post was despicable. If he'd wanted to know whether there was any post for him, he should have asked me. All he had to do was phone me and . . . I should have made sure that he'd left his key before walking out on me, I reflected, again thinking of changing the lock. The last thing I wanted was Alan wandering into my house whenever he felt like it. There again, I loved the idea of having a voyeur.

As Alan was lurking in the house, I thought that I should take advantage of his spying on me. Mary's beautiful young body spread out on the lawn, her hairless sex crack seemingly smiling at me, I knew that this was an opportunity to shock Alan. But, was that what I wanted? After ten years of enduring his crazy mind games, I'd thought that I was finally rid of my husband. If I continued to play his weird games, I'd never be free of him. He'd always be there, lurking, watching, spying. He obviously didn't shock easily. And, in my stupidity, I wasn't going to give up easily.

'I really enjoyed last night,' I said rather loudly for Alan's benefit. 'As you said, Mary, only a girl knows how to pleasure another girl. Alan was useless in bed.'

'So, are we going to do it again?' she asked hopefully, propping herself up on her elbows and grinning at me.

'Completely useless,' I continued. 'He'd fumble about, fuck me from behind once a week ... I've never known such a useless man.'

'Shall we do it again now?' Mary persisted excitedly.

'Yes, why not?' Lowering my voice to a whisper, I smiled at her. 'You can lick me, but I don't think I can reciprocate.'

'You've changed your tune,' she trilled. 'After all your comments about not being a lesbian and –'

'Keep your voice down,' I said. 'The neighbours might hear you.'

'I am the neighbours,' she returned with a giggle. 'Would you like me to lick you now? Would you like to come?'

'Yes,' I breathed softly, reclining on the grass with my legs wide apart. 'I want you to give me what Alan could never give me.'

I was doing this was for Alan's benefit, I thought as she settled between my thighs and kissed my fleece-covered outer lips. I wasn't a lesbian. I was doing this purely to shock Alan. The feel of Mary's wet tongue running up and down my open sex crack sending quivers through my womb, I again told myself that I wasn't a lesbian. Mary loved licking my clitoris and sucking my sex milk out of my vagina, and I enjoyed her intimate attention. But, although she'd brought me the best orgasm I'd ever experienced, I wasn't a lesbian. A tongue is a tongue, I mused as she parted the swelling lips of my vulva and licked my open sex valley. Male or female, a tongue is a tongue.

Pondering on shaving my pussy as Mary drove her tongue deep into my tightening vagina, I wondered what Alan was thinking. Perhaps he was wishing that we'd stayed together, I thought dreamily. He could have sneaked home from work and watched me having sex with Mary. He might have taken more interest in me sexually if he'd been turned on by watching another girl lick me to orgasm. Would I have allowed Paul to fuck me while my husband watched? It was pointless reflecting, I decided. It was too late, the marriage was over.

'You taste wonderful,' Mary breathed, lapping up my flowing sex milk. 'God, I love the taste of pussy milk.'

'I've only tasted sperm,' I said. 'I have no idea what pussy juice tastes like.'

'Perhaps you should find out,' she whispered huskily. 'Perhaps you should experiment, live a little and enjoy yourself for a change.'

'No, I – I don't think so.'

The sun warming my naked body, I closed my eyes and tried to lose myself in Mary's intimate attention. She was good, I mused languorously. She knew exactly what to do, exactly how to pleasure a girl. Alan could never have brought me such pleasure, I reflected, recalling his weekly fucking. Mary was soft, warm and gentle in her girl loving. But this was a female licking and sucking between my legs. I wanted to lose myself in my arousal, in her beautiful mouthing and sucking. I had to relax, I thought as she slipped her fingers deep into my creamy-wet vaginal duct and sucked my erect clitoris into her wet mouth. This was sex for the sake of gratifying sex.

Gasping, writhing, I dug my fingernails into the soft grass and arched my back as I neared my orgasm. I could feel my sex milk pumping out of my finger-bloated vagina, my clitoris beginning to pulsate within Mary's gobbling mouth. Opening my legs to the extreme, allowing her better access to the most intimate part of my trembling body, I let out a cry of pleasure as she pressed a fingertip against the tight brown ring of my anus.

'No,' I breathed shakily as her finger drove into the tight duct of my rectum. 'Mary, please . . .'

'Relax,' she murmured through a mouthful of vulval flesh. 'Relax and allow me to love you.'

'No, not there,' I gasped as her finger drove deep into the hot shaft of my rectum. 'God, no.'

She pressed her fingertip harder against my anal ring, finally defeating my sphincter muscles and impaling me. I could feel her finger deep within the tight sheath of my rectum, massaging me there, waking sleeping nerve endings. I'd not wanted this, but . . . but what? I mused as she bent and twisted her finger. I should have stopped her, I thought as she fingered my most private duct. I should never have stripped off and allowed her to have lesbian sex with me. Had I no control over my inner desires?

The incredible sensations driving me wild, I let out a cry of ecstasy as my orgasm exploded within my pulsating clitoris. Mary's fingers pistoning my rhythmically contracting vagina, repeatedly thrusting into my tightening rectal duct, her wet tongue sweeping over the sensitive tip of my orgasming clitoris, she sustained my amazing climax as I gasped and shook violently beneath the summer sun. Lost in the ecstasy of my lesbian-induced pleasure, I imagined licking Mary's vaginal crack, tasting her cream and sucking her ripe clitoris to orgasm. But I wasn't a lesbian.

Again and again, waves of orgasmic bliss rolled though my naked body. I could hear the squelching of my sex milk as she fingered me, the slurping of her

70

mouth as she sucked me. I could feel my anal sphincter muscles gripping her finger as she pistoned my sensitive bottom-hole. I wanted to shave my pussy, I wanted to drink from her vagina, finger her little bottom-hole, suck her clitoris into my mouth and take her to orgasm ... Did I have lesbian tendencies? Or was it that I wanted to shock Alan? Whatever was goading me to reciprocate and suck the pink nub of her solid clitoris to orgasm, I knew that I was weakening. Just once, I mused dreamily as my pleasure began to subside. To taste her creamy sex milk, suck her erect clitoris ... Just once?

Teasing the last ripples of sex from my erect clitoris, slowing her pistoning fingers, she brought me down gently from the most fantastic orgasm I'd ever experienced. I was shaking uncontrollably, whimpering in the aftermath of my lesbian-induced pleasure, and I knew that this wouldn't be the last time I gave my body to her. Licking the sensitive tip of my receding clitoris, massaging deep within my sex ducts, she knew exactly what to do and when to do it. *Only a girl knows how to pleasure another girl.*

'Was that nice?' Mary asked me, her fingers leaving my inflamed sex holes as she sat upright. 'Was it a good one?'

'God, yes,' I gasped, my head lolling from side to side, my naked body trembling uncontrollably. 'That was amazing.'

'I'll do that for you any time you want. The thing is ... It doesn't matter.'

'What were you going to say?'

'Licking you makes me feel so horny, Helen. Horny and ... and very much neglected.'

'I know,' I sighed. 'But I can't ...'

'I feel like I do when I have sex with Tom. I'm always left yearning, wanting.'

The time had come to return the sexual favour, I knew as she lay back on the grass and parted her slender legs. Gazing at the puffy lips of her hairless vulva, her inner labia protruding invitingly from her young sex crack, I noticed a globule of opaque liquid glistening on her pink folds. What did her milk taste like? I mused, again glimpsing Alan out of the corner of my eye. I'd never thought to taste my sex juices. Alan used to enjoy drinking from my pussy, but I'd never dreamed of tasting my own pussy milk.

Settling beside Mary, I leaned over her naked body and sucked her ripe nipple into my hot mouth. Obviously delighting in my intimate attention, she gasped and writhed as I swept my wet tongue over her sensitive milk teat. I couldn't deny that I was also enjoying the experience as I squeezed and kneaded the firm mound of her mammary sphere. Her breasts were small, but well-rounded and hard with beautifully pointed nipples standing proud from the dark discs of her areolae. Sucking hard, mouthing on her sensitive breast bud, I slipped my hand between her parted thighs and stroked the smooth flesh of her outer lips. I was becoming weak in my lesbian arousal.

'God, yes,' she breathed as I ran my fingertip up and down her opening valley of desire. Her lubricious juices of lust wetting my finger, I again wondered what she tasted like. Most men enjoyed lapping up pussy cream, I reflected. And I'd always loved the taste of sperm. Was vaginal milk so very different? Massaging the erect bulb of her clitoris with my fingertip, I wanted her to come. Unable to bring myself to lick her, I could at least bring her pleasure by taking her to a massive orgasm.

'Please,' she breathed as she writhed on the soft grass. 'Please, suck me.' Ignoring her request, I continued to massage the solid nub of her clitoris. I wanted to suck her and taste her but, despite my soaring arousal, I couldn't commit the lesbian act. Alan was still there, hiding, spying, and I knew that I had to do more than masturbate Mary. What did she taste like? I pondered for the umpteenth time. There was only one way to find out, I finally decided. Her ripe nipple leaving my mouth as I sat upright, I moved down and settled between her parted thighs.

Examining her hairless mons, the wet crack of her beautiful pussy, I parted her swollen outer lips and gazed at the intricate folds of inner labia. Her clitoris was huge, stretching its pink hood to the extreme. Her fleshy inner lips unfurling, her pussy milk flowing from her open love hole, I knew that I couldn't miss this opportunity to experience lesbian licking. Just this once, I thought dreamily. Taking the plunge, I kissed the hairless cushions of her outer lips. But I still couldn't bring myself to taste her cream. I could massage her clitoris, finger her tight vagina . . . But I couldn't push my tongue into her sex hole and lap up her vaginal milk. Was there something wrong with me? A tongue is a tongue, so . . .

'I need to come,' she murmured huskily. 'Helen, I need to come.' Parting her outer labia further, I licked my lips. I knew that I had to do this to shock Alan. I had to commit the lesbian act to . . . Why did I want to shock Alan? I wondered. My mind in turmoil, I couldn't determine whether I was about to lick another girl's pussy because I wanted to, or because I was trying to prove something to my husband. Mary was waiting patiently for the caress of my wet tongue, the explosion of orgasm. Alan was no doubt awaiting my lesbian sex act but . . . Hesitating, I didn't know what to do.

Finally pushing my tongue out, plucking up the courage to lick the most intimate part of Mary's young body, I tasted the wet inner folds of her sex crack. Tangy, creamy, arousing ... Her juices were like a drug, and I knew that I was hooked as I lapped fervently between the swollen lips of her vulva. Breathing in the scent of her feminine intimacy, I also knew that Mary and I would enjoy a lesbian relationship for some time to come. She didn't want her husband, I didn't want mine, so what better solution was there other than lesbian love? Was I a lesbian? As I opened her vaginal hole and pushed my tongue into the tight sheath of her pussy, I finally stopped worrying about it.

Moving up Mary's drenched sex valley, I sucked the solid protrusion of her erect clitoris into my mouth and snaked my tongue around its base. She writhed again, gasping beneath the summer sun as I tended to her feminine needs as only another girl could. Lapping, sucking, slurping, I couldn't get enough of her young pussy. Wondering what I'd become as I took her closer to her orgasm, I drove two fingers deep into her tight sex sheath and massaged her hot inner flesh. I was bisexual, I decided as her vaginal muscles tightened around my pistoning fingers. Hard cocks, wet pussies ... Did I want to be bisexual?

Mary came with a violent shudder and a scream of lesbian pleasure. Her pussy milk gushing from her hot vagina as I fingered her, her clitoris pulsating beneath my sweeping tongue, she clung to tufts of my long black hair as I licked and sucked between her open sex lips and sustained her climax. I didn't care about Alan, what he was thinking. All I cared about was giving Mary the pleasure she'd given me. Sixty-nine? I pondered, imagining our naked bodies entwined in lesbian lust, writhing on the lawn as we sucked and licked each other's orgasming clitorises.

The heat of Mary's thighs warming my ears, her hands clutching at tufts of my hair, I knew that, whether I wanted it or not, whether I was a lesbian or not, I wanted Mary's young body.

'Wow,' she breathed as I sucked the last ripples of orgasm out of her deflating clitoris. 'God, Helen. You really know how to please a girl.'

'I'm glad you enjoyed it,' I said, slipping my wet fingers out of her tight vagina and licking my lips.

'Did you enjoy it?'

'Yes, yes very much,' I replied for Alan's ears, the taste of her sex cream lingering on my tongue.

'We'll do it again, then?'

'Yes we will.' Smiling at her, I settled by her side and again glimpsed Alan hiding behind the dining-room curtains. 'We'll definitely do it again.'

'I can't believe that, at long last, I've found a girl to –'

'Don't say too much,' I interrupted her. 'There might be someone in the garden next door. This is our secret, Mary.'

'Yes, of course. I dread to think what Tom would say if he found out about us.'

'What would you say if you discovered that he'd been unfaithful?'

'I suppose I'd accept it,' she sighed. 'I'm no good to him. Not in bed, anyway.'

'He might understand if you had a girlfriend.'

'We did talk about splitting up,' she confessed. 'He knows that I prefer my own sex and I can't give him what he wants. We were going to go our separate ways, but ... Well, we came up with another idea. Also, we have a nice home and we live comfortably so we might as well stay together.'

'What other idea?'

'Just something to keep us both happy.'

'Have you ever thought about sharing a girl with him?' I asked her hopefully.

'What do you mean?'

'Say you knew a bisexual girl who was up for a bit of fun. She could please you both, couldn't she?'

'Funnily enough, Tom and I . . . He thought that I was seeing a girl behind his back, which I wasn't. His idea was for me to bring her home and . . . Anyway, I wasn't seeing anyone.'

'Why don't you suggest it to him?' I asked her, my clitoris stirring at the thought of three in a bed.

'What, you mean . . .'

'You, Tom and me.'

'God,' she breathed. 'You'd want sex with Tom?'

'I'm discovering the real me. I'm bisexual, Mary. To put it bluntly, I like cocks and pussies.'

'I'll have to give it some thought,' she said, grabbing her clothes. 'I can't believe that you'd want to do something like that.'

'Neither can I,' I returned with a giggle as I leaped to my feet and dressed. 'The things I've got up to since Alan walked out have amazed me.'

'I'll ask Tom when he gets home. Actually, Tom and I have a little secret.'

'Oh? What's that?'

'It's nothing important. I'll mention your idea to him, OK?'

'That's great. Just say that we were talking and we came up with the idea. You don't have to tell him that we've had sex.'

'I'd better get back, Helen. Thanks for a lovely time.'

'Thank *you*,' I said with a giggle.

'I'll see you later. I'll let you know what Tom says.'

Finishing dressing as she left, I glanced at the dining-room curtains but couldn't see Alan. Reckoning that he'd gone, I walked into the kitchen and made myself a cup of coffee. That was that, I reflected, not quite able to believe that I'd had full-blown lesbian sex. I'd taken another step along the path to my inevitable debauchery. Debauchery, common whoredom? What lay at the end of the path? I wondered. Sexual gratification? Or tears? I was playing with Tom and Mary's marriage, poking my nose, and my body, into their private affairs. One thing was for certain: I was treading a dangerous path.

I should never have suggested having sex with Tom and Mary, I mused. I was turning into a whore. Having sex with Paul was different. He was single, and I'd split up with my husband. When Alan had walked out on me, I'd not planned to have a relationship with anyone. Although I'd known that sex would inevitably rear its beautiful head at some stage, I suppose I'd envisaged going with a single man, beginning a real relationship.

What I'd suggested to Mary was obscene. Sucking on Tom's cock while she licked my pussy and sucked my clitoris to orgasm . . . The notion turning me on, sending my arousal sky high, I imagined Tom's cock shafting my pussy while I sucked Mary's clitoris to orgasm. The feel of another girl's finger deep inside my bum, massaging my inner rectal flesh, had driven me wild with passion. Would she like to lick me there? I pondered, imagining her wet tongue slipping into my anal hole. Anilingus with another girl?

'God,' I breathed, realising the depth of my depravity. Tom and Mary had been to several of our barbecues and we'd got on quite well. But I'd never dreamed that I'd have sex with them. What was their little secret? I pondered. Did they share girls? To have them both attending my feminine needs would be . . .

I couldn't deny that it would be an amazing experience. What if Alan watched us? Sod Alan, I thought, taking my coffee into the lounge. Alan could take his peculiar mind games to hell.

Sitting in the armchair, I was acutely aware of my wet pussy. Mary had been amazing, I reflected as I sipped my coffee. Her fingers, her tongue . . . Licking and fingering her to orgasm had also been an amazing experience, and one that I'd never forget. Should I shave off my pubic curls? I mused, recalling the soft smoothness of her hairless sex lips. Should I have sex with Mary and Tom? My mind in turmoil again, I didn't know what I wanted. What on earth was their little secret?

Five

After a day spent job hunting, I was feeling despondent. I'd not realised how low the pay was for shop
assistants and bar staff. The problem was that I'd
been used to Alan earning a good salary. I'd been
spoiled, got used to having plenty of money, and now
I was broke. To take a menial job would just about
cover the rent and the bills, but leave me with nothing
for clothes or going out. I was beginning to worry
about money, and I didn't like it. Alan would come
back to me if I asked him, but I'd be admitting defeat.
Besides, I couldn't endure another moment of his
mind games. Taking him back wasn't an option.

I'd not seen Alan for a couple of days, and there'd
been no sign of Paul. Tom and Mary had kept out of
my way and I began to wonder whether they'd
decided against sharing my naked body. It was
probably just as well, I thought. The idea of Tom
shafting my tight pussy from behind while I licked
Mary's creamy-wet crack turned me on no end, but I
wasn't a common whore. Although I'd derived immense sexual gratification from my exploits, there
were limits.

Wondering whether Alan had found another
woman and moved on in life, I knew that I had to
move on. The time had come to make some definite

plans for the future. Living alone in a large house was nice, but I began to wonder whether I should take in a lodger. Maybe two lodgers, I mused as a knock sounded on the back door. The idea of having someone in the house didn't appeal to me, but at least it would bring in some cash.

'Hi, Tom,' I said, opening the door. 'I haven't seen you for a while. Have you been in hiding?'

'No, no,' he replied with a chuckle as he stepped into the kitchen. 'I've been pretty busy at work. But I have today off, so I intend to relax.'

'I wish I had a job,' I sighed. 'I need to earn some money, but . . . I won't bore you with that.'

'What sort of work are you looking for?'

'Anything that pays well. I don't need to earn a fortune, just enough to pay the bills. Do you know of anything?'

'No, sorry. Why don't you go into modelling? Contact one of the men's magazines and –'

'Tom, I'm not a whore.'

'You don't have to be a whore,' he returned, grinning at me. 'I've often thought that, if I were a good-looking woman, I'd earn money from my body. I don't mean prostitution.'

'I'm pleased to hear it.'

'Seriously, Helen. You could earn yourself a fortune. You're attractive, slim, sexy . . .'

'Flattery will get you everywhere, Tom.'

'A friend of mine is a photographer and he seems to do pretty well. He does nude stuff and . . . Would you like me to ask him about it?'

'I'm not good enough,' I sighed. 'Besides, I'm too old. How's Mary?'

'Ah, that's what I came to talk to you about.'

'I thought you'd come round for sex?' I quipped.

'Are you offering?'

'Maybe. Tell me about Mary, first.'

'We're having a barbecue this evening and she wants you to join us.'

'Thanks, I'd like that.'

'Nothing formal, just a few friends and . . . I've just had an idea,' he said, rubbing his chin pensively. 'I'm in line for promotion and I'm doing pretty well financially.'

'And?'

'You want to earn some money, right?'

'Are you going to pay me for sex?' I asked him with a giggle.

'No, no. The thing is, Mary's been talking about getting an au pair girl or someone to come in and do some cleaning.'

'Why doesn't she do her own housework?' I returned. 'I mean, she doesn't go out to work so . . .'

'She's going to study for a law degree, so she'll be kept busy. Helen, I'm not trying to belittle you by offering you a cleaning job. If you're not interested . . .'

'I am interested, Tom. But, earning a few pounds as a cleaner won't pay the bills.'

'It's not only cleaning. There's ironing, cooking . . . Why don't you talk to Mary about it?'

'I suppose I could do it as a fill-in job, just until I find something decent.'

'Mary's bought a maid's outfit.'

'A maid's outfit?' I echoed, frowning at him. 'What on earth has she bought it for?'

'She's hoping to get an au pair, and she reckons that a maid's outfit would be suitable. You know about her liking for her own sex, Helen. I reckon that she wants a pretty girl around the house dressed in a uniform. Would you mind wearing that?'

'Me? Wearing a maid's . . .'

'Don't worry, she won't want sex with you,' he said with a chuckle. 'It's just her little fantasy. I'm out at work all day and she's stuck in the house and she gets lonely. To have someone come in every day would help her out and . . .'

'I don't know, Tom,' I sighed, trying to conceal my delight. 'It all sounds rather weird to me. I can't imagine myself trotting around your house in a maid's uniform.'

'Give it some thought, Helen. We have to go out for an hour, so I'll leave the uniform on the patio table. Just in case you want to try it on.'

'Try it on? Look, I'm not a cleaning woman or a maid. And I certainly don't want to prance about wearing a silly uniform so that Mary can indulge in her fantasy.'

'Sorry, maybe I shouldn't have suggested it. It was only a thought. OK, I'll see you later. We're starting the barbecue at about six o'clock. But, you can come over any time you like.'

'All right, I'll think about it. The maid's outfit, I mean.'

'Really? That's great. Mary would be delighted if you –'

'I'll think about it, Tom. I didn't say I'd do it, OK?'

'OK. Well, I'll see you later.'

As he left, I felt my stomach somersault. The thought of wearing a maid's uniform exciting me, I knew that Mary would want sex with me. She'd want to lick my pussy crack, suck my clitoris to orgasm and . . . My excitement rising, I knew that my duties would include tending to her lesbian needs as well as doing her housework. And I'd get paid for it. She obviously hadn't asked Tom about sharing my body, which was a little disappointing. There again, I didn't really want to go down that road. I'd enjoy Tom's beautiful cock and Mary's tight little pussy, I decided. But not together.

The maid's uniform fitted me perfectly. The black skirt was so short that I hardly had to bend over to display my white cotton panties, and the top accentuated my cleavage beautifully. I was looking forward to starting my new job, but I'd have to wait until Tom wasn't around. Mary would hardly make a move towards me with her husband there. My panties soaking up my pussy milk as I imagined Mary slipping her wet tongue into my hot vagina, I felt a quiver run through my womb. When I'd returned to my house after my sex duties, Tom would call round and fuck me. A maid, a sex slave to Mary and her husband . . . Wondering how much they intended to pay me, I was about to take the uniform off when the phone rang.

'It's me,' Mary said excitedly. 'Have you come to a decision?'

'Oh, er . . . Yes, I . . . I have,' I replied hesitantly.

'And?'

'I'll take the job, Mary. About the money –'

'Can you start now?' she trilled.

'Well, I suppose I could.'

'That's great. Does the uniform fit you?'

'Yes, I've got it on.'

'OK, come round now and you can start.'

She was so excited that she hung up before I could ask her about the money. But, whatever the pay, I reckoned that the job would be fun. Hoping that Tom had gone out, I locked up and went round to Mary's back door. My tight little panties were wetting with my copious flow of pussy milk at the thought of a young lesbian gazing at me as I worked. Would she order me to lick her sex crack? I mused.

83

Would she kneel before me and pull my drenched panties down and suck my outer lips and tongue my love hole?

'Come in,' she invited me, opening the back door. 'Wow, Helen. You look great.'

'Thanks,' I breathed, stepping into the kitchen.

'You look really sexy, Helen.'

'Mary, about the money.'

'We'll talk about that later. First of all, I have to tell you the rules.'

'Rules?' I breathed. 'What do you mean?'

'I want you to call me madam.'

'Madam? Mary, I really don't think . . .'

'And I don't want you to wear panties.'

'I'll take my panties off, but I'm not calling you madam.'

Her smile fading, she frowned at me. 'I wouldn't want to have to use this,' she said sternly, taking a thin bamboo cane from the worktop. 'You'll call me madam at all times, Helen. Now, take your panties off.'

Realising that this was part of her fantasy, I felt my clitoris stir as I slipped my juice-dripping panties off. There was no way I'd allow her to cane me, but the notion excited me. Would she like me to bend over and take a severe caning like a naughty little schoolgirl? I pondered. Standing before her with my naked pussy barely concealed by my short skirt, I wondered what Alan would think if he could see me. I also wondered where he'd got to. He'd not been to the house or spied through the lounge window for a couple of days, and I thought that he might have given up on me. It was a shame really, I mused as Mary admired my naked thighs. I'd rather enjoyed his voyeurism.

'You may begin by washing those cups,' Mary instructed me, pointing to the sink with the cane.

'OK,' I replied, standing at the sink. 'I'm going to enjoy –'

'Don't speak unless you're spoken to,' she snapped, tapping my naked buttocks with the cane. 'And, don't forget to call me madam.'

'Yes, Madam,' I breathed.

There was obviously far more to Mary than met the eye. In all the years I'd known her, I'd never have guessed that she was into this sort of fantasy. I'd had no idea that she was a lesbian, let alone a dirty girl who enjoyed playing at mistress and maid. Taking my panties from the worktop, she held the wet crotch to her face and breathed in my girl-scent. She really was a horny little thing, I thought happily. But I still had no idea how much she intended to pay me for my duties. Was this a real job, or simply a game?

'The master will be down in a minute,' she enlightened me.

'The master?' I murmured, turning and facing her. 'Do you mean Tom? Mary, I thought that you wanted me to –'

'Naughty girl,' she hissed, swiping my naked buttocks with the cane.

'Bloody hell,' I shrieked. 'Mary, for God's sake –'

'Madam,' she returned, again swiping my stinging buttocks with the thin bamboo. 'I will not tolerate disobedience. You will call me madam at all times, do you understand?'

'Yes, Madam,' I replied, unable to believe that she'd caned my bare bottom.

'I'm warning you, girl,' she continued. 'Step out of line, and you'll be punished most severely.'

I enjoyed playing the game, but I wasn't going to allow her to cane me. My naked buttocks stinging like hell, I wondered what Tom thought about her peculiar fantasy. He'd obviously employed me to be

Mary's plaything, but had he realised that she'd order me to take my panties off and then swipe my bare bottom with a cane? Finishing the washing up, I was sure that Mary hadn't told him about our lesbian affair. And I was certain that he'd not told her that he'd fucked me. They were an odd couple, I reflected. But, as long as she didn't use the cane again, I'd be happy to play the game.

'Very nice,' Tom said as he walked into the kitchen a little later. 'Is she behaving herself?'

'Yes, she is,' Mary replied. 'After her training, I'm sure she'll be fine.'

'Obedience and discipline are of paramount importance,' he breathed. 'If she doesn't shape up, a damned good caning will correct her wicked ways.'

Discussing me as if I wasn't there, Tom and Mary, my master and mistress, left the kitchen and went into the lounge. Although I knew that this was a game, I was beginning to feel a little uneasy. They were playing their roles rather too seriously for my liking, and I pondered on leaving. I'd already received two swipes of the cane, and wasn't going to take any more. *A damned good caning will correct her wicked ways* ... Deciding to put an end to the game before things got out of hand, I tried to open the back door to make my escape. To my amazement, it was locked.

'In here, girl,' Mary called.

'Yes, Madam?' I replied, scurrying into the lounge.

'There's a duster on the table. Get on your hands and knees and dust the shelves below the television.'

Grabbing the duster, I felt my arousal soar as I took my position on the floor and jutted my naked bottom out. They could see my bare buttocks, my swollen vaginal lips bulging between my slender thighs, I knew as I began cleaning the shelves. This was only a game, I reminded myself. But, why had they locked the back door? I wasn't in any danger, was I? They were my neighbours, and I knew that I had no need to worry. I was overreacting, I decided. They'd probably locked the door for security reasons rather than to imprison me.

'I'll prepare the correction room,' Tom said, walking into the hallway.

'Mary,' I breathed, wondering what the hell the correction room was as Tom climbed the stairs. 'I don't know what you have in mind, but I'm not going to –'

'Silence, girl,' she hissed, pushing me down with her foot as I tried to stand up. 'I've already told you that you're not to speak unless you're spoken to. You'll be earning fifty pounds for working a couple of hours. There's the cash on the windowsill. If you don't want the job, leave now.'

'I'll stay, Madam,' I said, amazed by the amount of money she'd offered me.

'Good. Now, get upstairs and we'll begin your training.'

I had no idea what to expect as I followed Mary up the stairs. The correction room? I thought anxiously as she directed me to the back bedroom. Begin my training? Fifty pounds for two hours was well worth having, especially if I was to work every day. But I was sure that they couldn't afford that sort of money. No matter how well Tom was doing, he couldn't afford to pay me fifty pounds every day. Three hundred and fifty a week? With that sort of money coming in, I'd be more than happy.

'The box is ready,' Tom said as Mary led me into the room.

'Good,' Mary replied. 'Are you sure that you still want the job?' she asked me.

'Er . . . Yes, Madam,' I breathed softly, gazing at a large wooden box resembling a dog kennel.

'In that case, we'll begin your training.'

What sort of people were they? I mused. I couldn't believe my eyes as I gazed around the room. A row of hooks on the wall supported whips, leather belts, chains, handcuffs . . . An assortment of vibrators lined a shelf and there was a leather-topped table in the centre of the room. In all the years I'd lived next door to Tom and Mary, I'd had no idea that they had a sex room in their house. Not once had they even hinted that they were into perverted sexual acts. Realising that I didn't know them at all, I followed Mary's instruction and dropped to my knees and crawled into the dog kennel.

My head emerging through a hole at the far end of the box, I began to worry as Mary lowered a length of wood across the back of my neck. It was like being in stocks, I thought anxiously. Unable to back out of the box, I realised that my skimpily-covered body was completely defenceless, vulnerable to their every perverted whim. The game had gone too far, but I daren't protest for fear of receiving the cane or the tails of a leather whip across the naked orbs of my bottom. What the hell had I got myself into? I pondered fearfully as someone lifted my maid's skirt up over my back and parted my knees.

'Tom is going to fuck you,' Mary announced as a matter of fact. 'You can't escape, so there's no point in struggling.'

'I've been looking forward to this,' Tom said. 'After all these years living next door to the horny little slut, watching her, admiring her young body, picturing her sweet little crack . . . At last, I'm going to fuck her tight little cunt.'

He'd obviously not told Mary that he'd already

fucked me, I mused. And, no doubt, she'd not told him about our lesbian exploits. They were a weird couple, I again thought as my firm buttocks were parted wide. What had made them think that I'd want to join them in their sex games? Had Tom thought that I was a slut who'd be up for anything? Or had Mary decided that I was a lesbian and would jump at the chance to play the part of her maid? Shit, I thought. I *had* jumped at the chance. But, I'd not expected this.

Listening to movements behind me, I let out a rush of breath as fingers parted the fleshy cushions of my pussy lips and slipped deep into my wet sex sheath. The idea of being abused heightening my arousal as the fingers massaged my hot inner flesh, I again wondered what Alan would think if he could see me. He was missing my most degrading sexual act yet. A husband and wife sexually using and abusing me to satisfy their perverted lust? Alan was missing out, big time. It was a shame really, I thought. The thought of him watching me would have added to my pleasure.

The fingers left my tightening vaginal duct and I closed my eyes as Tom slipped his swollen knob between the creamy-wet petals of my engorged inner lips. What the hell was Mary thinking? I wondered as his bulbous knob journeyed along my hot sex sheath to my ripe cervix. Had they discussed the idea of sharing my imprisoned body? I could feel Tom's balls against my mons, his knob pressing against my cervix, as I pondered on the incredible situation. I couldn't believe that these people were my next-door neighbours. We'd chatted over the garden fence, been to their place for drinks . . . And now I was in their sex den.

As Tom withdrew his solid cock and rammed into my drenched pussy, I reckoned that I was on to a winner. Earning good money for playing the role of a maid was far better than serving in a shop or behind a bar, and far more exciting. Prostitution, I mused. Receiving cash in return for allowing Tom to fuck me, I was a prostitute. It had been such a short time since Alan had walked out on me, I reflected. Never in a million years would I have believed that I'd have sex with Tom, let alone lesbian sex with his lesbian wife. And now I was on my hands and knees in the dog kennel with Tom's cock embedded deep within my hot vagina while his wife watched. What the hell would Alan think if he could see me now?

'She's a tight-cunted little slut,' Tom breathed, grabbing my hips and repeatedly driving his huge cock deep into my sex-drenched vagina. 'I'm going to enjoy having her working for us. I'm going to enjoy fucking her little cunt every day.'

'And I'm going to enjoy training her,' Mary rejoined. 'By the time I've finished with her, she'll jump to attention at the snap of my fingers.'

They must have planned this, I thought as Tom shafted my contracting vaginal duct with his rock-hard cock. He must have gone running back to Mary after he'd fucked me and told her of his idea. She'd then seduced me, completing the second part of their dirty plan. I'd always thought them to be an innocent young couple, faithful and loyal in the early years of their marriage. How wrong I'd been. How deep did their depravity run? I pondered as Mary said that she'd suck Tom's spunk out of my vagina once he'd finished using me.

'Her little bottom-hole looks tight and inviting,' Mary breathed huskily. 'I'd love to slip my tongue into her bottom and taste her.'

'You've always had a thing about girls' bum-holes,'

Tom returned with a chortle. 'Would you like me to fill her arse with spunk?'

'Mmm, yes please. I'll suck your spunk out of her bum and . . .'

'God, I'm coming,' Tom announced as his cock shaft swelled within the tight sheath of my vagina. 'I'm coming.'

I could feel Tom's sperm flooding my vaginal cavern as he gripped my hips and increased his penile shafting rhythm. Fingers ran up my inner thigh as my body jolted with the crude vaginal pistoning. Working their way slowly towards my swollen pussy lips, I knew that it was Mary's sensual touch as she massaged the solid nub of my clitoris. The squelching sound of my sex juices and Tom's sperm resounding around the room, my tensed body rocking back and forth with the crude shafting of my inflamed vagina, I let out a cry of pleasure as my clitoris exploded in orgasm.

A blend of sperm and girl-juice streaming down my inner thighs, my clitoris pulsating in orgasm beneath Mary's massaging fingertips, I knew that I'd be working for my master and mistress on a permanent basis. No doubt Alan had thought that I'd end up broke and beg him to come back to me. Fifty pounds a day? I'd be far from broke. My body shaking wildly as I rode the crest of my orgasm, I couldn't believe the immense pleasure my master and mistress were bringing me. Another first, I thought in my sexual delirium. I'd enjoyed lesbian sex, and was now delighting in having two people attend my feminine needs. There was nothing I needed Alan for now.

Tom continued his vaginal pistoning, his spunk-flow seemingly never ending as his heavy balls battered my mons. Mary's fingertips expertly massaging my orgasming clitoris, her husband's cock pumping sperm deep into my sex duct, never had I known such incredible sexual pleasure. Perhaps Alan and I should have brought someone into the marital bedroom to share our fun? I reflected. Perhaps Paul would have joined us in our bed and spiced up our sex lives.

As Tom drained his swinging balls and Mary massaged the last ripples of sex from my deflating clitoris, I again wondered where my new life was taking me. My orgasm receding, I shuddered my last shudder and breathed heavily in the aftermath of my incredible coming. I'd got what I'd wanted, I mused. I was free of Alan, I was earning money, I'd found immense sexual gratification ... And yet a nagging thought bothered me. I was a prostitute. I'd committed adultery, I'd enjoyed lesbian sex, group sex, and had now plunged head first into prostitution. Did I need to label myself? I wondered as Tom withdrew his deflating cock from my sperm-flooded vagina. I was happy, so what was the problem? But, where was my life taking me?

As Mary pushed her head between my thighs and lapped up the hot sperm flowing from my open vaginal entrance, I felt my clitoris swell again. Expertly licking between the engorged inner lips of my pussy, tonguing my hot sex sheath, sucking out her husband's spunk, she certainly knew how to pleasure a girl. I could feel her hot breath against my vulval crack, her long blonde hair tickling my inner thighs as she worked on my swollen clitoris and sucked at my vaginal entrance. I was being paid for this, I reflected. Prostitution ... Was that so bad?

Listening to the slurping and sucking sounds of sex as Mary drank from my hot vagina, I became aware of movement in front of me. Raising my head and opening my eyes, I gazed at Tom's solid cock waving from side to side as he knelt before me. I was amazed that he'd stiffened so quickly after shafting my tight vagina and pumping my pussy full of his sperm. He was all man, that was for sure. I parted my full lips as he ordered me to suck his cock. Taking his bulbous knob into my mouth, I ran my wet tongue over its silky-smooth surface and breathed heavily through my nose.

Gobbling on his swollen knob, sinking my teeth gently into his veined shaft as Mary tongued my vaginal hole, I pondered on their relationship. Why have a den of debauchery if Mary didn't want sex with Tom? Did they invite couples round for evenings of depraved sex? Or had they created the room purely for my visits? The feel of Mary's wet tongue sweeping over the brown ring of my anus as she yanked the cheeks of my firm buttocks wide apart was heavenly. My juices of desire flowing freely from my gaping sex duct, my clitoris stirring beneath its pink hood, I needed to come again. But questions were nagging me, bothering me.

'Her bottom tastes beautiful,' Mary breathed as she tongued fervently at my anal hole. 'Two beautiful girlie holes to lick and suck. What more could a young lesbian ask for?'

'And what more could a man ask for other than a horny slut's hot wet mouth?' Tom rejoined.

Tom's cock twitched and his knob swelled as I gobbled and sucked like a babe at the breast, and I knew that he wasn't far off his second coming. My entire body quivering, my womb rhythmically contracting, I'd never enjoyed sex so much in all my life. Even with Alan in the early days of our relationship, sex had never been like this. But I'd thought that I'd been in love in those distant days. We'd never fucked, we'd only made love. This was cold loveless sex for the sake of sex. No strings, no ties, no strange moods or mind games . . . This was hardcore illicit sex. Had I found my niche in life?

My mouth flooding with fresh spunk as Tom shuddered and gasped, I breathed heavily through my nose and snaked my tongue around his orgasming knob. I knew that this was my destiny, and I knew that I was now hooked on crude sexual acts. If Alan could see me now, I thought for the umpteenth time as my mouth overflowed and spunk dribbled down my chin. Where was he? I wondered. Was he at work? Perhaps he was trying to find a flat to rent? Or was he planning his next voyeur session? One thing was certain, there was no way he'd be watching my crude act with Tom and Mary.

'God, that was amazing,' Tom gasped as he withdrew his spent cock from my sperm-bubbling mouth. 'Did you enjoy that, girl?'

'Yes, Master,' I replied, licking my sperm-glossed lips.

'Can you manage another spunking, Tom?' Mary asked him, her wet tongue slipping out of my well-salivated bottom-hole. 'I'd like you to fill her arse for me.'

'Please,' I breathed. 'Tom, I don't want –'

'My God,' Mary gasped. 'The insolent bitch dared to speak. The filthy little whore dared to protest . . . And she didn't call you master.'

'You'd better deal with her,' Tom said sternly. 'Deal with her most severely.'

'I'm extremely disappointed,' Mary sighed. 'Not to worry, it's nothing a good whipping won't put right.'

'No, Madam,' I breathed, shakily. 'Please, let me go now. I've played the game and now I want to –'

'Played the game?' she echoed, clambering to her feet. 'I don't employ you to play games, girl.'

'The leather strap or the cat o' nine tails?' Tom asked her. 'Which do you think would fit the crime?'

'The leather strap,' Mary replied. 'A few lashes of the strap should correct her wicked ways.'

Yelping like a dog as the first lash of the strap landed squarely across my tensed buttocks, I knew that there was no escaping my gruelling punishment. With the stock-like wooden bar across the back of my neck and my buttocks jutting out, I was completely defenceless, unable to halt the crude abuse of my trembling body. Squeezing my eyes shut as the leather strap again flailed the stinging flesh of my clenched buttocks, I squirmed and begged my master and mistress for mercy. My cries only served to drive Mary on. She chuckled wickedly and repeatedly brought the strap down across the burning flesh of my naked buttocks with deafening cracks.

A gush of hot urine streaming down my inner thighs, splashing onto the floor between my knees, I'd never been so humiliated in all my life. Tom laughed about my pissing myself as the cracking of the strap resounded around the sex den. Calling me a filthy slut, Mary increased her lashing rhythm, flailing my twitching buttocks harder until my stinging flesh numbed. Tom laughed and said that I'd have to lap up my piss from the floor. What the hell had I got myself into? I again wondered fearfully. The stinging sensation fading, all I could feel was a warm glow as the heat penetrated my flesh and my mistress continued with the merciless thrashing.

'Let that be a lesson to you,' she said, finally halting the assault. 'Now, Tom, as I was saying before the rude little slut interrupted me. I'd like you to fill her arse with spunk.'

'Of course,' he said eagerly, taking his position behind me. 'There's nothing I'd like more.'

I could feel Tom's bulbous knob stabbing at my well-salivated brown ring as he held my glowing buttocks wide apart. I daren't protest, I knew as his glans slipped past my defeated anal sphincter muscles and peered into the dark heat of my rectal canal. I'd never experienced anal sex, never even dreamed of taking a huge cock deep into my rectum. I'd not wanted this, but . . . My tight tube stretching open to capacity as his shaft entered me, I could feel his bulbous knob sinking deep into the very core of my trembling body.

Tom withdrew his rock-hard penis slowly, and then rammed his shaft deep into my anal canal. My body jolting with every thrust of his solid cock, my rectal duct inflating and deflating with the crude shafting, I wondered when I'd be released from the dog kennel. How much longer could Tom go on fucking my sex holes? I wondered in my exhaustion. I couldn't take much more, I knew. My anal ring rolling back and forth along his veined shaft, my bowels pummelled by his bulbous knob, I could feel my anal duct burning.

From a twee housewife to a common whore, my transformation over such a short period of time had been incredible. Fucked, spunked, fingered, thrashed, licked and sucked, used and abused . . . How much deeper would I plunge into the pit of depravity? How much deeper did I want to plunge? I'd never considered myself to be oversexed but, now, I craved crude sexual acts and gratification. Although I couldn't take much more of Tom's shafting, I didn't want him to stop. I'd become a slut.

My rectum finally flooding with Tom's sperm, his creamy lubricant easing the pistoning of his solid cock within my tight anal cylinder, I listened to the squelching sounds of crude sex. His lower belly repeatedly slapping the rounded cheeks of my glowing buttocks, his swinging balls battering my mons, he shafted me with a vengeance as Mary talked about sucking his spunk out of my arse. They were the crudest people I'd ever known. But, enjoying the debased sex, craving more vulgar acts, wasn't I as crude?

Tom finally slowed his anal fucking to a gentle pace. His balls drained for the third time, his shaft deflating within my sperm-laden rectum, he stilled his cock and allowed his knob to absorb the wet heat of my bowels. The delicate tissue of my inflamed anal ring hugging the root of his sperm-slimed rod, I was sure that he'd not be able to give me another shafting. Virile as he was, I knew that he couldn't raise another erection.

'I'm thirsty,' Mary said eagerly as Tom withdrew his flaccid shaft from my spunked rectum with a loud sucking sound. 'Let me suck your cream out of her little bum-hole.'

'Go ahead,' Tom said, moving aside as Mary took her position behind me. 'Suck her arse dry.'

Parting my glowing buttocks to the extreme, opening the once sacrosanct entrance to my rectal duct, Mary locked her lips to my anus and began her crude sucking. I could feel the sperm leaving my anal tube as she repeatedly sucked and swallowed. A cocktail of spunk and girl-juice oozing from my vaginal opening and streaming down my inner thighs, I knew that I'd reached the bottom of the pit of depravity. As Mary's tongue entered my rectum, licking the wet walls of my anal canal, Tom knelt before me and offered his dripping knob to my gasping mouth. I could plunge no deeper into the mire of debauched sex, could I?

Parting my lips, I took Tom's purple plum to the back of my throat and sank my teeth gently into his swelling shaft. His fleshy rod tasted bitter, tangy, salty. Would he shaft my inflamed rectum again? My thoughts were riddled with filth. But I couldn't help myself, I knew as I savoured the heady taste of his slimed cock. I was desperate for crude sex, hooked on obscene sexual acts. My transformation from a loyal and faithful wife to a common slut was complete.

To my amazement, Tom managed to flood my mouth with another load of creamy spunk. With Mary sucking sperm from one end of my trembling body and her husband filling me from the other end, I knew that I'd discovered my sexual heaven. My clitoris responding beneath Mary's massaging finger-tips, I was fast nearing another heavenly orgasm. How many times could I come? I mused in my sexual ecstasy. How much more crude sex could I endure? How many times could Tom come?

'You're a filthy slut,' Tom breathed, rocking his hips and fucking my mouth as his balls drained. 'A dirty filthy little slut.'

'She's a tasty little slut,' Mary rejoined, her tongue leaving my bottom-hole and moving down to my gaping vaginal entrance.

'I'm going to spunk your mouth every day,' Tom said, clutching my head and repeatedly ramming his swollen knob to the back of my throat as his spunk flow began to stem. 'I'll fuck all three of your tight holes every day. You're a filthy slut, and you'll be treated like a filthy slut.'

Tom's words firing my libido, I imagined donning my maid's uniform every day and visiting the sex room. A filthy slut? I mused. He was right, I was a filthy slut. As he slipped his cock out of my sperm-brimming mouth, I swallowed hard. I'd had all three holes fucked and spunked, I mused as Tom released the wooden bar and ordered me to get out of the box. Fucked, spunked, fingered, licked, whipped, used and abused . . . Slut. Prostitute. Whore.

Clambering to my feet with sperm gushing from my inflamed vagina, I leaned against the wall to steady my trembling body. Dizzy in the aftermath of debauched sex, I needed to rest. My body aching, quivering uncontrollably, I hoped that the beautiful abuse was over as Tom left the room. Grinning at me, Mary ordered me to collect the money from the lounge and leave. Although I was exhausted, I felt a little disappointed. I'd desperately needed another orgasm, but my master and mistress had finished with me. They'd satisfied their lust for crude sex, for the time being.

'Be here tomorrow at ten o'clock,' Mary instructed me as I followed her down the stairs. 'And I want you shaved, do you understand?'

'Yes, Madam,' I murmured, grabbing the cash from the lounge.

'If I find one trace of a pubic hair, you'll be whipped. Do you understand?'

'Yes, Madam.'

'Good,' she breathed, leading me into the kitchen and opening the back door. 'Now, get out.'

Taking my panties from the work top and heading for the safety and security of my house, I couldn't believe what I'd been through. My buttocks stinging, sperm streaming down my inner thighs in rivers of milk, I was completely exhausted. Closing the back door, I went into the lounge and flopped onto the sofa and tried to come to terms with what I'd endured. I'd earned fifty pounds, I thought happily. But I'd also behaved like a common whore. *You're a filthy slut, and you'll be treated like a filthy slut.* Recalling Tom's words, I again wondered what Alan would think of me if he discovered the shocking truth. Whore, slut, tart ... Closing my eyes and drifting in sordid dreams as sleep gripped me, I was sure that Alan was moving on in life. He wouldn't bother me again, would he?

Six

It was mid afternoon when I was woken by a noise. Sitting upright on the sofa as sleep left me, I looked up at the ceiling as I heard a dull thud upstairs. Slipping my panties on, I knew that it was Alan poking about in my bedroom. What the hell was he looking for? I wondered angrily. I should have changed the front door lock. I was about to shout and confront him when I heard him descending the stairs. I didn't want to answer a barrage of questions about my maid's uniform, so I lay on the sofa and feigned sleep as he entered the room.

Watching him through my eyelashes as he leaned over and pulled my short skirt up, I wondered what he'd think of my sperm-soaked panties. It was none of his business, I reminded myself. This was my life, and he was no longer a part of it. And, this was my house. His audacity amazed me as he pressed his fingertips into the swell of my wet panties. I didn't want him in my house, let alone lifting my skirt up and groping between my legs. He obviously hadn't moved on, I reflected as he massaged my vulval lips through the wet material of my panties. Would he ever leave me in peace?

I couldn't believe what he was doing as he unzipped his trousers and hauled out his erect cock.

Standing by the sofa, towering above me, he ran his hand up and down the length of his veined shaft. Surely, he wasn't going to wank and spunk over me? I wondered. What the hell did he think he was playing at? He'd always been a peculiar man, but this wasn't like him at all. Had my maid's uniform turned him on? I mused. Or had the feel of my spunk-soaked panties sent his arousal soaring?

Breathing heavily, he stood with his cock above my head and increased his wanking rhythm. What would he say if I opened my eyes and asked him what the hell he thought he was doing? Didn't he think that his spunk raining over my hair and face would wake me? I didn't know what to do, whether to throw him out of the house or wait to see just how far he'd go. He'd not had a chance to play his voyeur games for a while, and I reckoned that his libido had soared out of control. He'd probably been hovering outside the lounge window hoping to watch me get fucked. Seeing me sleeping on the sofa, he'd taken the opportunity to search my bedroom and then . . . And then spunk over me?

Moaning softly, stifling his gasps, he finally pumped out his white spunk. The male liquid splattering my long black hair, raining over my face, I somehow managed to remain perfectly still. Parting my lips slightly, I allowed his spunk to splatter into my mouth. I'd not thought that I'd ever taste my husband's sperm again. Salty, creamy, fresh . . . He'd never given me a facial. In the early days of our marriage, I'd loved sucking his spunk out of his cock, but I'd never enjoyed a good facial. Another first, I reflected as his sperm-flow began to stem.

He was weird, I thought as he brought out the last of his sperm. Searching my bedroom, wanking and spunking over me . . . How far would he go? I again

102

wondered. How far did I want him to go? I had to admit that, although it was weird, I was enjoying this particular game. I'd never seen him wank before, I'd never known him to be so sexual. Finally unable to keep still as his spunk landed on my eyelids, I sat upright and wiped my face with the back of my hand.

'God,' I breathed as he dashed out of the room. 'What the hell . . .' Hearing the front door close, I decided not to change the lock. I didn't want Alan wandering into the house and searching my bedroom, but I rather liked the idea of him spunking over me. I'd feign sleep again, I thought, climbing the stairs to the bathroom. Washing my face, I imagined pretending to be drunk. Alan would come into the lounge and find me on the floor with my legs apart and my crack open. He'd fuck me in my drunken stupor and fill me with his spunk. Was that what I wanted? I was supposed to be moving on in life, I reminded myself as I went into my bedroom.

I was about to change my clothes and do the washing when I noticed that the linen basket had been moved. What the hell had Alan been looking for? I wondered, tipping the dirty clothes onto the bed to sort through them. There wasn't one pair of dirty panties in the pile, and I immediately realised that Alan had taken them. He was weird, to put it mildly. What the hell did he want my soiled panties for? Perhaps he wanted to sniff them while he wanked, I thought as the doorbell rang.

Trotting down the stairs, I wondered whether Mary had come round to check up on me. Maybe Tom wanted to give me another anal shafting. Looking down at my maid's uniform as the bell rang again, I imagined Paul lifting my short skirt and fucking me. My mind was riddled with thoughts of crude sex and, again, I couldn't believe how much I'd changed since Alan had walked out on me. Finally opening the door to find Alan standing on the step, I felt despondent. What the hell did he want now? Did he want to wank and spunk over me again? He had a bloody nerve.

'Yes?' I breathed. 'What do you want?'

'I was just passing,' he replied, looking me up and down. 'Are you all right? You look –'

'I've never been better,' I cut in as he followed me through the hall to the lounge. I had no idea what to say as I ran my fingers through my spunked hair. 'I'm rather busy, so . . .'

'What's that white stuff in your hair?' he asked me. 'And why are you wearing that uniform?'

'I went to a fancy dress party last night. I didn't get home until this morning and I haven't had time to change.'

'That's not spunk in your hair, is it?' he persisted.

'It's hand cream, Alan,' I returned. 'I squeezed the tube and it splattered over me. Not that it's any of your business.'

'Don't be like that, Helen,' he sighed, plonking himself in the armchair. 'I've only called round for a chat, just to make sure you're OK. You could at least be civil.'

'Civil? You come round here asking me whether I have spunk in my hair, and you expect me to be civil?'

'I'm sorry, I was only joking.'

'Well, I don't find it funny. Anyway, what do you want? Have you found a flat yet?'

'No, not yet. I'm staying at my mum's for a while. So, what have you been up to? Have you done anything interesting?'

'Interesting?' I echoed, recalling my time with Tom and Mary. 'No, not really.'

'Have you got a man friend?'

'Alan, I don't want to talk about my private life. We're getting divorced and –'

'It seems funny sitting here in my old armchair chatting with you. We had some good times together, Helen. It's a shame that it ended.'

'Yes, it is a shame. I can't remember how many times you ended it by walking out on me.'

'I know, but we always got back together.'

'Not this time, Alan. What is it you want from me? It seems that I'll never be rid of you.'

'I miss you, Helen. Shall I tell you what went wrong?'

'I know what went wrong,' I sighed. 'Your peculiar moods and . . .'

'I reckon that we should have worked on our sex life. I miss having sex with you, making love with you. Do you miss sex?'

'No, I don't.'

'You have got a man friend, then?'

'Alan, I'm busy. I don't want to talk to you about sex. Or anything else, for that matter.'

'OK, I'll leave you to get on,' he said, leaping to his feet and heading for the hall. 'As I said, I was just passing and thought I'd make sure that you're all right.'

'Of course I'm all right,' I snapped, following him to the front door. 'I hear that you met Tom in the pub the other evening.'

'Yes, we had a few beers and a chat.'

'What did you chat about?'

'I thought you didn't want to talk to me?'

'I just wondered what Tom had to say.'

'Nothing, really. I told him about my new girl-friend and we had a few beers.'

'You've found someone?'

'Yes, I have. Are you jealous?'

'Far from it, Alan,' I breathed, opening the front door. 'If anything, I'm pleased.'

'She's good in bed, Helen. She loves –'

'I'm sure she is. Good bye, Alan.'

Closing the door as he left, I couldn't understand how he'd had the audacity to spunk over me and then chat to me as if nothing had happened. But there was no understanding Alan. He was deranged, weird, peculiar . . . He was also uncharacteristically sexual. Stealing my dirty panties and wanking over me? Was that something he'd wanted to do during our marriage? Perhaps he was right and we should have worked on our sex life. There again, there was nothing we could have done to save the marriage. Other than seek help for his weird psychological problems.

After a shower, I changed into a miniskirt and blouse and made myself a sandwich. The morning's events with Tom and Mary had been amazing, exciting, and extremely satisfying. And Alan's spunk raining over my face had fired my arousal. But I now felt bored. The evening looming, I had nothing to do, nowhere to go, and I began to wonder whether I should invite Paul round for sex. Hadn't I had enough sex for one day? I reflected. No, I could never have enough sex. Sure that Alan was planning to spy through the lounge window that evening, I wanted to shock him. Two men? I pondered. Two cocks fucking my sex holes, spunking in my mouth and . . . What the hell was I turning into?

Pondering on Tom and Mary's sex room, I still found it difficult to believe that I'd known them for so long and yet I'd had no idea what they were like. They'd always come across as a quiet couple. I'd been amazed by Tom's revelation that his wife was a lesbian and . . . They must have planned my seduction, I again thought. Tom had called round to test the water, make sure that I was up for sex. And then Mary had come to see me and enticed me into lesbian sex. It was a good job that Alan didn't know what they were like. Knowing him, he'd be round there trying to screw Mary. Either that or wank over her and give her a facial.

The evening fast approaching, my despondency rising, I was about to phone Paul when the doorbell rang. Standing by the lounge window, I gazed through the net curtains expecting to see Alan hovering on the step. To my relief, it was the lad from next door. He was about eighteen and not bad looking. But, what did he want? I didn't really know the neighbours on that side as they'd only recently moved in. Perhaps he'd come to invite me round for a drink with his parents, I mused, heading for the hall. Perhaps Alan had sent him round to fuck me?

'Hi,' I breathed, smiling at him as I opened the door.

'Oh, hi. I'm sorry to trouble you. I've kicked my football over the fence.'

'We'd better go and look for it,' I said, eyeing his tight jeans. 'I'm Helen, by the way. Come through to the garden.'

'Pleased to meet you. I'm Dave. Sorry we've not been round to introduce ourselves. It's just that mum and dad are always working.'

'That's OK. I should have been round to your place, but I've been rather busy.'

'And I'm sorry about the football. Actually, it was my mate,' he sighed, following me out to the patio. 'I told him not to kick it so high, but he wouldn't listen.'

'It doesn't matter,' I said with a chuckle. 'The garden's become a mess since my . . . I just haven't had the time to do anything out here.'

'I've been doing our garden,' he said, retrieving his football from beneath a bush. 'Mum and dad work long hours, so I've been elected as the gardener.'

'They're lucky to have you. I wish I had someone to –'

'I'll have a go,' he interrupted me. 'I'm at college and I could do with some extra cash.'

'That would be great, Dave. If the garden's left for much longer, it'll become a jungle.'

'I enjoy gardening. I'd love to have a go.'

'I can't afford to pay you much, I'm afraid. You see, I'm single and ... What I mean is, I don't have much money.'

'A couple of quid an hour would do. It's better than nothing.'

'OK, two pounds an hour.' A wicked idea coming to mind, I grinned at him. 'I don't suppose you're free this evening?'

'I'm free now. I'll go and get changed and I'll be back'

'Good. You can go through the bushes at the end of the garden rather than go round to the front door. There's a hole in the hedge.'

'Right, I'll be back in a while.'

Watching him disappear into the bushes, I knew that I was onto a good thing. Young, fresh, muscular, good looking ... Dave was going to be my next sexual conquest. I was beyond caring about such labels as slut and prostitute. Whatever I'd become, I was enjoying my life to the full. With money coming in from my job with Tom and Mary and my rent halved, I had no need to worry about finances. And I now had a fit young gardener working for me. Things were looking good, I thought happily.

Returning to the house, I slipped my panties off in readiness to seduce young Dave. Did he like older women? I pondered as I tossed my panties onto the kitchen work top. Was he a virgin? I had experience, I thought gleefully. I knew how to initiate Dave into the delights of crude sexual acts, I knew exactly what to do with his solid cock. Shit, I thought. I had a hell of a lot of experience. I could feel my pussy milk seeping between the engorged inner lips of my sex crack as I returned to the garden. The summer air wafting up my short skirt, cooling my vulval flesh, I felt sexually alive as never before. Had Dave ever tasted a girl's vaginal cream? My clitoris swelling at the thought of the young lad's tongue entering my wet sheath, I grinned as he emerged from the bushes wearing shorts.

'Hi, Helen,' he said as he walked across the lawn. 'I'm ready.'

'So am I,' I breathed huskily.

'Where would you like us to start?'

'Us?' I breathed. 'What do you mean?'

'My mate's coming to give me a hand. His name's Brian.'

'Oh, I see. Er . . . How about doing some weeding?' I asked him. 'There are plenty of tools in the shed.'

'Right, I'll get started.'

'I'll sit here on the patio and enjoy the evening sun. I might even have a sleep. I was up late last night.'

'I won't disturb you,' he said as I lay on the sun bed.

Brian emerged from the bushes wearing shorts and nothing on top. He was a muscular lad with a crop of blond hair, and I couldn't help wondering how big his cock was. The evening wasn't going to be dull after all, I mused happily, reclining on the sun bed and parting my thighs just enough to expose the crack of my vulva. No man would escape me, I decided. No visitor to my house would leave without quenching my thirst for sexual gratification. Parting my thighs further, I waited in anticipation for one of the boys to spot my tight pussy crack. To suck on two swollen knobs and gulp down two loads of teenage spunk would be heaven, I thought dreamily. Things certainly were looking good.

Brian nudged Dave and whispered something to him, and I knew that my pussy slit had been noticed. The evening sun warming me, I half closed my eyes and watched my potential lovers through my lashes. Overwhelmed by a feeling of wickedness, desperate to commit the most degrading sexual acts imaginable, I allowed my thighs to part further. The boys whispered and sniggered, but I doubted that they'd make a move. Wondering how to entice them, to seduce them, I closed my eyes fully as Dave walked across the lawn towards me.

'Are you sleeping?' he whispered. Remaining silent, I wasn't sure what to do. He was obviously eyeing my pussy crack, but he might not dare to touch me there for fear of waking me. Stirring, moaning softly through my nose, I parted my thighs wide. He obviously thought that I was in a deep sleep as he stroked the swollen lips of my vulva. Running his finger up and down my slit, he began to massage the solid nub of my clitoris. The time had come to instigate crude sex, I decided.

'Oh,' I gasped, opening my eyes and lifting my head.

'I was just . . .' he began, backing away. 'I thought . . .'

'I know what you were just doing,' I said, smiling at him. 'Now that you've started, you'd better carry on.'

'What? You mean . . .'

'I mean, carry on with what you were doing to me.'

He obviously couldn't believe his luck as I lay back and parted my thighs to the extreme. As Brian settled one side of the sun bed and Dave the other, I felt a quiver run through my contracting womb as they ran their hands up and down my inner thighs. My arousal climbing to frightening heights, I couldn't believe how well things were going, and I began to wonder whether Alan had set this up. But I was sure that he knew nothing about it. He wouldn't have been in touch with the lad from next door and arranged my seduction, I knew as fingers slipped between my pussy lips and drove into the wet heat of my vagina. Alan couldn't even spy through the lounge window without my seeing him, let alone set me up with two teenage lads.

Hands slipping beneath my blouse and kneading the firm mounds of my breasts, fingers massaging deep inside the hugging sheath of my hot vagina, my solid clitoris caressed by more fingers, never had I known such exquisite sensations. My entire body trembling as the boys expertly tended my most feminine needs, I knew that this was only the beginning of an evening of rampant sex. Two teenage boys with rock-hard cocks to satisfy me, Tom and Mary's sex den next door . . . I'd definitely found my niche in life.

'How far do you want us to go?' Dave asked me.

'As far as you like,' I murmured dreamily. 'I'm yours for the taking.'

'Wow,' he breathed. 'You're some woman.'

Again thinking back over the short time since Alan had walked out on me, I thought my transformation inconceivable. I'd almost forgotten about my young body, my firm breasts and my tight pussy. Having been virtually neglected for years, used as a partner in psychological war games, I'd rarely given sex a

111

thought. Wearing drab clothes, concealing my feminine form, I'd stagnated beyond belief. Mary wasn't stagnating, I thought as more fingers entered the tight sheath of my vagina. And Tom wasn't playing mind games. Sharing their bodies with others, enjoying all aspects of sex to the full, they made a good couple.

Recalling my teenage years as fingers unbuttoned my blouse and lifted my bra clear of my firm breasts, I thought of my first sexual experience. A teenage lad, fumbling in his inexperience, had taken me behind the bushes on the common and pulled my knickers down. He'd never seen a pussy crack before and I felt proud to show him. He touched me, ran his fingers up and down my crack and made me quiver all over. And now, all these years later, two teenage lads were exploring my hot body. Did they know what to do? I mused dreamily. Were they experienced in the fine art of pleasuring a girl?

'Are you any good at sucking cock?' Dave asked me unashamedly.

'I think I'm good,' I replied. 'Why don't you find out?'

'Both at once?' Brian rejoined.

'OK, both at once.'

Sitting upright as the boys stood either side of the sun bed, I watched them tug their shorts down. Their beautiful organs catapulting to attention, their heavy balls rolling, I couldn't believe how big their cocks were. My mouth watering, I licked my lips and ordered them to pull back their foreskins and show me their purple knobs. Eagerly complying with my dirty request, exposing their ripe plums, they moved closer and offered their knobs to my open mouth.

I wasn't surprised to hear a noise emanate from the house as I grabbed a solid cock in each hand. Alan was obviously lurking, watching, spying. He'd not seen me enjoying two cocks before, and I couldn't help but grin as I noticed the dining-room curtain move. I again pondered on changing the front-door lock, but I was in two minds. Wanking the boys' rock-hard shafts, I kissed each swollen knob in turn. I loved the idea of Alan watching me, but it was getting out of hand. Wandering into the house whenever he liked, rummaging though my clothes and stealing my dirty panties ... Where would his voyeurism end? In tears?

Pushing my tongue out and tasting each purple plum, I knew that Alan had a perfect view of my debauched act. But I didn't know what he was thinking. From the day he'd first spied through the lounge window and watched me masturbate, I'd had no idea of his thoughts. I'd been his loyal and faithful wife for ten years. Did he feel no jealousy? He'd lost his wife, his home ... And all he'd gained was the pleasure of watching me get fucked and spunked by different men. I didn't understand him. There again, I'd never understood him, his thoughts, his peculiar ways. What did he want, what was his goal? Did he aim to spend the rest of his life watching me suck cocks and get fucked? I no longer cared what Alan did or thought, but my intrigue was growing.

Taking the two purple knobs into my sperm-thirsty mouth, I savoured the beautifully salty taste. The boys gasped, their legs visibly wobbling, as I ran my wet tongue around their swollen cock-heads. My view of Alan had been blocked by Brian, but I knew that he was still there. Was his cock hard? Was he wanking? For some reason, I wanted to let him know that I knew of his voyeurism. I wanted him to know that I was deriving immense pleasure from distressing him. But, was he distressed? I reckoned that he was enjoying this as much as I was.

I knew that, at some point, my intrigue would get the better of me and I'd confront Alan. What the hell would he say? I pondered as I gobbled and mouthed on the lads' beautiful knobs. Would he try to deny it? He couldn't deny wanking and shooting his spunk over me, I knew. That was the extent of his sex life, I mused as the boys neared their orgasms. Alan hadn't found another woman, he wasn't enjoying sex with anyone except himself. Wanking, that was his sex life. Wanking as he watched me enjoying my sex life was all he had left.

My mouth flooding with the boys' fresh sperm, I moaned softly through my nose and repeatedly swallowed hard. The two orgasming knobs bloating my mouth, stretching my lips wide, spunk overflowing and running down my chin, I wanked the solid cock-shafts and gobbled for all I was worth to sustain the trembling boys' pleasure. This was real sex, I thought in my frenzied gobbling and swallowing. This was something I could never have had with Alan.

Draining the last of the spunk from the boys' heaving balls, a thought struck me. Alan was always hanging around my house. He let himself in, went through my post, stole my panties, spied through the lounge window at me, hid in the dining room . . . He must have been living nearby, I mused. His mother lived miles away, a good hour's drive. Alan wouldn't sit in his car around the corner and keep walking to the house. He may have taken some time off work to spy on me, but I instinctively knew that he was living nearby.

'You're amazing,' Dave said, breaking my reverie. 'With you living next door, I'm going to be . . .'

Slipping the knobs out of my mouth, I looked up at Dave. 'Living next door to me, you'll be at my beck and call,' I interrupted him. 'You're my gardener, you work for me.'

'The best job I could wish for,' he said with a chuckle, nudging his friend.

'I'd like you to get on with the gardening now,' I said, licking my sperm-glossed lips.

Grinning as the lads pulled their shorts up and got back to work, I savoured the taste of their teenage sperm lingering on my tongue. My arousal soaring high, I decided to order them to fuck me before they left. But, first, I wanted to deal with Alan. Should I confront him? I pondered. Should I walk into the dining room and ask him what the hell he thought he was doing? There again, I knew Alan of old. He'd only come out with some lie or other, say that the front door was open and he wanted to speak to me about something.

Wandering into the kitchen and grabbing the phone, I knew that I was now playing silly mind games as I pretended to make a call. Alan would have no trouble hearing me from the dining room as I made out that I was talking to a friend. But I'd not formulated a plan and didn't really know what to say. Chatting about the weather and arranging a shopping trip into town, I came up with an idea.

'Yes, I would take Alan back,' I said rather too loudly. 'The thing is, he now has someone else. I don't know who she is, but he said that he has another woman. No, he didn't say any more that than. That's what I thought. I reckon that he's been seeing her for a long time, that's why he left me. OK, I'll be in touch. Yes, I will. Bye.'

Replacing the receiver, I had no idea what my plan was. What was I trying to achieve? Alan now thought that I wanted him back and he'd pester me rather than leave me alone. I was becoming confused in my

115

confusing game, lost in some kind of fantasy world. Tom and Mary's sex room seemed like a fantasy, and I wondered whether I was dreaming. Would I wake up to find Alan next to me in the marital bed? The taste of sperm on my red lips was proof enough that this was no dream.

Watching the boys through the kitchen window, I again wondered where my life was taking me. Alan was hiding in the dining room, I'd just sucked two teenage cocks and swallowed a deluge of fresh sperm ... There was no disputing the fact that I was a fully-fledged slut, but that didn't bother me. It was the future that concerned me. Alan's continual spying, searching the house, stealing my dirty panties ... Hearing the front door close, I knew that he'd made his escape. I also knew that, within minutes, he'd ring on the bell and say that he just happened to be passing.

It had been a long day and I'd enjoyed some incredibly crude sex. But I still wanted more. Was there no quenching my insatiable thirst for spunk? My clitoris stirring within my wetting sex crack, my nipples rising proud from my areolae, I knew that I'd have to have the boys before the evening was over. Their hard cocks fucking my tight little pussy, filling me with their creamy spunk ... Would they like to arse-fuck me? As I wandered into the hall, the doorbell rang. I took a deep breath.

'Yes?' I sighed, finding Alan on the step.

'I was just –'

'Passing?' I cut in.

'Yes, that's right.'

'And you thought you'd call in to make sure that I'm all right?'

'Well, yes. Actually, I need to talk to you.'

'What about?'

'The future.' He walked past me into the hall and went into the lounge. 'I think it's time to discuss the future,' he said, turning and facing me as I followed him.

'What future?' I asked him. 'What are you talking about?'

'Helen, I know that you want me back. I've heard that you –'

'Alan, I –'

'Please, just listen to me. I know that you want me back so there's no point in denying it. I heard it from the horse's mouth, so to speak.'

'Well, you heard wrong.'

'I know what you've been up to since we split up. I know about the men you've been entertaining.'

'Men? What men?'

'Helen, let's not play silly games.'

'You're a fine one to say that,' I quipped.

'Yes, I know. Look, we were good together. With the way you are now, we could be even better.'

'Alan, I have no idea what you're talking about. The way I am now?'

'You know what I mean. I've seen you, Helen.'

'Seen me doing what? Look, I have things to do. I don't know what you're talking about or what it is you want.'

'I want us to get back together.'

'No,' I returned firmly. 'I put up with you for years. Your funny moods, your weird mind games, walking out on me . . . That's the last thing I want.'

'Can we at least talk about it?'

'What, your funny moods? No, we can't. I think you'd better leave, Alan.'

Following him to the front door, I couldn't understand why I'd played such a stupid game. All I'd done was given him hope, encouraged him. I had no real direction in life, I mused, opening the door for him. Once the divorce was through, I'd be rid of him for good. I'd change the door lock and keep the lounge curtains drawn. Closing the door as he left, I slid the bolt across. The game had come to an end.

Returning to the garden, I was disappointed to find that the boys had gone. Maybe they'd heard me talking to Alan and had thought it best to leave. I'd ruined what could have been a good evening, I reflected dolefully. No, Alan had ruined what could have been a brilliant evening. But I'd had a good day, enjoyed plenty of hard cold sex, had my fill of fresh spunk ... Tomorrow would be even better, I was sure. I'd be working for Tom and Mary, earning another fifty pounds – and enjoying several massive orgasms.

Opening the fridge, I eyed the bottle of chilled white wine. I'd stop drinking tomorrow, I decided, taking the bottle and pulling the cork. It was only wine, I mused, filling a glass. It wasn't as if I was turning into an alcoholic. I was a nymphomaniac, I thought, chuckling inwardly. But not an alcoholic. It was a shame that Alan had never enjoyed pubs, I reflected. We could have walked down to the local on summer evenings and met people, made some new friends. There again, who'd want to become friendly with Alan?

Whatever I'd become, however deep I'd plunged into the pit of depravity, I was enjoying my life. I'd got to know Tom and Mary very well, I thought, again recalling my time in their sex room. Had they set the room up just for me? I wondered. Or did they invite other people round for evenings of debauchery? Mary had said that they were more like brother and sister. She'd lied to me, tricked me ... They'd both lied through their teeth, I reflected. But I wasn't complaining. Apart from Alan and his continual games, my life was looking good. I'd no longer allow him to play his games, I thought, locking up and climbing the stairs. His voyeurism had come to an end. And my sex life had just begun.

Seven

I was about to don my maid's uniform and start work at Tom and Mary's house when I found a letter on the doormat. It was from Alan's solicitor. Even though Alan had said that he'd wanted us to get back together, he was obviously still going ahead with the divorce. But that was his peculiar way, I reflected. This was all a big bluff and he no doubt hoped that I'd take him back before the divorce proceedings had reached the point of no return. Things were moving on, so I went into town and found myself a solicitor.

She was a nice woman, understanding and very helpful. She said that I'd have no worries about the house as it belonged to my grandmother. There was no way that Alan could get his hands on the property. Although I already knew that, it was nice hearing it from a professional person. We'd have to share the furniture, but that didn't bother me. Knowing Alan, he'd not want anything from the house.

Walking home, I felt that I'd achieved something. Rather than doing nothing while Alan was seeing a solicitor, I'd made a positive move towards ending the marriage. The next step was to have the front door lock changed so I rang a local locksmith the minute I got home. He said that he could fit me in at four o'clock, giving me plenty of time to earn another fifty pounds by playing Tom and Mary's sex games. Changing into my maid's outfit, I felt that I'd taken control of my life. The divorce was going ahead, Alan would no longer be able to walk into my house uninvited, and I was earning reasonable money. And, I had a couple of fit young gardeners.

I finally got to Tom and Mary's at eleven o'clock. Mary was furious and asked me why I was an hour late. I tried to explain about the solicitor, but she ranted and raved and wouldn't let me get a word in. I didn't see that it really mattered about the time, but she said that she had things to do and didn't want to have to stand around waiting for me. I could hear Tom moving around upstairs and reckoned that he was preparing the correction room for my visit. Was I to be thrashed?

Mary was wearing a red miniskirt and she looked extremely attractive. But she was far from the sweet girl next door I thought I'd known for several years. With the mood she was in, I wondered whether to forget the job and go home. There was no way I was going to be whipped again, I decided as I was about to leave. Grabbing my arm and ordering me to go upstairs, Mary seemed to have forgotten that this was a game.

'Mary, I don't want the cane or the whip,' I dared to say.

'Madam,' she snapped. 'You'll call me madam. You turn up an hour late and then you dare to –'

'I'll go,' I said, pulling away from her. 'I couldn't help being late. You're obviously taking the game too far, so I'll go.'

'You'll do no such thing,' she hissed, again grabbing my arm. 'Your money is on the windowsill in the lounge, and you're going to earn it. Now, get up to the correction room.'

Climbing the stairs, I knew that I couldn't turn down fifty pounds. What with the locksmith and the solicitor to pay, I was in desperate need of cash. I'd be back at home within a couple of hours, I mused as Mary almost pushed me into the correction room. During my last visit, I had enjoyed the sex, the beautiful orgasms. But it was the cane and the leather whip that worried me. To be paid for two hours of crude sex was amazing, but I didn't want a gruelling thrashing. I'd give this one last chance, I thought as Mary closed the door. If they treated me badly, I'd never return.

'About bloody time,' Tom breathed, looking me up and down. 'Now that you're here, you'd better get into the box.'

'We've lost a whole hour,' Mary mumbled as I crawled into the dog kennel. After placing the wooden bar across my neck as I took my position, she pulled my head up by my hair. 'Did you shave?' she asked me.

'I – I was –'

'There's one way to find out.'

Releasing my hair, she moved behind me and yanked my short skirt up over my back. What with sucking the boys' cocks and Alan coming round the previous evening, and then having to find a solicitor, I'd forgotten about shaving my pubes. Mary would probably have a go at me, I thought as she tore my panties from my trembling body. Would she cane me? I felt financially trapped in my new line of work. I needed the money, but I couldn't endure the thrashings. If I'd been used for sex, I'd have been happy to dress up as a maid and play the sex games. But I had bills to pay, and had no choice other than to work for Tom and Mary.

'I told you to shave,' Mary growled, holding the

122

tops of my thighs apart. 'You turn up late, you're insolent, and you don't follow my instructions.'

'I'm sorry, Madam,' I breathed softly.

'Sorry? It's no good being sorry, girl. With today's money, you'll have earned one-hundred pounds. The least you could do is –'

'Shall I use the cream?' Tom cut in.

'Yes, use the cream,' Mary replied. 'This will be more time wasted. But I want her sluttish little cunt bald and smooth.'

As Tom massaged cooling cream into my outer sex lips and the fleshy rise of my mons, I wondered why Mary kept on about the time. Why did the time bother her so much? And why wasn't Tom at work? I instinctively knew that something wasn't right as my master and mistress waited for the depilating cream to do its job. How could they afford to pay me so much? Were they running some kind of sex business and making a lot of money? Something didn't add up, but what?

Mary finally washed away the cream and my pubic curls and dried my naked vulva. Praying that I wasn't going to get the cane as she stroked my hairless pussy lips, I let out a gasp as a finger slipped deep into my wet vagina and massaged my hot inner flesh. A second finger entered my anus and, as it drove deep into my tightening rectum, I felt my clitoris swell and my juices of lust flow. My muscles gripping the pistoning fingers, I loved the crude abuse of my helpless body. But I was still fearful of a cruel thrashing.

'The boys you sucked yesterday,' Mary said. 'Did you charge them?'

'What boys, Madam?' I asked her, wondering how on earth she knew about my escapade in the garden.

'You know very well, so don't lie to me,' she returned. 'Did you charge them?'

'No, Madam.'

'Have you arranged to see them again?'

'They're going to do the garden for me, Madam.'

'You'll charge them in future. You'll charge them thirty pounds each and share the money with me. Do you understand?'

'But, Madam –'

'You work for me, girl. I'll not have you moon-lighting. They're going to do your garden, and Tom is going to do your arse,' she said with a chuckle.

As her fingers slid out of my contracting sex ducts, I again wondered how she knew about the boys. My patio was secluded, there was no way she could have seen me from her house or garden. Unless she'd pushed her way into the bushes dividing our gardens, she couldn't have seen me. Massaging cooling cream into my anus, Mary told Tom that I was ready for his cock. I'd enjoyed the feel of his beautiful penis shafting my rectal duct the previous day, and was looking forward to another bowel spunking. But something was bothering me, nagging me from the depths of my mind. What the hell was it?

The feel of Tom's bulbous knob pushing against my tight anal ring sending quivers through my womb, I let out a rush of breath as he drove his granite-hard cock deep into my hot rectal passage and impaled me fully. His solid penis was big, filling, and opened my tight sheath to capacity. As he withdrew his length and again rammed into me, it felt as if his knob had gone deep into my stomach. He seemed far bigger than before, but I reckoned that I must be tighter and perhaps not so relaxed for some reason. Fear of the whip?

'I'll do her tight little cunt in a minute,' Tom gasped as he increased his anal pistoning rhythm. 'Fill her sweet little cunt with spunk.'

'And her mouth,' Mary said eagerly. 'And then she can give me a good licking.'

My body rocking back and forth with the crude anal fucking, I felt Mary's fingers open my hairless vaginal lips and stroke the solid nub of my expectant clitoris. I'd missed so much sexual pleasure during my marriage, I reflected as my clitoris pulsated and my womb contracted. It wasn't just Alan and his weird moods that I'd had to endure, but neglect. The weekly fucking from behind, the weekly spunking followed by snoring . . . Ten years wasted.

But the monotony and boredom of marriage was now far behind me. The routine had gone, and my days were now full of surprises and immense sexual gratification. I still had no idea where my life was taking me, but my concern for the future was fading. I had two fit young gardeners to tend the flowers, and my feminine needs. Paul was only a phone call away, and I had the pleasure of Tom and Mary's crude sexual abuse. What more could I ask for? I mused dreamily as Tom increased his anal shafting and Mary sank at least three fingers deep into my spasming sex sheath. But there were still questions nagging me, bothering me. Where were Tom and Mary getting money from? Where was Alan living and –

'Here it comes,' Tom announced, grabbing my hips and fucking my arse with a vengeance. His creamy offering lubricating my anal cylinder, easing the crude pistoning, he repeatedly drove his orgasming knob deep into my spunk-flooded bowels. My vaginal muscles gripping Mary's thrusting fingers, my clitoris exploding in orgasm, I let out a cry of pure sexual ecstasy as my entire body shook wildly.

'Filthy slut,' Mary breathed as a deluge of hot liquid gushed from my urethral opening and streamed down her hand. 'Dirty filthy little whore.'

'We'll give her the whip,' Tom rejoined. 'Teach the filthy bitch a lesson she'll never forget.'

'No,' I gasped in the grip of my massive climax. 'No, please . . .'

'You'll get the whip,' Mary cut in, repeatedly ramming her fingers deep into my contracting vagina. 'You arrived late, you hadn't shaved . . . You'll be whipped until you scream and beg for mercy.'

My orgasm peaking, another gush of vaginal cream and hot golden liquid issuing from my burning sex valley, I'd known all along that Mary wouldn't allow my bad behaviour to go unpunished. She'd been dying to administer the whip or the cane since she'd first seen me dressed in my maid's outfit. And she'd already given me my first taste of the leather strap. Why did she need excuses? I wondered fearfully as Tom drained his swinging balls and finally slipped his deflating penis out of my inflamed rectum. Why the threats? Unless she'd wanted me to wait, I reflected. Make me wait make me sweat.

'Now do her tight little cunt,' Mary said with a chuckle as she slipped her fingers out of my aching vaginal duct. 'Fill her dirty little cunt with sperm and I'll suck it out of both her holes.'

My orgasm barely over, I couldn't believe Tom's virility as the fleshy pads of my vulva were stretched wide apart and he rammed his swollen knob deep into my sex-drenched vaginal sheath. His glans pressing against the hard softness of my cervix, his solid shaft opening my vagina to capacity, he again grabbed my hips and began his fucking motions. At least two fingers slipped into the gaping hole of my anus and drove deep into my sperm-flooded bowels as Tom fucked me, and I knew that Mary couldn't resist abusing my most private duct.

My body again rocking with the enforced fucking, the squelching sounds of my vaginal juices resounding around the sex room, I knew that I'd have to rest before Tom fucked my gasping mouth. There was no way I'd be able to entertain my young gardeners, I thought, imagining their cocks fucking the two holes between my legs. Two cocks? Was that what I really wanted? Debased, debauched in my whoredom. What the hell had I become?

Tom's second load of spunk came quickly, and I again pondered on his staying power. He was an incredible man, a man of great virility. Mary would have been a very lucky girl, had she not been a lesbian. They had a peculiar relationship, and I wondered how long their marriage would last. Sharing my body, each loving and using my vagina in their own way, they were no doubt satisfied. And I couldn't deny my satisfaction. Although I was behaving like a common whore, I was deriving immense sexual satisfaction from my visits to my neighbours' house. Would I be visiting them in years to come?

'Before I whip her, I want to use the anal speculum,' Mary said as Tom again withdrew his spent cock from my trembling body. 'I want to stretch her tight little arse open so wide that she'll –'

'God, no,' I protested as she grabbed something from a shelf. 'Please . . .'

'Tom, please gag her mouth with your cock.'

'My pleasure,' Tom said with a wicked chuckle as Mary moved behind me. 'This'll stop her screams,' he added, kneeling before me with his rock-hard cock in his hand.

Forcing his wet knob into my mouth, he held my head and rocked his hips slowly. There was no escaping the crude mouth fucking, or the imminent opening of my anal canal. All I could do was endure the abuse of my body and pray that I wouldn't be whipped or caned. Mary chuckled wickedly as she settled behind me and yanked the firm cheeks of my bottom wide apart. This was it, I thought squeezing my eyes shut as Tom's knob glided back and forth over my tongue. I'd had Tom's cock shafting my rectal canal, and now my once-sacrosanct tube was to be stretched wide open by an anal speculum.

The cold steel instrument entering my sperm-lubricated anal canal, Tom's knob fucking my mouth, I breathed heavily through my nose and waited apprehensively for my tight rectal duct to expand. Sucking on Tom's swollen knob as Mary began to open my rectum, I couldn't stop thinking about the whip. Tensing the sensitive flesh of my naked buttocks as I imagined a leather strap flailing me there, I again vowed not to work for Tom and Mary if they thrashed me. I loved the anal shaftings, the vaginal spunking and the mouth fucking, the multiple orgasms . . . But I wasn't into pain.

My mouth flooding with creamy sperm as Tom shuddered and gasped, I felt my rectal duct stretch open. Repeatedly swallowing hard, gulping down the fresh spunk, I again squeezed my eyes shut as the speculum opened my anal canal further. How far did Mary intend to go? I wondered anxiously. The delicate tissue of my anal ring painfully stretched, I knew that she'd be peering deep into my rectal tube. This wasn't lesbian love, this was crude sexual abuse of my tethered body. I should never have believed her lies of love and closeness.

'Suck it all out,' Tom instructed me, stilling his throbbing knob within my gobbling mouth 'Use your tongue, whore. Suck it all out.'

'I'll leave the speculum in place,' Mary said as she continued to open my rectal sheath. 'She'll be ready for another arse fucking in a while.'

Swallowing the remnants of Tom's creamy sperm,

I knew that I couldn't endure another anal fucking. I needed to rest, recover after the crude abuse of my young body. How the hell was Tom going to manage another erection? I wondered as he slipped his deflating cock out of my spermed mouth and stood up. He'd fucked and spunked all three of my holes, and there was no way he'd be able to pump me full of his cream a fourth time.

Kneeling on the floor with her rounded bottom cheeks only inches from my face, Mary ordered me to lick her anal inlet. I gazed wide-eyed at her small brown hole as she reached behind her back and yanked her buttocks wide apart. I couldn't do it, I couldn't bring myself to lick her bottom-hole. Pushing my tongue into her vagina and lapping up her girl cream was one thing, but there was no way I could tongue her rectal duct. Tom noticed my hesitation and held my head up as Mary moved back. My nose between her bottom cheeks, her anal ring pressing against my pursed lips, she again ordered me to lick her there.

'Do it, girl,' she snapped. 'Behave like the slut you are and lick my arse out.'

'If you don't,' Tom began, grinning at me, 'you'll have your pussy lips whipped.'

'Please, I can't,' I breathed. 'I'll do anything but . . .'

'You'll tongue-fuck her arse or you'll have your tits caned,' he threatened me. 'Do you know what it's like to feel the cane across your nipples? Have you ever had your inner lips and your clitoris caned? I suggest you do as you're told, my girl.'

Pushing my tongue out until the tip pressed against Mary's brown tissue, I closed my eyes as the bitterness played on my taste buds. I didn't want this, I thought anxiously as I pushed my tongue into her tight hole. My knees on the urine-wet carpet, the speculum painfully stretching my anal tube open, my tongue embedded deep within Mary's rectum, I knew that I could sink no further into the pit of depravity. This was worth more than fifty pounds, I decided. Before returning to the sex room, I'd demand a pay rise.

Leaving me to tongue Mary's anus, Tom moved behind me and slipped his fingers deep into the constricted sheath of my vagina. My aching sex holes bloated, I hoped that he couldn't raise another erection and force me to endure his fourth penile shafting. Slurping at Mary's anus, savouring the bitter taste of her rectal canal, I was still in fear of the whip. I hadn't wanted this, I reflected. I'd been happy to play the role of Mary's maid, suck her clitoris to orgasm and allow her to lick me, but I'd not wanted to sink this low into the mire of obscene sex.

Tom slipped his fingers out of my tight vaginal sheath and, to my great relief, removed the speculum from my aching rectal tube. I could feel my anus gaping wide open, the passageway to my inner core laid bare before my abuser. Mary shuddered and swivelled her hips, aligning the dripping entrance to her vagina with my mouth. I tasted her cream, tongued her sex hole and nibbled on her inner lips. I'd soon be released, I was sure. I'd be paid for my debauchery and allowed to go home and rest.

'No,' I gasped through a mouthful of vagina flesh as I felt Tom's swollen knob enter my inflamed rectum. 'No. Please, no more.'

'We've barely started,' Tom returned with a chuckle. 'Besides, you're not leaving here until you've had a damned good whipping.'

His knob driving deep into the wet heat of my bowels, I again pondered on his virility. How many times could he fuck me and spunk me? He must have been some sort of superman, I mused. A sex machine. Aligning her erect clitoris with my mouth, Mary ordered me to suck her to orgasm. Once she'd come and Tom had pumped out his fourth load of spunk, I was sure that the session of debauchery would be over. They couldn't go on for ever, could they?

Tom came quickly. His sperm flooding my bowels, he held my hips tight and repeatedly rammed the entire length of his solid penis deep into my trembling body as Mary reached her climax. Sucking and licking her pulsating clitoris as Tom rocked me with his crude anal shafting, the squelching sounds of sex filling my ears, Mary pumped her vaginal cream over my face as I mouthed on her orgasming clitoris. My body was awash with sperm and girl-juice, and I desperately needed to take a shower and rest after my incredible ordeal. But it wasn't over yet.

Mary finally collapsed on the floor, shaking uncontrollably in the aftermath of her climax, and Tom withdrew his spent cock from my inflamed anal canal. Exhausted, my master and mistress were in no fit state to whip me, I was sure. Sperm flowing from my gaping anal hole, my body trembling, all I wanted to do was go home. I'd had more than enough cold sex for one day, I thought as Mary clambered to her feet and moved behind me. I'd given my body completely, and I'd certainly earned my money.

The first lash of the whip flailing my naked buttocks with a loud crack, I yelped like a dog. I couldn't believe what Mary was doing as she again brought the leather strap down across my tensed buttocks. The game had gone too far. What the hell had possessed her to thrash me like this? The pain permeating my clenched bum cheeks, the deafening crack of the whip resounding around the room, I begged and pleaded for mercy. But she ignored my cries and repeatedly lashed my stinging buttocks as I involuntarily released a gush of hot urine.

Her wicked chuckles echoing around the sexual torture chamber, she continued with the gruelling thrashing. My buttocks felt as though they were on fire, and I knew that I couldn't endure the lashing for much longer as another gush of hot liquid streamed down my inner thighs and splashed onto the carpet between my knees. Again and again, I yelped with each lash of the whip. This wasn't a game, I thought fearfully. No matter how much money Mary paid me, I wasn't going to endure this sort of treatment. The leather strap catching the backs of my thighs, my whole body jolting, I again begged her to stop.

'That will do for now,' she said, finally halting the punishment. 'In future, I expect you to arrive at ten o'clock sharp, do you understand?'

'Yes, Madam,' I whimpered, vowing never to set foot in her house again.

'I'm feeling hungry, Tom,' she said. 'Pass me the banana, please.'

As she knelt behind me and parted the burning cheeks of my bum, I knew what she was about to do. How much more of this could I take? I wondered anxiously as she pushed the peeled fruit past my anal sphincter muscles. The banana entering the fiery sheath of my rectum, opening my inflamed tube, I hoped that this was the final degrading act I'd be forced to commit before I'd be given my freedom and allowed to go home. The fruit sinking deeper into my anal duct, I couldn't believe Mary's decadence as she locked her lips to my anus and sucked hard.

I could feel the banana sliding out of my sperm-flooded anal canal as she sucked and slurped, and I wondered what sort of girl she was. A filthy whore, I thought as she ate the banana. A common slut, a tart, a . . . But, wasn't I as bad? I mused. I was being paid for this, I reminded myself. A prostitute paid to commit lewd sexual acts. Mary had talked about love after our first sexual encounter in my lounge. This wasn't love. This was vulgar sex for the sake of sex.

'It's broken in half,' she said, slapping my burning buttocks with the palm of her hand. 'Tom, give me another banana.'

'Of course,' he replied, moving about behind me.

'I'll eat this one out of her cunt,' Mary said, giggling as she parted the hairless pads of my vulval crack. 'If it breaks in two, I'll thrash her bottom again.'

The banana driving deep into my sperm-drenched vagina, the end of the cold fruit pressing hard against my cervix, I closed my eyes as she locked her mouth to my gaping sex hole and sucked hard. Would it snap in two? I wondered anxiously, trying to relax my vaginal muscles. I couldn't take another whipping, I knew as I felt the fruit sliding out of my sex duct. I could feel the other banana deep inside my rectum. It would eventually turn to pulp and come out, so I had no need to worry. But this abuse of my young body, this degrading act, this vulgar . . . Never again, I vowed as she swallowed the hot, creamy fruit. Never again, would I lower myself to commit such corrupt acts of filth.

'Mmm,' Mary breathed through her nose as she slurped and sucked between my swollen vaginal lips. 'She's very hot and wet.'

'I like to see you enjoying yourself,' Tom said. 'You, girl,' he snapped, lifting my head up by my hair. 'Are you enjoying yourself?'

'Yes, master,' I murmured.

'You like having all your holes fucked and spunked, don't you?'

'Yes, master.'

'Tell me how much you like it. Tell me that you long to feel my cock fucking your arse.'

'I ... I long to feel your cock fucking my arse, master.'

'You won't be late tomorrow, will you?'

'No, master.'

Mary slurped and gobbled and sucked my vaginal entrance until she'd eaten the creamy fruit. They were both perverts, I thought as she clambered to her feet. In all the years I'd known them, I'd never once dreamed that they were ... But I was no better, I again reminded myself. The things I'd done, the things I'd allowed people to do to me, I was no better than Tom or Mary. Maybe I was worse, I reflected. I'd taken money in return for cold sex. I'd sold my body for crude sex. Had the Devil bought my soul?

'Release her, Tom,' Mary finally ordered her husband.

'What about the clamps?' he asked her, removing the wooden bar from the back of my neck and helping me out of the box.

'We'll save the clamps for tomorrow,' she breathed as Tom helped me to my feet. 'I have plans for her sweet little tits. But they can wait until tomorrow morning.'

Opening my blouse and easing my firm breasts out of my bra, she tweaked each nipple in turn. I swayed on my sagging legs, clutching my burning buttocks as she sucked on my ripening milk teats. My inner thighs wet with a blend of sperm and urine, I looked down at her pretty face as she suckled like a babe. We could have had something together, some sort of loving lesbian relationship, I mused. Only a girl knows how to pleasure another girl.

Barely able to speak, my head spinning, I wondered whether she'd been talking about nipple clamps. Plans for my tits? What the hell did she intend to do to me? There would be no tomorrow, I thought as she slipped my erect nipple out of her mouth and stood upright. I couldn't endure the whip again. The thrashing, the crude fuckings . . . Never again would I visit the correction room.

'Go now,' she ordered me as Tom opened the door. 'And don't forget to be here on time tomorrow.'

'Yes, Madam,' I murmured, staggering to the door and making my way downstairs.

'We have a little surprise lined up for you,' Tom said, following me into the lounge. 'Actually, it's a big surprise. When you get here tomorrow . . . No, I won't spoil it.'

Ignoring him, I grabbed the money from the windowsill and made my escape through the back door. Surprise? I mused as I headed for the safety of my house. The only surprise would be my not turning up at ten o'clock, or at any other time for that matter. Closing and locking the back door, I went into the lounge and flopped onto the sofa. Exhausted, my body still trembling, my buttocks burning a fire-red, I tried to relax and calm myself after my incredible ordeal.

Mary wasn't simply a lesbian, I reflected, aware of the banana embedded deep within my inflamed rectum. She was a sexual deviant, a complete pervert. And Tom was . . . Tom was a bloody sex machine. At least I had some money to pay the locksmith, I thought, lifting my skirt and gazing at the hairless lips of my abused pussy. What the hell had I allowed those people to do to my poor body? I wondered, eyeing my wet inner thighs. Whipped, fucked, used and abused . . . Never again.

Climbing the stairs to the bathroom, I managed to ease the pulped banana out of my rectal duct. How

135

crude could a girl be? I mused, massaging my stinging buttocks. And what plans did she have for my tits? They wouldn't involve me again, I swore as I turned the shower on. In future, her plans for me would go no further than dreams. Like Alan, she'd lost me – for good.

After a shower, I dressed in a miniskirt and blouse and sat in the garden. My buttocks were still stinging, but I knew that the pain would soon fade and my pubic hair would eventually grow and veil my most private parts. My body would eventually return to normal, but the memories of my ordeal would never fade. I'd find myself a proper job, I decided as I reclined on the bed chair and drifted off to sleep beneath the afternoon sun. The divorce was going ahead, I'd never go to Tom and Mary's house again, and everything would return to normal.

I was woken at four o'clock by the doorbell. I thought for a minute that it might be Alan, but it was the locksmith. He was a good-looking young man with dark swept-back hair and a suntanned face. But he was there to change the lock, I reminded myself as I dragged my eyes away from his bulging jeans. He wasn't going to become another of my sexual conquests. I had to change my thinking, I decided as he worked. I had to drag my thoughts away from sex and return to some kind of normality. But I was sure that his cock was big and his balls were full.

The lock changed, I paid him and sent him on his way before my lewd desires got the better of me. I'd have loved to have pulled his cock out and sucked his purple knob to orgasm and swallowed his fresh spunk. But I wasn't a whore, was I? I had to get out of the house for a while, I thought. Fresh air and a little exercise was what I needed to blow away the cobwebs, and the lewd images looming in my mind. Sex, orgasms, sperm, vaginal milk, fingering, fucking, whipping . . . Leaving the house, I knew that I had to clear my thoughts.

Walking through the park, I listened to the birds singing in the trees. After my ordeal with Tom and Mary, I was beginning to feel calm and tranquil. The smell of sex leaving me as I breathed in the fresh air, I once more vowed never to set foot in my neighbours' correction room again. I didn't want to lead a life of debauchery and whoredom. Noticing a young woman pushing a pram, I blamed Alan for our broken marriage. We could have been happy, normal, I reflected. I'd never contemplated divorce. Always doing my best to please Alan, I'd thought that we'd build our home together and eventually have a family. But that was never to be. What with Alan's weird ways, we were destined to drift apart.

Noticing a young couple holding hands as they watched the ducks on the pond, I realised that Alan and I had never been close. The housework and cooking, the mind games and threats of splitting up, had only been punctuated by the weekly fucking. We'd never been close, we'd never been in love. I'd been more like a mother to Alan, I reflected. I'd cooked and ironed his shirts, looked after him, listened to his complaining . . . That wasn't marriage. It was a living hell.

Things had changed beyond recognition, I mused as I relaxed on a bench. What had I wanted? I wondered, closing my eyes as the sun warmed me. Love? Lust? I'd not known what I'd wanted after marriage. I supposed that no one knew what life held in store for them after the break-up of their marriage. I'd not wanted anything in particular. Apart from escaping Alan's mind games, I'd not given the future a thought. Prostitution? That was what I'd become, I thought dolefully. A prostitute. Whether I'd wanted it or not, that's what I'd become. But that was about to change.

Eight

I'd slept well and was up early to find the sun already hot in a clear blue sky. It was going to be a good day, I was sure as I walked into town to do some shopping. Tom and Mary could go to hell and, with the new lock fitted, Alan wouldn't be snooping around my house. At long last, I felt free. Although I was going to have to find a job and earn some money, I felt that I was moving in the right direction. I'd made some horrendous mistakes, wandered down a road to incredible decadence, but was now back on track.

'Hello,' someone called from behind me as I lugged my shopping up to my front door.

'Oh, hi,' I said, turning as the man who lived opposite walked up the drive.

'Enjoying the sunshine?'

'Not really,' I replied, opening the front door. 'It's a lovely day, but I've had to do the shopping. How are you keeping?'

'I'm fine, thanks. Actually, I'm glad I've bumped into you.'

'Oh?'

He rubbed his chin and smiled at me. 'To be honest, this isn't a coincidence. I've been looking out for you.'

'Well, here I am,' I said, forcing a laugh.

'I was wondering whether you'd like to come over to my place this morning?'

'Er . . . Well, that's very nice of you but . . .'

'Only for an hour or so,' he persisted. 'And I'll pay you, of course.'

'Pay me?' I breathed, wondering what on earth he was talking about.

'As you know, I live alone. I find loneliness difficult to cope with at times and I'm not too good around the house. I saw you in your maid's outfit the other day and thought it might be nice if you came over for an hour now and then to help me out.'

'Oh, I see,' I breathed, wondering how he'd seen me dressed in my uniform. He was a nosey old man, always looking out of his window or leaning on his front gate, and I reckoned that he must have seen me going to Tom and Mary's. 'To be honest, I'm not sure whether I can fit you in,' I said.

'That's a shame,' he sighed.

Wondering why he thought that I was a real maid, I hoped that he'd not heard anything about my other little business. What had given him the idea that I was a cleaning woman? I could have been going to a fancy dress party or . . . There was no way he'd know anything about Tom and Mary's sex room, I was sure of that. Deciding to play this by ear, it occurred to me that Alan might have been talking to him.

'I really need someone to come in and do a little cleaning,' he persisted. 'There are quite a few elderly people around here, so I suppose you get pretty busy. How long have you been in business?'

'Er . . . Not long. I suppose I could come over for an hour,' I finally agreed. 'To be honest, I need the money.'

'That is good news. It's not heavy work, just vacuuming and dusting and general cleaning.'

'Yes, that's fine. I'm Helen, by the way.'

'Derek,' he said, smiling at me. 'I heard that your husband left you. It must be difficult making ends meet.'

'I threw him out,' I returned. 'He was no good to me, so I threw him out.'

'I'm sorry that things didn't work out for you.'

'Things *have* worked out,' I said with a chuckle. 'I finally got rid of my husband. Er . . . Will ten o'clock be all right?'

'Yes, that's fine. I'll have the kettle on ready for coffee.'

'I'm not sure what to charge as you're a neighbour.'

'Charge your normal rate, Helen,' he said. 'Just because I live opposite, I don't want any concessions.'

'OK, that's very nice of you.'

'Good, that's settled. I'll see you later, then.'

'Yes, yes I'll see you later,' I breathed as he walked away.

I knew that he wasn't short of money and decided to charge him ten pounds for an hour's cleaning. If he needed me to call two or three times each week . . . Shit, I thought, dumping the shopping on the kitchen table. I didn't want to be a bloody cleaning woman. But it was better than enduring sexual abuse at Tom and Mary's house. Dressed in my maid's outfit, I might get a few elderly male customers. Charge them ten pounds for cleaning, and give them a little excitement by flashing my knickers, and I'd probably do quite well. No knicker flashing, I decided as I put the shopping away. I wanted to move away from sex. Flashing my knickers to old men wasn't on the agenda.

I felt that bumping into the old man was an omen. Although I'd not wanted to become a cleaning

141

woman, I'd wanted to get away from sex and prostitution and find a proper job. Maybe I could earn a half-decent living from cleaning, I mused. Five clients each day would bring in fifty pounds, and the work wouldn't be too bad. It wasn't a fortune, but it was better than selling myself for sex. Feeling a lot happier as I changed into my maid's outfit, I imagined Alan trying his key in the front-door lock. He'd immediately realise that I'd had the lock changed and, hopefully, leave me in peace.

With the time approaching ten, I slipped my overcoat on and wandered across the road to the old man's house. It was a beautiful day, far too warm to wear a coat. But I didn't want the neighbours seeing me dressed as a maid. As Derek had said, there were quite a few elderly people living in the area and I didn't want faces peering through net curtains and the local gossips firing up. Hoping that Alan wasn't lurking somewhere as I rang the doorbell, I felt positive about the future. I'd have to build up a list of clients, but I was sure that the old man would recommend me to his friends and I'd soon be earning some cash. Ten o'clock. Tom and Mary would be expecting me, but they were going to have a long wait.

'Come in,' Derek said as he opened the door. 'Why the coat?' He looked me up and down. 'It's a very hot day.'

'I don't want the neighbours seeing my uniform,' I replied, stepping into the hall. I slipped my coat off and threw it over the banister. 'Right, where would you like me to start?'

'Well, that's up to you. Where do you normally start?'

'Er . . . The kitchen, I suppose.'

'Helen, about your other services,' he began, following me through the hall to the kitchen. 'I was just thinking that –'

'Other services?' I echoed, wondering what the hell he knew about me. 'What do you mean?'

'I've heard that you ... How can I put it? I've heard that you offer other services.'

'What?' I gasped, holding my hand to my mouth.

My hands trembling, my heart racing, I couldn't believe what I was hearing. Other services? Sure that Alan had spoken to him, told him that I was on the game, I didn't know what to say. The last thing I wanted was the neighbours discovering that I was a prostitute. The two young lads were all right. I knew that they wouldn't go blabbing to the neighbours, so it must have been Alan.

'What other services?' I said again.

'Don't get annoyed, Helen. I've heard that you offer services to men.'

'Where the hell did you hear that? Who told you?'

'Well, it was Tom.'

'Tom? What the hell has he been saying about me?'

'Nothing, really. Look, forget that I mentioned it.'

'Right, Derek. I want the truth. Tell me exactly what Tom said about me.'

'He just said that you offer services to men.'

'And?'

'Well, we were talking about this and that ... He said that your husband had left you. I said that you were a fine-looking girl and would soon find yourself another man. And then he said ... No, I said that I ...'

'The truth, Derek. You're making this up as you go along. I want the truth.'

He brushed his crop of grey hair back and stared at me. 'You're the girl in the box, aren't you?' he said.

'What box?' I asked him, unable to believe that Tom had told him everything.

'At Tom's place. You're the girl in the box. I thought I recognised you yesterday when I was there.'

'You were there?'

'Well, yes. You see, I'm a client.'

'A client?

My head spinning, I felt dizzy in my confusion. A client? The old man had been there, in the sex room when I'd been in the box and . . . This was one hell of a revelation, I mused angrily. Revelation? It was a bloody bombshell. If the old man was a client, then . . . Shit, I thought, holding my hand to my head. He must have fucked me. He must have knelt behind me and fucked my cunt and my arse and . . . Vowing to strangle Tom and Mary, I stared hard at Derek.

'I think you'd better tell me everything,' I said. 'Start from the beginning, and tell me everything.'

'About a year ago, I started going over to Tom and Mary's. I went to their sex room once a week for . . . for sex with a young girl. I'm a regular client and, when I recognised you in the box, I thought I might cut out the middle man, so to speak.'

'Cut out the middle man? Bloody hell, this is a nightmare,' I gasped. 'How much did they charge you?'

'Fifty pounds. There are usually three of us and –'

'Three men? Three men, besides Tom?'

'Yes, that's right. We each take turns to . . . The thing is, Tom has told us to say nothing about this. We don't speak when we're there because he likes to make out that he's the only man in the room. And he doesn't want the girls to know who we are.'

'Girls? God, how many girls work for him?'

'I know of four, including you. I shouldn't have said anything. I thought you knew, you see. I thought you –'

'Shut up,' I snapped. 'I'm trying to think.'

Sitting at the kitchen table, I again held my hand to my head. Everything was falling into place. Tom was no sex machine. There'd been several men taking turns to fuck me. That's how Tom could afford to pay me, I reflected. He was charging the men fifty pounds each, and then giving me fifty. He was a bastard, I thought angrily. And Mary was a cunning little bitch. I'd been conned big time. Wondering how to get my own back on the evil couple, I couldn't believe that Tom and Mary had been running a brothel. Who were the other girls? I wondered. More to the point, who were the other clients? Were they neighbours? Did they see me in the street and snigger behind my back? This was worse than a nightmare, I thought, imagining that Alan might be a client.

'Have you ever seen Alan there?' I asked Derek as he poured two cups of coffee.

'Your husband? No, no I haven't.'

'Who are the other clients?'

'I don't know them. They're not from round here. Helen, I wish I hadn't said anything. I thought you knew about –'

'They were selling me for sex,' I breathed pensively. 'And I knew nothing about it.'

'You must have realised what was going on?'

'I knew nothing about the other men. I thought that it was just Tom and Mary. I thought that it was a sex game we were playing. I had no idea that I was actually on the game.'

'I've really put my foot in it, haven't I?' he sighed.

'No, you haven't. I'm glad that you told me, otherwise I might have gone there again and . . . Who are the other girls? Do you know them?'

'No, I don't. It's difficult to see who it is in the box. That's the idea, of course. As Tom says, anonymity is the name of the game. I thought I recognised you,

145

but I didn't say anything to Tom. What will you do now?'

'I'll kill him,' I hissed. 'And I'll strangle that little bitch of a wife of his.'

'His wife?' he said, looking at me as if I was mad. 'No, no . . . Mary is his sister.'

'What? His sister? Shit, this gets worse by the minute. And, the whole thing is becoming clearer by the minute.'

'How did you get involved with them?'

'It's a long story,' I sighed as he passed me a cup of coffee. 'And one that I don't want to go into. Suffice to say that I had no idea that they were selling me for sex.'

'I'm sorry, Helen.'

'Don't be sorry, it's not your fault. When are you next due there?'

'Not for a couple of days. I go twice a week.'

Sipping my coffee, I wondered what on earth to do. Although I'd vowed never to set foot in their house again, I wanted revenge. *Cut out the middle man*, I mused, recalling Derek's words. Three clients a day at fifty pounds each? A wicked plan coming to mind, I grinned. Why not work from my own house and steal the evil couple's clients? My mind was made up. I was going into business as a prostitute. And, not only would Derek be my first client, but he'd lure the other clients away from Tom and Mary.

'You'll come straight to me twice a week,' I instructed Derek. 'Do you understand?'

'Er . . . Yes, yes that's fine.'

'And you'll tell the other clients to come straight to me.'

'I don't know them, Helen.'

'Then, you'd better find out who they are.'

'I sort of know one of them,' he confessed. 'I'll contact him and tell him, OK?'

146

'OK. So, you are sure that my husband never goes to Tom and Mary's?'

'I've never seen him there.'

'That's good.'

'Helen, I'm worried. You won't tell Tom about this, will you? I mean, if he finds out that I've . . .'

'You steal his clients for me, and he'll never know,' I assured him.

'OK, I'll do my best.'

'Right,' I said, finishing my coffee. 'Would you like to visit me tomorrow?'

'I'd love to,' he replied eagerly.

'Good. Be at my house at ten o'clock tomorrow morning. And bring fifty pounds with you.'

'Yes, yes I'll be there.'

I donned my coat, left his house and crossed the road. I was fuming, and determined to ruin Tom and Mary's business. If I had to resort to prostitution to destroy them, then so be it. Although I'd vowed to move away from crude sex and live a normal life, things had changed drastically. I'd been used and abused, sold for sex . . . Closing the front door, I heard someone banging on the back door. I knew that it was Tom as I dumped my coat on the banister and walked through the hall to the kitchen. I didn't want him to know that I'd discovered his game, and quickly formulated a plan as I opened the door.

'Sorry,' I said, holding my stomach. 'I've been really ill.'

'Oh, right,' he sighed. 'You could have let us know.'

'I was about to call you. I got changed into my uniform ready to come round, but I'm just not up to it. I should be all right tomorrow.'

'Well, I suppose it can't be helped. OK, I'll go and tell Mary.'

'I'm sorry, Tom.'

'No, no it's OK. You get well and I'll see you tomorrow.'

After closing and locking the door, I made my plans. Even if Derek did find out who the other girls were, there was no way I'd employ them. Why share the cash with others? I ruminated. I could easily entertain the men on my own. I'd set up a special room, I decided. A room similar to Tom and Mary's with whips and . . . No, I wasn't going to endure the whip. Wondering whether all the clients were the same age as Derek, I went up to my bedroom and slipped out of my maid's uniform. I had no need for silly costumes, I thought as I stepped into a miniskirt and grabbed a white blouse from the wardrobe. It was my eager young body that the men wanted, not a silly uniform.

Gazing out of the window at Derek's house, I again found it difficult to believe that he'd been visiting Tom and Mary for a year or so. It was amazing to think that there was a brothel next door, and I'd had no idea. Recalling the lies Mary had told me about her having to marry Tom to please her parents, I again vowed to get my own back. Tom had said that he'd met Mary though another girl and . . . They were a conniving, lying, evil pair.

They'd planned the whole thing, I mused. From the minute they'd discovered that Alan had walked out on me, they'd homed in on me. First, Tom had moved in with his plans of seduction. And then Mary had seduced me. They'd tested the water, discovered that I was up for lesbian sex as well as heterosexual, then they'd asked me to work for them as a maid and . . . and they'd sold my body for sex to other men. Like a fool, I'd fallen for the scam.

Noticing Alan slipping up the drive, I shook my head and sighed. He was the last person I wanted to see, let alone speak to. At least he couldn't get into the house, but I didn't want him forever lurking and spying. What the hell did he want? I wondered as the doorbell rang. Making my way down the stairs, I decided that I would speak to him one last time. I'd tell him to get out of my life once and for all, and stay out. Opening the door, I gazed at the pathetic figure standing on the step. He was grinning like a naughty schoolboy, and I knew that he had something planned. No doubt it was something to annoy me, as usual.

'Is there any post for me?' he said, stepping past me into the hall.

'No,' I stated firmly. 'Alan, I'd prefer it if you waited to be invited into my house rather than just walk in.'

'Sorry, I just wanted to know about the post.'

'There isn't any, so you may as well go.'

'Have you found a job yet?'

'Yes, I have. Have you any other questions before you leave?'

'Don't be so cold, Helen. I've only called round to ask about the post.'

'You could have phoned me.'

'I was passing, so I thought I'd call in.'

'Where are you living? I only ask because your mum's place is miles away and yet you always seem to be passing my house.'

'I've . . . I've found a flat nearby,' he said, obviously lying.

'That's nice for you. So, you now have a flat and a woman.'

'A woman? Oh, yes, yes I have.'

'Do you see much of Tom and Mary?'

'Not really. I meet Tom for a beer now and then, but that's about it.'

'You don't like pubs, Alan. At least, you never did.'

'Things have changed,' he said, grinning at me. 'I have a social life now.'

'For someone as unsociable as you, that's quite amazing,' I quipped.

'Helen, let's at least be friends,' he whined. 'OK, so the marriage is coming to an end. But we can still be on speaking terms, can't we?'

'We are speaking, Alan. It's just that I don't like you turning up here unannounced every five minutes.'

'I've only been here a couple of times since we split up.'

'Look, I have a lot to do today,' I sighed as the phone rang. 'Is there anything else you want?'

'No, no. I only wanted to check the post. You get the phone and I'll leave you to get on.'

'Close the door behind you,' I called, heading for the lounge.

Grabbing the phone as the front door closed, I frowned. The line was dead. Must have been a wrong number, I thought, moving to the window and watching Alan walk down the drive. He seemed to be happy enough, I reflected. Although I didn't believe that he had a flat or a woman, he'd at least said that the marriage was coming to an end. The end of an era, I thought happily. The end of ten years of marriage. And the beginning of . . . The beginning of my own business?

Again thinking that I'd vowed to move away from prostitution, I knew that it was my only option. Apart from getting even with Tom and Mary, I needed the money. And it would be decent money, I mused. Spending all my time cleaning for a few pounds wouldn't get me anywhere, whereas selling my body for sex would bring in a small fortune.

There was nothing wrong with prostitution, I tried to console myself. Sex was sex. Getting fucked by my husband or another man ... What the hell did it matter?

Noticing a man hovering outside Tom and Mary's house, I flung the window open and called out to him. Was he a client? I wondered as he walked up my drive. I could hardly ask him. He was in his sixties with sparse grey hair, and I was sure that he'd been about to call on Tom and Mary. If he was a client, then this was a stroke of luck.

'Are you all right?' he asked me, standing by the window.

'Sorry, I thought I knew you,' I replied. 'Are you going to Tom's place?'

'Er ... Yes, yes I am. They're friends of mine.'

'What time is your appointment?'

'Eleven o'clock. I mean ... I don't have an appointment. I just said that I'd call around eleven.'

'Why don't you come in for a minute?' I said, smiling at him. 'I think we have something to talk about.'

'Do we? I don't know you, so ...'

'It'll only take a minute,' I cut in, closed the window and dashed into the hall. Opening the front door, I again smiled at him. 'Please, come in.'

'Well, I ... I suppose so,' he murmured, stepping into the hall. 'What's this all about?'

'To be honest, I don't know how to say it. Er ... I'm running my own business from home.'

'Yes?'

'Come into the lounge,' I said, closing the front door. 'You see, I'm building up my clients and ...'

'What sort of business are you running?'

'The same business as Tom and Mary.'

'And what business would that be?'

151

'Sex,' I blurted out.

'I see,' he breathed, settling on the sofa.

'You're obviously a client of theirs and . . .'

'And you want me to come here instead of visiting them?'

'Yes, yes that's right.'

'What would be the benefit of that? I can see that it would benefit you, but how would it benefit me? Will you charge me less?'

'No, I'll charge the same,' I said boldly. 'But I'll be offering a better service. Firstly, you won't have to share me with other men. When you visit me, there'll be no one else here.'

'Go on.'

'Secondly, I won't be stuck in a wooden box. You'll have proper access to my body to do with as you wish.'

'I must admit that I never liked the idea of Tom's box. He called it, anonymity but I'd rather see the girl properly. OK, I'm interested.'

'Good. I'm Helen, by the way.'

'I'm Frank. There is just one thing.'

'Yes?'

'I'm heavily into anal sex. Is that a problem with you?'

'Far from it,' I replied with a giggle. 'I love anal sex. I'm afraid I haven't prepared a room yet. I don't have any equipment or . . .'

'All I want is your bum,' he cut in with a chuckle. 'If you'd like to bend over the back of an armchair, I'll give you a damned good anal shafting.'

Rising to his feet, he reached into his jacket pocket and tossed fifty pounds onto the coffee table. Easy money, I thought happily, slipping my panties off and hoisting my skirt up. This was real prostitution, I mused anxiously. A total stranger paying me to shaft my bottom? Although I'd not wanted this, I was

152

beginning to think that it was meant to be. After years of boredom and frustration with Alan, I was now enjoying sex to the full. A stranger, a friend, my husband . . . It didn't matter who the man was. Sex is sex, I again mused.

Leaning over the back of the armchair with my feet wide apart and my naked backside jutting out, I could feel my juices of desire seeping between my engorged inner lips and trickling down my thighs. Parting my firm buttocks, the man scooped a handful of lubricant from my sex valley and massaged the cream into my anal ring. The sensations were heavenly, and I quivered as I waited expectantly for his solid penis to enter me.

He said nothing as he pressed his bulbous knob hard against the delicate tissue surrounding my anal hole. I could hear him breathing deeply, moaning softly, as he pushed his knob past my defeated anal sphincter muscles. His swollen glans opening me, journeying along my tight rectal duct, he drove his cock slowly into the very core of my trembling body. Finally impaling me completely on his rock-hard shaft, his heavy balls pressing against the hairless lips of my vulva, he held my hips and allowed his huge knob to absorb the inner heat of my bowels.

He withdrew slowly, gently, until the brown tissue of my anal ring hugged the rim of his helmet. To think that I was being paid to receive such immense pleasure was incredible. Cut out the middle man, I mused dreamily, as my client began his slow rhythmical shafting. Tom and Mary would be waiting, looking out of the window and wondering where the man had got to. Frank was now my client, I thought happily as he increased his anal shafting. And Derek, the man over the road. That was two customers I'd stolen. How many more were there?

Not only had Tom and Mary lost two clients, but they'd lost me. According to Derek, they had some other girls working for them but, with no clients, things were going to gradually fall apart and the business would end up somewhat fruitless. I felt no guilt for destroying my neighbours' money-making venture. After all, they'd used and abused me, and they deserved no less that ruination. To sell me for sex like that was evil, I mused. But I'd make sure that their business ended in tatters.

'You're a tight-arsed little whore,' Frank breathed as his swollen glans repeatedly sank deep into the heat of my bowels. 'I've always loved fucking tight little bottom-holes.'

'Then you've come to the right place,' I quipped.

'I might even call three times each week, if that's all right with you?'

'You call as many times as you like, Frank. My bum will always be open for you.'

Three times each week? I pondered as he fucked me with a vengeance and neared his climax. At fifty pounds a time? That was fine by me. I wasn't bothered about being labelled a prostitute. After all, a cock was a cock, I thought for the umpteenth time. Whether it was my husband's cock shafting my bottom or a stranger's, it made no difference to me. The only difference was that strangers paid me. My clitoris swelling, my vaginal milk streaming from my neglected sex hole, I was thinking how well things had turned out when I turned my head and happened to notice Alan spying through the window.

Shit, I thought, wondering whether I'd ever be rid of him. Didn't he go to work any more? He was always lurking, hanging around my house and spying on me. Had he lost his job? He must be living nearby, I decided as Frank announced his imminent coming.

It seemed that, every time I looked out of the window, Alan was there. Creeping up the drive, hiding behind bushes, gazing through the lounge window like a peeping Tom . . . He must have found a flat close by, which was all I needed. And he must have lost his job. Either that, or he'd taken a hell of a lot of time off work.

'Yes,' Frank gasped as his cock swelled to an incredible size and his creamy spunk flooded my bowels. 'You're a naughty little schoolgirl,' he breathed. 'A dirty filthy little girl. I'll put you across my knee and pull your navy-blue knickers down and spank you. I'll finger your sweet schoolgirlie bottom-hole and . . .'

Losing himself in his fantasy as he shafted my sperm-flooded rectum, his swinging balls battering my shaved pussy lips, he was obviously enjoying his first visit to my house. If this was all he wanted, just a quick anal fuck, I'd be rid of him in no time at all. Wasn't he into anilingus? I pondered. Didn't he enjoy straight sex or mouth fucking? He'd said that he was heavily into anal sex. If that was all he wanted for fifty pounds, that was fine by me.

Perhaps he'd recommend me to his friends, I mused as his sex cream overflowed and streamed down to my vaginal entrance. Three men a day at fifty pounds each? Four men, five men . . . The only limitation was my endurance. I could easily take three anal shaftings each day, I decided. And probably half a dozen or more cocks into my accommodating vagina. Grinning as I watched Alan gazing at me through the window, I reckoned that I could suck a dozen knobs to orgasm every day with no trouble at all. God, I thought as my body jolted with the crude arse fucking. I was turning into a sex machine.

155

'Naughty little girl,' Frank murmured. 'Dirty naughty little girl. I ought to finger both your tight little holes and then spank your bare bottom. I'll pull your school knickers down and give your bare bottom a damned good spanking.'

Listening to his muttering, I wondered what Alan was thinking as he pressed his face against the window and watched the crude anal fucking. Was he wanking? I mused as Frank stilled his deflating cock deep within my well-creamed rectal sheath. Was he splattering his spunk over the ground as he watched his wife take an anal shafting from an old man? One thing was for certain, I wasn't going to be free of Alan and his voyeurism.

'Perfect,' Frank breathed as his cock slipped out of my wet anal hole with a loud sucking sound. 'You're good, very good.'

'I'm glad you're pleased with me,' I said, hauling my trembling body upright. 'After all, I'm here to please.'

'I never did like that bloody box of Tom's,' he murmured, zipping his trousers. 'I like to stand up when I'm doing a girl's tight arse. The only thing I'm going to miss is the schoolgirl.'

'Schoolgirl?' I echoed, frowning at him as I pulled my knickers up my long legs.

'She wasn't a real schoolgirl,' he returned with a chuckle. 'But she wore a uniform and allowed me to spank her bare bottom.'

'I see,' I murmured pensively. 'I think I'm too old to wear a school uniform. But I'll bear your comments in mind.'

'Do you know of any teenage girls who might be interested?'

'Maybe. Leave it with me.'

'OK. Well, thank you for a most pleasant time. Er . . . Do you want me to ring you or shall I just call in?'

156

'Ring me,' I replied, grabbing a pen and writing my phone number of a piece of paper. 'And, if you have any friends who might be interested . . .'

'Maybe,' he said, chuckling as he winked at me. 'Leave it with me.'

'OK, Frank. I'll look forward to seeing you again.'

Leading him through the hall and opening the front door, I hoped that Alan wasn't still lurking outside. I was going to have to do something about Alan, but what? Watching Frank walk down the drive, I also hoped that Tom or Mary wouldn't see him leaving my house. There again, it was none of their business, I mused, closing the door and heading for the kitchen. If they were losing clients, then that was their fault.

It seemed strange to think that I'd called out of the window to a man I'd never seen before and invited him into my house for anal sex. It had all happened so quickly, I reflected. A business deal. He tosses fifty pounds onto the coffee table and I bend over the back of a chair and allow him to fuck my arse. Quick, easy, no ties . . . He was happy, and I'd earned fifty pounds. Rather a nice arrangement, I thought.

The doorbell rang as I filled the kettle, and I instinctively knew that it was Alan. His key no longer fitted the lock, so I had nothing to worry about. He could stand there ringing the bell all day, and I'd ignore him. He'd got his kicks from watching his wife enduring a beautiful anal fucking, so what more did he want? Knowing Alan, he'd want to stand over me and wank and splatter my face with his spunk. He could go to hell, I thought, pouring myself a cup of coffee.

Taking my coffee into the lounge as the phone rang, I was sure that it was Alan. Would he never give up? I thought angrily, imagining him hiding in

157

the bushes and calling me on his mobile phone. Eyeing the cash on the table, I grinned. Fifty pounds for a quick anal shagging, I mused in my decadence. I was going to do well, very well now that I was a single woman. But I had to get Alan out of my life. Grabbing the phone, I was about to tell Alan where to go when Mary's voice asked me how I was feeling. Had she seen Frank leaving my house? I pondered anxiously.

'I'm feeling a little better,' I replied. 'Hopefully, I'll be all right by tomorrow.'

'That's good. Have you had any visitors this morning?'

'Visitors?' I echoed, realising that the bitch had seen Frank. 'Er . . . No, why?'

'I thought I saw someone leaving your house earlier. It looked like a friend of mine and I just thought that . . .'

'Oh, yes, someone did call. He was selling life assurance, so I sent him on his way.'

'That's odd, because I'm sure I know him. Did he give his name?'

'No, he didn't. Look, I'm not feeling too good so . . .'

'All right, I'll see you tomorrow at ten o'clock.'

'Yes, yes that's fine.'

So, she had seen Frank, I mused as I replaced the receiver and sipped my coffee. She'd eventually discover that he was now visiting me for sex rather than going to her house, but there'd be nothing she could do about it. It was the customer's choice. Things were looking very good, but I still had Alan to deal with. Maybe he'd give up once we were divorced. There again, I doubted that he'd ever give up. Would I ever be free of him? At least he couldn't get into the house, I reflected as I finished my coffee.

Making my way upstairs to the spare room at the back of the house, I pondered on a sex den. Alan wouldn't be able to gaze through the window and watch my debauched acts. I'd be able to commit every perverted deed imaginable with my clients, and he'd remain totally oblivious. Feeling elated, I grinned. I had work to do, I thought happily. The furniture had to go, I'd need vibrators and handcuffs and ... and a whip?

Nine

I was up early and looking forward to Derek's visit at ten o'clock. I'd come up with a kinky theme for my business and had placed a table in the middle of the spare room. Tom and Mary's sex den with its wooden box was boring. Frank had said that he'd not liked the box because he wanted to see the girl he was screwing, which was understandable. My idea was a medical sex room. I'd covered the table with a rubber sheet, transforming it into my examination table. I still needed some equipment such as vibrators and speculums, but I had some latex gloves and candles which I was sure my clients would love to use when examining me.

Feeling nervous, pacing the lounge floor, I continually checked the time. Would Derek be happy with the sex room and my medical theme? I should have asked him what he liked, what he was into. My white cotton knickers hugging the freshly shaved lips of my vulva, my juices of desire seeping into the tight crotch, I felt as horny as hell. Gazing out of the lounge window as the time approached ten, I wondered whether Tom or Mary were keeping an eye out for their clients. They expected me to go to their house for a couple of hours of sex and debauchery. What would they do when they realised that I wasn't going to turn up?

I had to admit to feeling a little fearful of my neighbours. Not only had I left them in the lurch by not turning up for the second day running, but I was stealing their clients. What would they do? I wondered, again staring out of the lounge window. I didn't suppose for one minute that they'd take kindly to my setting up in competition with them, let alone stealing their clients. There again, if Frank and Derek said nothing to them, they'd never know of my sex den. But Mary had seen Frank leaving my house and she was bound to . . . My heart jumped as the phone rang, and I grabbed the receiver.

'It's ten o'clock,' Mary said. 'Are you coming round?'

'I'm still feeling a little queasy,' I lied. 'I was about to ring you.'

'OK, not to worry. Our sex room is coming to an end, so it doesn't matter.'

'Coming to an end? What do you mean?'

'We're moving next week, so I'm afraid you'll be out of a job.'

'Oh, I see,' I breathed, trying to conceal my excitement.

'It's Tom's work. He's been promoted and will be based in London, so we'll have to move. God knows what we're going to do with all the stuff in the sex room. The problem is that we're going to a small flat, so we'll have very little space.'

'That's a shame, Mary,' I breathed, unable to believe my luck. 'I was looking forward to coming round again.'

'If there's anything you want in the way of furniture, you're welcome to it. The flat is furnished, you see.'

'Yes, there may be one or two things I'd like.'

'If you feel up to it later, come round and have a look.'

161

'Yes, I will.'

'All right, I'll see you later.'

This really was a stroke of luck, I mused, replacing the receiver and again looking out of the lounge window. Wondering whether Mary would give me the equipment from her sex room, I reckoned that my future was looking better than ever. She might even refer her clients to me, I thought happily. This was too good to be true. Again checking the time, I was beginning to think that Derek wasn't going to turn up. This was a good start, I thought, wondering whether to go over the road to see him.

The time dragged on. I waited until ten thirty before giving up on Derek. Something must have cropped up, I thought. If that was the case, then he should have let me know that he couldn't keep his appointment. Deciding to take Mary up on her offer, I locked the house and went round to her back door. At least I'd have the opportunity to get on with my sex room, I thought, imagining taking Mary's vibrators and speculums. And the whips?

I decided not to have a go at her about selling my body for sex. Although I'd initially been fuming, I didn't see the point in ruining my opportunity to get my hands on her sex equipment. Besides, if it hadn't been for Tom and Mary, I'd have never set up in business. Vibrators, whips and canes, vaginal speculums . . . I'd soon have an amazing sex room of my own. And I'd be making decent money.

'Helen, come in,' she invited me, opening the door. 'How are you feeling?'

'A little better,' I replied, stepping into the kitchen. 'It must have been a stomach bug or something. So, you're moving away?'

'Sadly, yes. As I said, Tom's been promoted so he'll be based in London. I'm not looking forward to living in a flat, but it can't be helped. Is there anything in particular you want in the way of furniture? Or maybe you'd like the things from the sex room?'

'Well, I wouldn't mind a vibrator or two,' I said with a giggle. 'Perhaps a few things to remind me of you and Tom.'

'Come up and you can help yourself,' she said, walking into the hall. 'I'm going to miss the sex room. We've had some great times but . . . Oh well, all good things come to an end.'

'You certainly have a lot of gear,' I said, following her up the stairs into the sex room.

'Yes, and it all has to go.'

As Mary began emptying a cupboard full of speculums and vibrators, I was amazed by the amount of equipment she had. This was just what I needed for my new business venture. No doubt I'd make a lot of money, and receive immense sexual gratification from my clients. But I knew that I'd miss Mary's intimate attention. Selling my young body to old men for sex was despicable, but . . . but licking and sucking her clitoris to orgasm had been an incredible experience, and one that I'd miss very much. She was so young and attractive and sensual. Although I'd not enjoyed the whip, I knew that I was going to miss the fun and games.

'You're an incredible girl,' she breathed, standing before me and squeezing my breasts though the thin material of my blouse. 'I'm really going to miss you. I know that you didn't like my games, playing the role of my maid and –'

'I did, Mary,' I cut in. 'It's just that I didn't like the whip.'

'I got carried away,' she sighed. 'I love whipping girls' naked bums, and I got carried away. This might interest you,' she said, pointing to two wooden posts rising from the floor to the ceiling. 'Tom made it a while ago, but we've never got round to using it.'

'What are they for?' I asked her, running my hand over the smooth wooden posts.

'I'll show you, if you like. How about a little fun before I dismantle the room?'

'Well, I . . .'

'Just for old times' sake?' she persisted. 'Tom isn't here, so why not have a little lesbian fun with me?'

'OK,' I agreed, my clitoris swelling as I imagined Mary's tongue delving into my wet sex crack.

'Stand between the posts, and I'll show you how it works. I'm sure you'd love one last beautiful orgasm.'

'Yes, yes I would,' I sighed as my arousal began to soar.

Taking up position, I allowed Mary to lift my arms and cuff my wrists to the steel rings set at the top of the posts. Parting my feet, she cuffed my ankles to the bottom of the posts and then stood upright. I felt quite safe as she looked me up and down and smiled at me. Her long blonde hair cascading over her shoulders, her firm breasts clearly outlined by her white blouse, she really was an attractive young girl. Breathing in the scent of her perfume as she kissed my cheeks, I felt my stomach somersault. Tom was out, and we were going to enjoy one last beautiful lesbian encounter before she moved away.

'I wish I wasn't going away,' she breathed, stroking my cheek. 'What will you do about work? Getting a job and earning some money, I mean.'

'I don't know,' I replied dreamily as she slipped her hand up my short skirt and pressed her fingertips into the crotch of my wet knickers. 'I'll have to find something to bring in some cash.'

'What about the clients you stole from me?' she

asked me, cocking her head to one side. 'Surely, you'll earn enough money from them?'

'Clients?' I echoed shakily, frowning at her. 'I – I don't know what you mean.'

'The clients you stole from me, Helen. It's all right. I'm moving away so you're welcome to them.'

'How did you find out?'

'I saw Frank going to your house and I put two and two together. Is that why you've not been here? Were you afraid that I'd find out and . . .'

'Well, yes,' I confessed as she slipped her fingers between my knickers and my thigh.

'You are a silly girl,' she said with a giggle. 'Why were you afraid?'

'I thought . . . Well, I thought that you might whip me or something.'

'There's no might about it,' she hissed, tearing my knickers from my tethered body. 'You're in for the thrashing of your life.'

'Mary, no . . . Please . . .'

'You dare to steal my clients? You make out that you're ill when all along you were entertaining my clients? You little bitch.'

'We'll have to teach her a lesson,' Tom said, walking into the room and grinning at me. 'A lesson she won't forget for a long, long time.'

I'd been such a fool, I thought fearfully as Mary ripped my blouse from my trembling body. The evil couple had planned this. They weren't dismantling the sex room and moving away. Offering me the furniture, taking me up to the sex room . . . The whole thing had been planned. I couldn't believe how stupid I'd been by falling for their trick. As Tom ran a pair of scissors up the front of my miniskirt and tossed the garment aside, Mary cut my bra in two. Tethered to the wooden frame, my naked body completely defenceless, I knew that there was no escaping my captors.

Tom knelt before me and parted the hairless lips of my vulva and commented on the creamy juices seeping from my tight love hole. Slipping his thumbs into my hot sex sheath, he chuckled wickedly as he painfully stretched open my vaginal entrance. I had no idea what they had planned for me, for my naked body, but I knew that I was in for a horrendous time. Opening my tight hole further, Tom gazed into my vaginal canal and again chuckled.

'I reckon that you could fit two cocks in there,' he said.

'No,' I breathed, trying to imagine two massive penises driving deep into my tight pussy. 'Please, I –'

'Three, possibly?' Mary rejoined. 'Blindfold her and we'll bring in our client.'

'Certainly,' Tom said, grabbing a blindfold from the shelf and moving behind me.

'Anonymity,' Mary breathed. 'You'll never know who's fucked you, Helen. It could be Tom or a man living in the street. It could be –'

'No, please,' I again begged as Tom blindfolded me. 'Look, I'll work for you and –'

'It's too late, Helen,' Mary cut in. 'You had a job here, a good job. And you tried to put us out of business. Tom, ask our client in.'

Hearing movements behind me, I wondered who the hell the unseen man was. The door closed as fingers ran over the firm cheeks of my bottom and delved deep into my anal crease. Was it Derek? I pondered. A fingertip teasing the sensitive brown ring of my anus, I couldn't believe that I was back in Tom and Mary's sex room. How on earth had I been stupid enough to fall into their trap? More to the point, what did the future hold now? The last thing I wanted to do was advertise for clients. How would I ever get my business off the ground now?

The finger entering the tight duct of my rectum, my naked body trembling, I could hear the man behind me breathing deeply. I was enjoying the crude sex, the beautiful abuse of my tethered body, but I needed to know the man's identity. He didn't speak as Tom suggested that he ram his cock deep into my arse. Anonymity, I reflected. Were several of my male neighbours Tom and Mary's clients? Meeting men in the street, saying hello to neighbours, I'd never know whether or not they'd fucked me.

The man knelt behind me and yanked my buttocks wide apart and exposed my most secret hole. I could feel his hot breath within my anal crease, his tongue tasting my brown ring, wetting me there. Repeatedly running his wet tongue up my anal valley, lapping at my anal inlet, he finally pushed his tongue into my rectal duct and moaned softly through his nose. I knew that Tom and Mary were watching the forbidden act as the man reached between my parted thighs and thrust at least two fingers into the tight duct of my vagina.

'We'll give her a thrashing afterwards,' Tom murmured. 'How many clients are there?

'Four,' Mary replied. 'Five, if the new one turns up.'

'Why don't you try out your new nipple clamps?' Tom suggested, much to my horror.

'Now that is a good idea,' Mary returned, heading for the shelf.

The brown teats of my nipples were extremely sensitive. Nipple clamps? I couldn't endure such horrendous abuse of my helpless body. But I knew that this was only the beginning of my punishment. The cold metal biting into the sensitive brown protrusions of my breasts, I grimaced as Mary fixed what sounded like thin chains to the clamps. She then attached some kind of weights to the chains, chuckling wickedly as my nipples and areolae stretched into taut cones of flesh. With the pain permeating my milk teats, the firm mounds of my breasts, I let out a gasp as the man behind me pressed his bulbous knob hard against my tightly-closed anal ring.

I could feel the delicate brown tissue surrounding my anal inlet open as his knob entered me. As my anal ring closed slightly, gripping the rim of his helmet, I wondered how thick his penile shaft was. How long was his cock? How deep would he force his huge glans into the very core of my body? I'd come to love the sensations of anal sex. But I needed to know the man's identity. To be fucked and spunked by an unseen stranger was . . . I had no choice.

The weights swinging, painfully pulling on my sensitive breast buds as the man drove the entire length of his massive cock deep into my anal canal, I again grimaced and squeezed my eyes shut in the darkness of the blindfold. My anal duct inflating and deflating with the crude shafting, the swinging weights battering my stomach, I imagined another four or five men waiting in the wings to use and abuse my tethered body. How long was I to be cuffed to the wooden posts? I wondered fearfully. Tom had talked about two cocks forced into my tight sex duct. Would I be held prisoner until he'd witnessed the double shafting of my hot vagina?

The man behind me moaning softly, my anal cylinder lubricated with his gushing sperm, I listened to the squelching sounds of illicit sex as Tom and Mary chuckled. Could my vaginal canal accommodate two solid penises? I mused apprehensively. Tom would have his evil way, I was sure as my naked body rocked with the crude anal shafting. Sperm streaming down my inner thighs as my rectum overflowed, I knew that Tom wouldn't allow me my freedom until he'd committed the most perverse sexual acts imaginable on my tethered body.

The man's cock finally slid out of my inflamed anal duct with a loud sucking sound, and I listened to movements and whispering behind me. The door opened and then closed: the second client had entered the sex room. Did he plan to shaft my rectal sheath? I wondered anxiously. Or was he going to drive his erect cock deep into my wet vagina? The first man's sperm oozing from my inflamed anal eye, the weights pulling painfully on my sore nipples, I knew that I couldn't take much more. But I had no choice other than to endure the crude sexual acts.

As the second man unceremoniously rammed his rock-hard cock deep into my sperm-lubricated rectum, my trembling body was propelled forward by the thrust and I hung from the handcuffs like a rag doll. My head lolling forward as he began his fucking motions, the squelching of sperm resounding around the room, I stared at Tom as he lifted my head and removed the blindfold. He was naked, his cock standing to attention. He was going to force his solid shaft deep into the constricted sheath of my vagina and . . .

'Time for a double fucking,' Tom said, grabbing his cock by the base. 'That's all sluts like you are good for.'

'Give it to her, Tom,' Mary rejoined eagerly. 'Give her a damned good fucking.'

Saying nothing, I again squeezed my eyes shut as the man behind me stilled his penis deep within the wet heat of my rectum and Tom slipped his ballooning knob between the engorged petals of my cream-flecked inner lips. Another first in my journey of forbidden experiences, I mused anxiously as Tom's knob glided along my wet vaginal tube. My two sex holes bloated, stretched to capacity by the solid male organs, I thought that I was going to split open as the men began their pistoning.

Mary settled on the floor between my feet and ran her wet tongue up my inner thighs. She was a dirty little bitch, I thought as she eased a finger alongside Tom's solid cock and massaged the inner flesh of my vagina. She tried to force a finger into my rectum but, thankfully, the man's broad cock wouldn't allow her access. How far could my sex ducts stretch open? I wondered. Was it possible to fit two massive cocks into my tight vagina? Mary continued fingering my vaginal sheath and licking my inner thighs as the men fucked me, and I reckoned that she was hoping for fresh spunk to flow from my holes and drip into her mouth. She was a filthy little whore, I thought. There again, wasn't I?

The double fucking was amazing, the new and exciting sensations driving me wild, but I was still fearful of the whip. I was also fearful of Tom and Mary's intentions. Were they going to release me after my ordeal? They knew damned well that I'd never set foot in their house again, and they must have realised that I'd carry on with my business in competition with them. They couldn't hold me prisoner forever, I mused as the men's cocks swelled and stretched my bloated sex sheaths further. They'd have to release me at some point, wouldn't they?

Sperm flooding my inflamed rectal duct, filling my contracting vagina, I felt my clitoris swell and pulsate as the birth of my orgasm stirred deep within my womb. Swinging from my cuffed wrists as the men repeatedly drove their orgasming knobs deep into my abused body, I listened to Mary slurping between my legs, lapping up the overflowing spunk. Never had I experienced such crude and gratifying sex. Two rock-hard penises fucking the tight holes between my thighs? The beautifully obscene act was the height of decadence.

My orgasm erupting within my pulsating clitoris, I let out a cry of sexual satisfaction as my juices of lust gushed from my abused vagina. My naked rocking with the double fucking, the sounds of sex reverberating around the room, I thought that I'd never come down from my sexual heaven. Again and again, waves of pure sexual bliss crashed through my tethered body, shaking me to the core as my vagina again spasmed and pumped out another deluge of hot milky cream.

'God, yes,' Mary gasped, the blend of male and female orgasmic cream obviously raining over her pretty face. 'Fill her cunt and her arse and I'll suck it out.'

Riding the crest of my climax, my tethered body shaking uncontrollably, I couldn't believe the beautiful sensations of crude sex rippling through my womb. I could feel Mary's tongue lapping at my inner thighs, delving between the thrusting cocks and licking the stretched bridge of skin between my bloated sex holes as the men pumped me full of fresh spunk. Again and again, tremors of sexual ecstasy rocked my body as the cocks fucked me senseless and Mary lapped up the flowing spunk. Never had I experienced such amazing sex, and I knew that I was hooked on double fucking.

My nipples stretching painfully as the weights swung, my orgasm beginning to recede as the men drained their balls, I involuntarily released a gush of hot urine. Mary shrieked with delight as my golden liquid splattered her face. The deflating cocks finally leaving my spunk-flooded sex ducts, she licked and slurped between my thighs as the hot shower continued to rain over her. Tonguing my gaping vaginal opening, she sucked out the fresh spunk, drinking the creamy orgasmic blend from my trembling body.

The door opened and then closed as Mary moved to the gaping hole of my inflamed anus. Another client had entered the room, I knew as she locked her wet lips to my anal eye and sucked out the second load of hot sperm. Still apprehensive about the inevitable thrashing I was going to endure, I let out a rush of breath as Mary tongued my hot vagina and another swollen knob pressed hard against my spunk-wet anus. I loved the crude and obscene sex, but the thought of a severe thrashing was marring my pleasure.

The unseen man's penis gliding into my well-lubricated rectal duct, the sheer girth of his erect organ bloating my once-private sheath, he grabbed my waist and rammed his cock fully home. My anus burning, the delicate brown tissue stretched tautly around the base of the man's huge member, I couldn't take much more of the anal abuse. Who was the man? I wondered. Was he a neighbour of mine? Had I passed him in the street? I'd never discover the identity of my abusers, unless my own business got off the ground and they became my clients.

My tethered body rocking back and forth with the crude anal fucking, I was becoming more determined than ever to steal Tom and Mary's clients. Once I'd been given my freedom, I'd go over the road and talk to Derek. Why hadn't he turned up? Had Tom and Mary been to see him and threatened him? Was he the man behind me with his cock shafting my inflamed rectum? I'd complete my sex room, I decided. I'd offer my expert services to men, and put Tom and Mary out of business. But, first, I had to endure a gruelling thrashing.

'God, yes,' the man behind me murmured as his pistoning cock swelled within my anal cylinder. I was sure that I knew his voice, but I couldn't put a name to it. It wasn't Derek, I was certain as my rectum flooded with another load of creamy spunk. Who the hell was it? My arms high above in the air, my wrists cuffed to the wooden posts, I couldn't turn my head to look at my abuser. Who the hell was it? I again wondered as the squelching of sperm echoed around the room. Did I know him?

Mary finally slipped her tongue out of my contracting vagina and stood before me. Her face dripping with a cocktail of sperm, girl-cum and my golden liquid, she held my head and locked her wet lips to mine in a passionate kiss. The aphrodisiacal taste of my juices drove me wild as she slipped her wet tongue deep into my mouth, and I felt my clitoris swell again. My naked body hanging from the handcuffs, my arms aching, I breathed in the scent of Mary's sex-wet hair. Never had I been so aroused as I returned her lesbian kiss and sucked on her wet tongue. Three cocks? I mused dreamily in my sexual delirium. Two solid organs shafting my sex holes and one fucking my mouth?

The man fucking my inflamed rectum finally slipped his spent cock out of my anal hole. I'd lost count of how many rock-hard cocks had fucked me. Were there more men eagerly waiting in the wings? I pondered as Mary's mouth left mine and she moved back. How many more crude shaftings could I take? While a stream of spunk left my anal opening and coursed down my inner thighs, and with my naked body trembling uncontrollably, I watched Mary grab a thin bamboo cane from the corner of the room. This was it, I thought fearfully as she flexed the cane and grinned at me. I was in for the thrashing of my life.

'Disobedience,' she breathed, tapping the palm of her hand with the bamboo. 'I will not tolerate disobedience. It's no wonder that Alan couldn't put up with you.'

'Perhaps he should have given you a damned good thrashing now and then,' Tom rejoined. 'Had he instilled obedience in you, things might have turned out different.'

I tensed my bare buttocks as Mary moved behind my tethered body. Recalling her words, I wondered what on earth she was talking about. *It's no wonder that Alan couldn't put up with you.* Had Alan been talking to her? I wondered. What had he said about me, about our marriage? More to the point, had he been to Tom and Mary's house? God, I thought, imagining him to be a client of theirs. Had he stood behind me and shafted my rectal duct? I knew that Alan was a voyeur, but I was sure that he knew nothing about the sex room.

As the cane swished through the air and landed squarely across my naked bottom with a loud crack, I let out a deafening scream. All thoughts of Alan faded as the cane swiped my bum cheeks again. My pleading and begging for Mary to halt the gruelling thrashing only serving to drive her on, she again brought the cane down across the clenched cheeks of my stinging buttocks with a loud crack. My mind in turmoil, my buttocks burning, I began counting the times the cane flailed me. Six, seven, eight . . .

'Disobedient whore,' Mary hissed as I again cried out and begged for mercy. 'Filthy little slut.' Halting the punishment, she stood before me. 'You, my girl, are going to behave yourself from now on. I'm going to release you and allow you to leave. But there's a condition. You'll be back here this evening at seven o'clock. Do you understand?'

'Yes, yes I do,' I murmured shakily as relief engulfed me.

'You'll clean yourself up, wash the spunk out of your cunt and your arse, and be here at seven. If you don't turn up . . . I don't think you need me to tell you what will happen.'

'Seven o'clock, on the dot,' Tom said, releasing my wrists and removing the clamps from my distended nipples. 'If you're one second late, then you'll have your cunt thrashed.'

Lowering my aching arms as he released my ankles, I vowed never to return to the sex room. Grabbing my keys from the floor, I didn't bother to gather up my torn clothing. Naked, I left the room and bounded down the stairs to the back door and made my escape before they had a change of mind. The fresh air cooling my abused body as I dashed to my house, I was free at last. Sperm oozing from the burning eye of my anus, my stinging buttocks glowing a fire-red, my nipples aching like hell . . . Never again would I set foot in the evil couple's house.

After a shower, I went to bed and fell into a deep sleep. I dreamed my dreams of caning and whipping and double fucking and spunking. What the hell had happened to me, to my life? I wondered as I was woken several hours later by the doorbell. Slipping into my dressing gown, I went down to the lounge and peered through the net curtains. I'd expected to see Alan hovering on the doorstep, but it was Derek from across the road. A thousand thoughts swirled in the confusion of my mind. Had Tom and Mary spoken to him? Had he come to say that he didn't

175

want to become one of my clients? Feeling somewhat anxious, I finally opened the door.

'It's a shame about earlier,' he sighed. 'I was really looking forward to it. Are you able to fit me in now?'

'Earlier?' I echoed. 'What do you mean? Why didn't you turn up?'

'Well, you were busy,' he replied, frowning at me. 'I didn't think you'd want me turning up with Alan here.'

'Alan was here?' I gasped. 'Are you sure, Derek?'

'Of course I'm sure,' he returned with a chuckle. 'I may be getting on in years, but I can still recognise your husband.'

'You'd better come in,' I invited him, pulling my gown together. 'What time did he call round?'

'Just before ten o'clock,' he replied, following me into the lounge. 'You must have heard the doorbell because you let him in.'

'I didn't hear the doorbell, Derek. And I certainly didn't let him in.'

'In that case, he must have used his key.'

'He hasn't got a key. At ten o'clock, I was here, waiting for you. Alan didn't come into the house.'

'I saw him, Helen,' he sighed. 'That's why I didn't come over. In fact, he saw me and waved. The funny thing was that he looked rather guilty.'

'In what way?'

'He looked through the lounge window and then turned and noticed me. He waved and sort of hovered for a while before he went into the house.'

'I'm not surprised that he looked guilty. So, did you see him leave?'

'No, I didn't hang around. I went back to my place and sat in the garden.'

'I'm sorry about all this, Derek.'

'You'd better have the lock changed,' he said,

grinning at me. 'The last thing you want is Alan walking in when you're entertaining a client.'

'I've had the lock . . . Yes, yes I'll do that. I'll slide the bolt across in future.'

Hearing a noise upstairs, I knew that Alan was in the house. How the hell had he got hold of a key? I mused angrily. Remembering that I'd left the spare key on the hall table, I realised that he must have taken it when I'd answered the phone and left him in the hall. He was weird, I thought, wondering what the hell to do. Would I never be rid of him? Had he been in the house all the time? Had he been watching me sleeping? At least he'd not stood by the bed and wanked and shot his spunk all over me.

'I was really looking forward to this morning,' Derek sighed, breaking my reverie. 'I don't suppose you could fit me in now?'

'Can you come over in an hour or so?' I said, smiling at him. 'I have a couple of things to do.'

'Yes, that's great,' he trilled, checking his watch. 'I'll be here at seven.'

'OK, that's good. So, what are you into? Do you like straight sex or . . .'

'Domination,' he replied eagerly. 'I'd like you to be my school teacher and . . .'

'No problem,' I cut in with a giggle. 'I know exactly what you want.'

'OK, I'll see you in an hour,' he said, heading for the hall. 'I just hope that Alan doesn't turn up again.'

'He won't turn up,' I called as he let himself out.

Pacing the lounge floor, I wondered whether to climb the stairs and confront Alan. This was becoming too much, I thought as anger welled from the pit of my stomach. It was about time that I got him out of my life, for good. There again, the idea of my husband watching an old man fuck me was sending my arousal through the roof. I had no idea why I felt that way, but the notion of Alan watching an old man slide his cock deep into my wet cunt was turning me on. Cunt. I'd never liked the word. But, now? Crude sex, anal sex, double fucking, throat spunking, cunt licking . . . I was a common whore, a prostitute.

Hearing a dull thud on the ceiling, I knew that Alan was in my bedroom. What the hell was he up to? I wondered, imagining him wanking and splattering his spunk over my bed. Had he watched me go round to Tom and Mary's. Had he spied out of the window? More to the point, had he seen me come back naked with my bum glowing from a gruelling caning? I was supposed to be at Tom and Mary's at seven o'clock, I reflected. But I was about to entertain a client and earn some money. Would they come for me? Would Tom thrash my cunt? Tom and Mary could go to hell.

Ten

I'd lost the battle raging in my mind. I should have confronted Alan, thrown him out of the house, but I loved the idea of him watching Derek fucking me. I wanted my husband to watch another man's cock fucking me, I wanted him to listen to the sounds of crude adulterous sex. I was falling deeper into the pit of decadence, plunging further into the mire of my own debauchery. There was no turning back now, I knew as my clitoris stirred beneath its pink bonnet. I was a fully fledged slut. All this was Alan's fault, I mused. He'd driven me to . . . No, this was my doing. My new line of work, prostitution, and the mess I'd got myself into with Tom and Mary . . . It was my doing.

I'd been up to my bedroom and changed into a miniskirt and blouse in readiness for my client, and I'd noticed Alan hiding beneath the bed. He couldn't do anything properly, I reflected as I ran a brush through my long black hair. I'd clearly seen his foot beneath the end of the bed. He couldn't even play his voyeur games properly. What the hell was he trying to achieve? I wondered as I left the room and closed the door. A thought struck me as I descended the stairs. If Alan paid me, I'd perform for him, allow him to watch the abuse of my willing body. Should I sell myself to my husband for sex?

I closed and locked all the windows and the back door. This time, it wasn't to keep Alan out of my house. It was to keep Tom and Mary out. With the time approaching seven, I knew that they'd be waiting for me in their sex room. I also knew that, when I didn't turn up, they'd come round to get me. *If you're one second late, then you'll have your cunt thrashed.* I was safe enough in my house, I thought happily as I gazed out of the lounge window and saw Derek heading up the drive. Why was he wearing a long overcoat?

Although my sex holes were still inflamed from the crude double fucking and my buttocks were red-raw from the thrashing, I was looking forward to an hour of crude sex with Derek. Wondering how big his cock was as he rang the doorbell, I felt my juices of desire seep into the tight crotch of my white cotton knickers. My clitoris swelling again, I walked through the hall and took a deep breath. I was to be a dominant school teacher, I reflected. And Derek was a naughty little schoolboy. Should I grab a cane from the garden and thrash him?

'I'm sorry I'm late, Miss,' he said, grinning as he passed me fifty pounds.

'Get up to my room,' I snapped, slipping the notes beneath the letters on the hall table. This was obviously part of his game as he wasn't late at all. 'How dare you keep me waiting,' I bellowed as I closed the front door and followed him up the stairs.

Showing him into my bedroom, I stared open-mouthed as he slipped his overcoat off. He was wearing a school uniform. Complete with grey shorts and a blazer, a white shirt and school tie, he looked rather odd. But this was all part of his role-playing and, for fifty pounds, I was more than willing to play my part in his fantasy. Stifling a laugh as I looked down at Derek's knobbly knees, I wondered what the hell Alan was thinking. There again, being a complete weirdo, he was probably planning on getting himself a schoolboy uniform.

'Are you going to punish me, Miss?' Derek asked me hopefully.

'I have no choice,' I snapped, loving the game. 'You were caught wanking in the toilets. How many times have you been told not to do that?'

'But, I was only –'

'Be quiet. I want you to show me exactly what you were doing.'

'You want me to get it out, Miss?'

'Pull your penis out and wank it. I want to see exactly what you did so that I can decide on your punishment.'

For an ageing man, he had a thick and beautifully solid cock. His heavy balls hanging invitingly below the root of his shaft, I knew that I was going to enjoy running my own business. Fully retracting his fleshy foreskin and exposing his glistening purple knob, he began his wanking motions. I was desperate to suck on his knob, taste his salt and bring out his spunk. But he wanted to play his game, act out his schoolboy fantasy. He was my client, and it was my job to please him.

Standing in what was the marital bedroom, watching a man running his hand up and down his rock-hard cock . . . It was a strange feeling. And, to think that my husband was hiding beneath the bed, watching the proceedings, was a bizarre concept. The marital bedroom, I mused dolefully. What had happened to us? Why had Alan been hell bent on taking my smile away? But I was smiling again now. More than smiling, I was grinning. Alan now knew that I was a prostitute. He may have had his suspicions in the past, but he now knew that his once loyal and faithful wife was selling her body to old men for sex. And yet, I still had no idea what his thoughts were. What were his intentions? Did he plan to spend the rest of his days trying to watch me commit grossly indecent sexual acts? If that was the case then, to what end?

Derek ran his hand up and down his cock slowly, and I knew that he was going through the motions rather than wanking properly to bring out his spunk. He was saving his spunk for me, I thought excitedly. Where did he want to pump his sex cream? Did he want to fill my mouth? Or was he planning to pump his seed deep into the wet heat of my bowels, or the hot sheath of my contracting vagina? Would he come more than once?

'Stop it,' I instructed him. 'Having witnessed your disgusting act, I've decided on your punishment.' Lifting my skirt and parting my feet wide, I felt my womb contract, my stomach somersault. 'Kneel on the floor and suck my knickers,' I ordered him. 'You've made me wet, and now you'll suck my knickers clean.'

Taking his position, he mouthed and sucked eagerly on the creamy-wet crotch of my soaked knickers. Again, my clitoris swelled and my juices of desire oozed from my yearning vaginal hole. To think that I was being paid to receive such immense sexual pleasure was incredible. And to think that my husband was watching the crude act was bizarre. Prostitution, I mused dreamily as Derek bit and nibbled my swollen pussy lips through the wet cotton of my knickers.

I was a prostitute, but I was happy in my new line of work. I had what men needed, what men craved, so why not profit from their needs? After all, my pussy was designed to accommodate solid penises. My body was designed to be fucked, its vaginal throat swallowing creamy sperm into its womb. Was the tight sheath of my rectum designed to be fucked and spunked? Was my pretty mouth made for fucking?

'You're making me even wetter,' I said, parting my feet wider. 'The more cream you make me produce, the more you'll have to suck my knickers.'

Derek said nothing as he continued to suck on the drenched crotch of my knickers. Would he like my shaved pussy? I wondered as I felt my sex milk flowing from my vaginal entrance. There was no rush, I decided, revelling in the mouthing and sucking of my well-creamed knickers. To have a man kneeling on the floor, sucking the juices from the crotch of my knickers, was heavenly. I was in no hurry to have him pull my knickers down and go further. Besides, I wanted to tease him, drive him into a sexual frenzy, before allowing him the delights of my naked pussy.

This was the first time that I'd enjoyed slow gentle sex, I reflected. At Tom and Mary's, I'd been hurriedly fucked and spunked by several frenzied men. But, now, I was enjoying the intimate attention of a man. My arousal was soaring to frightening heights, and I wondered whether it was the thought of my husband being in the same room that was driving me wild. The marital bedroom, adultery, prostitution . . .

'May I pull your knickers down now, Miss?' Derek asked me, his expectant eyes looking up at my sex-flushed face.

'No,' I returned firmly. 'How dare you ask such a thing of your school teacher? You disgust me, boy. Have you no respect?'

'I'm sorry, Miss.'

'You will be,' I returned. 'You'll be extremely sorry for your vulgar manner. My knickers are getting wetter by the minute, so you'd better keep sucking them.'

Although I was teasing Derek, making him wait for the unveiling of my most private place, I was also teasing myself. How much longer could I deny myself the pleasure of his tongue delving deep into my hot and very wet cunt? I needed to feel my solid clitoris sucked into his mouth, his tongue sweeping over the sensitive tip ... Was I also teasing Alan? I pondered as I noticed him peering out from beneath the bed. Was he wanking beneath the once-marital bed?

For the umpteenth time, I thought how strange Alan was. Although we lived apart, he was still my husband. Had he no feelings of jealousy? Adultery was one of the main causes of heartbreak and divorce. The thought of one's partner having sex with another inevitably led to the destruction of marriages. Even though our marriage was already over, had Alan no feelings of resentment? I was blatantly giving my body to another man. While my husband watched, I was acting like a common whore with an old man. What the hell were Alan's thoughts?

As Derek sucked the crotch of my wet knickers, my sex-cream filtered by the thin cotton material, I knew that I could wait no longer for the relief of orgasm. My clitoris painfully swelling, my juices of desire flooding from my vaginal inlet, I felt my womb rhythmically contracting as my arousal shook my body to the core. I needed to come, I needed to feel my clitoris pulsating in orgasm within the wet heat of Derek's mouth.

'What are you doing?' I asked him, noticing his hand toying with his erect penis.

'I was just –'

'Just wanking, yet again?' I cut in angrily. 'For God's sake, boy. Will you never learn?'

'I'm sorry, Miss. It's just that I need to come.'

'You need to come?' I echoed. 'Your audacity amazes me, boy. Get behind me and suck my knickers.'

'Yes, Miss.'

He moved behind me and started sucking on the tight cotton covering my firm buttocks. I could feel the wetness of his saliva soaking my knickers as he ran his tongue up and down my anal crease. Gently sinking his teeth into the firm flesh of my buttocks through the thin cotton, he breathed deeply in his arousal. How much longer would I keep him waiting? I mused in my sexual frenzy. Deciding to allow him to go a little further, I ordered him to pull my knickers down so that the waistband was just below the orbs of my bum cheeks. He complied, yanking my knickers down eagerly and exposing the tightly closed valley of my bottom nestling between my rounded buttocks. Instructing him to lick my anal gulley, I let out a rush of breath as his tongue delved into the hot fissure.

My head spinning, dizzy with the sensations of crude sex, I swayed on my sagging legs as he licked the delicate tissue surrounding my anal hole. His breath warming me, his saliva wetting me, he pushed his tongue into my once sacrosanct hole and tasted the bitterness of my rectum. Little did he know that, earlier in the day, I'd been fucked and spunked there by several rock-hard cocks. Could he taste the lingering sperm? I wondered excitedly as he pushed his tongue deeper into the heat of my tightening rectum.

'You'll notice that I've been thrashed,' I said, more for Alan's ears than Derek's. 'Can you see the weals across my bottom?'

'Yes, Miss,' he replied, slipping his tongue out of my anal hole.

'I was tied up and caned for being a naughty little girl. Do you think I'm a naughty little girl?'

'Well . . . No, Miss.'

'You don't think I'm naughty for ordering you to lick my bottom-hole?'

'No, Miss.'

'You wouldn't be naughty and force your cock up my bum, would you?'

'Well, I – I think –'

'If I told you to fuck my bum, would you do it?'

'Yes, Miss.'

'Show me how you'd do it.'

Leaning on my dressing table with my feet wide apart, I jutted my naked buttocks out. I could see Derek in the mirror as he stood behind me. I could also see Alan's face peering out from beneath the bed as Derek parted the weal-lined cheeks of my bottom and exposed my brown anal hole. Pressing the swollen plum of his solid penis hard against my saliva-wet anus, he let out a rush of breath as my rectal throat swallowed his ripe plum.

After several anal fuckings at Tom and Mary's house, I'd not thought that I'd be taking another cock into my inflamed bottom-hole for some time. But I was hooked on anal sex. The feel of a swollen knob slipping into my anus, a veined shaft stretching my once-private duct wide open . . . The sensations were heavenly, and I knew that I'd be enjoying hundreds of anal shaftings during my work as a prostitute. Would Alan like to drive his solid cock deep into the very core of my open body and flood my bowels with fresh sperm?

I tried to imagine that it was Alan standing behind me as Derek pushed his hard penis slowly into my arse. But he'd never attempted crude sex, never suggested that we experiment in bed. For one who'd been almost asexual during his marriage, he was certainly enjoying his voyeurism. Had he been visiting Tom and Mary? I began to wonder. Had he been a client of theirs for years and had had no need for my young body? Alan wouldn't have cheated on me, would he?

The sensitive tissue of my anus dragging along Derek's veined shaft as he penetrated me, I felt a gush of pussy milk fill the crotch of my panties as he impaled me completely on his beautiful organ. I could still see Alan's reflection in the mirror. His eyes wide as he gazed at the crude coupling, I realised that it was his voyeurism that was driving me into a sexual frenzy. Apart from the beautifully physical sensations of a debauched arse-fucking, it was my husband's eyes upon me that fired my libido.

Holding my hips, Derek withdrew his slimed cock and rammed his knob deep into the dank heat of my bowels. Again, he withdrew, and then propelled his glans deep into the very core of my trembling body. Finding his rhythm, repeatedly thrusting his swollen knob into my bowels, he let out low moans of pleasure as he fucked me. I knew that he was nearing his long-awaited climax as he gasped and increased his pistoning rhythm. Sucking my creamy-wet knickers, tonguing my hot anal hole ... He was dangerously close to his orgasm.

'Naughty boy,' I breathed for Alan's benefit. 'You're a dirty, naughty little boy. If ever I catch you wanking in the toilets, your punishment will be to fuck my tight little arse. Do you understand?'

'Yes, Miss,' Derek replied shakily. 'I – I'm going to come.'

'No,' I snapped. 'I will not allow you to come. If

you fill my arse with sperm, I'll force you to suck the hot milk out of my tight cunt.'

'I – I can't stop it, Miss.'

'I'm warning you, boy. If you dare to –'

His spunk jetting from his throbbing knob and lubricating the illicit coupling, he fucked me with a frenzied vengeance. He was good, I thought languorously as I listened to the squelching sounds of anal sex. As old as he was, he knew exactly how to fuck a girl's arse. It was a shame that Alan had never been sexually adventurous, I reflected, again catching his reflection in the mirror. Why had he never taken it upon himself to treat me like a slut and arse-fuck me? Had he found sexual satisfaction in Tom and Mary's sex room? Maybe I, too, had been unadventurous in bed. Maybe he'd thought me too prudish to entertain such a beautifully vulgar act as anal intercourse and bowel sperming. Was he my neighbour's client?

As Derek repeatedly rammed his orgasming knob deep into my rectum and drained his swinging balls, I pondered on the next obscene act I'd instruct him to commit. The crotch of my knickers filling with my girl-milk, I decided that Derek would suck his own sperm out of my anus. Creamy and warm with a tang of bitterness . . . If he refused to drink from my rectal sheath, I'd make him bend over the bed and I'd thrash him, I mused in my rising wickedness. I had a leather belt in the wardrobe which would make an ideal whip.

His spent penis finally slipping out of my sperm-drenched anal canal with a sucking sound, he staggered back, gasping for breath in the aftermath of his coming. I could feel his sperm oozing from my inflamed anus and trickling over the small bridge of skin to my gaping vaginal entrance. The warm cream going to waste, I had an idea and grabbed a plastic bottle from the dressing table. Passing Derek the bottle, I let out a wicked chuckle.

'Ram it deep into my arse,' I ordered him. 'Push your spunk deep into my arse before it drains away.'

'Yes, Miss,' he replied obediently as he knelt behind me.

'Give me a good fucking with the bottle,' I breathed, leaning over the dressing table.

The bottle slipping into my well-lubricated rectum with ease, I gasped as Derek began his pistoning motions. I could hear the spunk squelching, feel the creamy liquid filling my hot bowels – and I could see Alan's face in the mirror as he watched the obscene act. My arousal soaring sky-high as Derek arse-fucked me with the plastic bottle, I felt decadent, dirty, filthy. Not only was I deriving immense sexual pleasure from my anal duct, but I was earning good money – dirty money. I was a dirty little slut, and I loved it.

'Stop now,' I ordered my pupil. 'Take the bottle out and suck out your spunk.'

'But, Miss –'

'Do it,' I hissed, reaching behind my back and yanking my firm buttocks wide apart as he slipped the bottle out of my rectum. 'Suck your spunk out of my arsehole, or you'll be in severe trouble.'

The feel of his lips locked to my anal ring sending quivers through my contracting womb, I breathed deeply as he sucked hard. I could hear him swallowing his own sperm, gulping down the creamy mixture as he drained my anal duct. This was sex in all its crudity, I reflected as Derek drank from my bottom-hole. Could I sink much deeper into the mire of decadence? I mused. Vulgar, obscene, vile . . . Beautiful.

I allowed him to suck and slurp at my anal entrance until my clitoris was painfully swollen and in dire need of licking to orgasm. Turning, I leaned back on the dressing table and ordered my pupil to tug my very wet knickers down with his teeth. Like an obedient dog, he moved in and pulled the thin cotton material down, exposing the hairless lips of my vulva. His eyes widening, his face grinning, I knew that he liked my shaved pussy.

'Lick my cunt,' I instructed him in my rising sexual frenzy. 'Lap at my cunt crack like a filthy dog.'

My body trembling, my heart racing, I closed my eyes as he repeatedly swept his tongue up the entire length of my valley of desire. My vaginal milk flowing in torrents, pouring into the crotch of my knickers, I listened to the slurping and sucking as my clitoris began to pulsate in the beginnings of orgasm. My womb rhythmically contracting, I could wait no longer for the relief I craved. Pulling my outer sex lips up and apart, exposing the full length of my solid clitoris, I ordered Derek to ram his fingers deep into my hot cunt and suck my pleasure bud into his mouth. Throwing my head back, I let out a long low moan of sexual ecstasy as he complied and almost sucked my pulsating clitoris out of its socket.

'God, yes,' I breathed shakily as my orgasm erupted and sent wonderful tremors of sex throughout my quivering body. His fingers pistoning my contracting cunt, my clitoris pulsating wildly within his hot mouth, I released a gush of orgasmic milk as my climax peaked and gripped my body. Whimpering, shaking uncontrollably, I thought that I'd never come down from the summit of my orgasm as Derek forced at least three fingers deep into my contracting vagina. Waves of pure sexual ecstasy repeatedly rocking my stretched body, I whimpered in my sexual delirium. My mind blown away on the wind of lust, I finally let out a scream of girl-pleasure as my swollen clitoris reached another orgasmic peak and the juices of desire gushed from my fingered cunt.

'No more,' I finally managed to gasp. 'Stop, stop . . . Please, no more.'

'Was that all right, Miss?' Derek asked me, slipping his fingers out of my burning cunt.

'Yes, yes,' I gasped, my head lolling forward, my long black hair veiling my sex-flushed face. 'Dirty boy,' I murmured, clinging to the dressing table as my legs sagged beneath me. 'Dirty, filthy little boy.'

Sitting back on his heels and looking up at me, Derek grinned like a Cheshire cat. He was obviously pleased that he'd pleased me. He was good, I had to admit as I felt another gush of vaginal cream issue from my gaping sex hole. Looking down at the soaked crotch of my knickers, white cotton material stretched between my slender thighs, I couldn't believe how much lubricant I'd produced. Had Alan enjoyed watching me in the grip of my multiple orgasm? I mused dreamily. Had he wanked beneath the once-marital bed and creamed the carpet with his spunk? Although I was exhausted in the aftermath of my coming, I wanted to shock Alan. I wanted him to discover what a dirty little whore I'd become since he'd walked out on me.

'Do you like my hairless cunt?' I asked Derek. 'Do you like my shaved cunt lips?'

'Yes, Miss,' he replied enthusiastically.

'You'd like to fuck my wet cunt, wouldn't you?'

'Yes please, Miss.'

'In that case, take my wet knickers off.'

He pulled my soaked knickers down and slipped them off my feet with an urgency that pleased me. I liked his eagerness, his desire to please, and I reckoned that he'd become my most satisfying client. This was far better than being clamped in Tom and

Mary's wooden box, I reflected. They might have had a successful business, but I was going to offer the clients far more varied and gratifying sex than they could ever dream of. Wondering where they were as I placed my foot on my dressing table, I thought it odd that they'd not hammered on my back door. Perhaps they'd given up on me, I thought as Derek focused on my gaping vulval valley.

'Stand up and fuck my cunt,' I ordered him. 'I want to feel your cock deep inside my cunt, do you understand?'

'Yes, I do, Miss,' he replied, leaping to his feet with his erect cock sticking out of his shorts. 'I understand only too well.'

'Take your shorts off, boy. I want to see and feel your balls when you fuck me.'

After slipping his shorts off, he stood before me with his organ standing to attention, rising above his heaving balls like a monument to the male species. He was big, I again mused happily as I eyed his thick veined shaft. I knew that Alan would have a perfect view of his swollen knob slipping between the engorged petals of my inner lips. He'd witnessed more than enough of my debauchery to realise that I was a dirty adulterous slut. But I had to commit one more act of sexual depravity.

Derek's knob slid into my sex-drenched vaginal canal with ease. I let out a gasp as he rammed his cock-head deep into my quivering body. He withdrew, then thrust into me again with such force that I almost keeled over backwards. He was good, I again mused as he found his thrusting rhythm. Had Alan been this good, I might have taken him back. There again, it wasn't only the sex that had lacked in our relationship. Where Alan was concerned, normality was non-existent.

My cervix repeatedly battered by Derek's huge knob, my lower stomach rising with each thrust of his solid cock, I knew that I'd soon reach another mind-blowing orgasm. I could see Alan watching from beneath the bed as my client fucked me, and I again wondered what his thoughts were. He could clearly see Derek's cock pistoning my tight pussy, the old man's balls bouncing as he neared his climax. Was Alan jealous?

My spasming vagina flooding with spunk, the creaming liquid spurting from my fucked holes and running down my leg, I shuddered as my own orgasm erupted within the pulsating nub of my clitoris. His pussy-wet shaft massaging my swollen sex button as he fucked me, he increased his rhythm and sustained my incredible pleasure. He was thinking of my satisfaction as well as his, which pleased me. Kissing my neck, biting my ear lobe, he held me close as he drained his swinging balls. This was more like making love than fucking, I thought dreamily. But Derek was a paying client, and love didn't come into it. Would I ever fall in love?

'Enough,' I finally gasped. His cock slid out of my spermed cunt and he leaned on the dressing table to steady his trembling body. 'You're a good boy,' I panted. 'A very good boy.'

'And you're a wonderful teacher, Miss,' he returned with a chuckle.

'If you're caught wanking in the toilets again, you'll be in trouble. Do you understand?'

'Yes, Miss.'

'Right, you may go now.'

Pulling his shorts on as I recovered from my amazing orgasm, he couldn't stop grinning. He'd enjoyed his time with me, and I was sure that he'd be back for many more sessions. If he only called twice each week, I'd earn four hundred pounds each month, I mused happily. And that was only from one client. Watching Derek straighten his clothes and grab his overcoat, I thought that he wasn't bad looking for his age. He was a good client, and I reckoned that he'd bring me new customers. After my ordeal at Tom and Mary's, I was beginning to feel positive again. I was also feeling extremely sexually gratified.

'I'll see you soon,' Derek said, opening the bedroom door. 'I must say that coming here is far better than visiting Tom and Mary's sex room.'

'Er ... Yes,' I said, realising that Alan was listening. 'I'll see you out.'

Ushering him down the stairs, I wondered whether Alan had known what Derek was talking about. He must have done, I reflected. Tom and Mary's sex room? He'd realise immediately that they were running a brothel. Although I enjoyed performing in front of my husband, I could see that there were going to be problems. There was already a problem: he was stuck beneath my bed. What did he intend to do? He could hardly stay beneath the bed and would have to make his escape before long. But, with me in the house, it wouldn't be easy for him.

Helping Derek with his overcoat, I saw him out and closed the front door. I needed a shower, I decided as sperm oozed from my sex holes and trickled down my inner thighs. I climbed the stairs, went into the bathroom and locked the door. Alan was now free to leave. Having satisfied his thirst for voyeurism, he could now make his escape. Wondering what his long-term plan was as I washed the spunk and girl-juice from my sex crack, I realised that I'd never shock him. In fact, the more crude sexual acts I committed, the more he'd want to watch.

After a shower, I slipped into my miniskirt and blouse and went into the spare room. A medical examination room, I pondered. I was about to have a look on the internet for some sex toys when the front doorbell rang. This was all I needed, I thought as I bounded down the stairs. What the hell did Alan want now? But what if it was Tom or Mary? I slipped into the lounge and peeped through the net curtains. There was a young blonde girl hovering on the step, and I instinctively knew that this had something to do with the wicked couple next door. Had she been sent to lure me into the sex room? I mused as I walked down the hall and opened the door.

'Hi,' she said softly, her full lips furling into a smile. 'Do you mind if I come in for a minute?'

'Who are you?' I asked, eyeing her tight T-shirt clinging to the mounds of her small breasts. 'What is it you want?'

'I need to talk to you,' she replied. 'It's about working for you.'

'Working for me?'

'I work next door, if you see what I mean? I overheard them talking and . . .'

'You'd better come in,' I invited her, closing and bolting the front door once she had stepped into the hall.

I led her into the lounge and ordered her to sit on the sofa. Her blonde hair framing her fresh face, her slender legs emerging from beneath her red miniskirt, I reckoned that she was no older that eighteen. With blue eyes and succulent red lips, she was stunningly attractive. But, what the hell did she want? More to the point, had Tom and Mary sent her? Eyeing her naked thighs, I imagined the tightly closed crack of her teenage pussy. Had she shaved? I mused, standing with my back to the mantelpiece as she toyed nervously with her hair.

'Well?' I breathed, cocking my head to one side and staring at her. 'You overheard them talking?'

'They – they were talking about you setting up in business,' she began uneasily.

'Please, don't make me prompt you every five seconds,' I sighed. 'Just tell me what it is you want.'

'I've been working for Tom and Mary for two months. I don't like the way things are going and I was wondering whether I could work for you?'

'I see. What is it that you don't like?'

'The wooden box, for a start. And the way Mary thrashes me. She loses control and canes me until –'

'How much do they pay you?'

'Twenty pounds for a session.'

'I'm Helen, by the way.'

'Angela,' she breathed.

'OK, Angela. You certainly look the part. I can pay you the same, but I don't have many clients. In fact, I only have two.'

'I can bring some of the clients with me,' she proffered excitedly.

'I was hoping you'd say that. OK, I think we have the beginnings of a deal. How many clients do Tom and Mary have?'

'At least ten. I know how to get in touch with a couple of them. Of course, I can't do anything about the client who lives there.'

'Lives there?' I echoed. 'Someone lives with Tom and Mary?'

'Yes, so I can hardly bring him along as a client.'

'What's his name?'

'They call him Suds. I don't know his real name. The thing is . . . I have nowhere to live.'

'Now comes the catch, I suppose?'

'I'm living at home with my parents, but . . .'

'You want to live here, with me? Is that what you're trying to say?'

'Mary said that I could move into her house but, if I'm working for you ... I was hoping that I could move in with you.'

I didn't recognise the brand of perfume she was wearing, but it was beautiful, aphrodisiacal. Her long blonde hair shining in the light from the window, her eyelids fluttering, her pink tongue peeping between the fullness of her red lips ... I knew that I was weakening in my rising arousal. Repeatedly telling myself that I wasn't a lesbian, I couldn't imagine resisting the delights of her young body. Firm, fresh, curvaceous ... I had no control over my desires.

'All right,' I agreed, again eyeing her slender thighs and imagining the sweet crack of her teenage pussy. 'I'll have to work things out, financially. I mean, you can't live here for nothing.'

'No, no of course not. Shall I go and get my things?'

'You want to move in now?'

'Well, yes, if that's all right?'

'Er ... No, not now. I have to get a room ready and ... Move in tomorrow morning, OK?'

'OK.'

'I'll tell you what I'll do. We'll have a trial, a one-week trial. If I don't want you here after a week, you'll leave.'

'That's fine. I'm sure you'll be happy with me. Apart from the work, I can cook and do housework and –'

'This is getting better by the minute,' I interrupted her.

'This is great,' she trilled, rising to her feet. 'I'll see you in the morning.'

'I'll be here,' I said, seeing her to the door. 'By the way, don't tell Tom and Mary.'

'God, no,' she gasped. 'That's the last thing I'd do.'

I closed the door after her and returned to the lounge. Butterflies fluttered in my stomach, and I wondered what the hell I'd agreed to. But it was only a trial, I reflected. If we didn't get on, if I felt that she was in my way or ... Her perfume lingering in the air, I knew that we'd become friends. Intimate friends? My heart racing, my stomach somersaulting, my clitoris swelling expectantly, I felt my juices of desire seeping into the tight crotch of my panties. Where would she sleep? I mused dreamily. In my bed with me? My life was taking a new direction. A new and exciting direction? Or was I treading dangerous ground again?

Eleven

Up bright and early, I'd slept well and was feeling refreshed and looking forward to Angela's arrival. It would be strange having someone living with me, I mused as I munched my marmalade on toast and sipped my coffee. Living with Alan had been a nightmare. But, hopefully, living with Angela would be both financially rewarding and sexually satisfying.

Again, I felt that I was at last moving on in life. Although Alan was always lurking, spying, I'd come to terms with his weird ways. Apart from his voyeurism, which I thoroughly enjoyed, he wasn't part of my life anymore. If he wanted to watch men fucking me, using and abusing my body, that was fine by me. The divorce was in the hands of solicitors, and it was only a matter of time before the marriage was terminated. What would Alan do then? I wondered. Would he still sneak into my house and watch me entertaining my clients?

I'd heard nothing from Tom and Mary, and reckoned that they'd given up on me. After all, they could hardly drag me out of my house and force me into their sex room. Recalling Angela's words, I wondered who was living with them. Suds? I mused. It was obviously a nickname, but one that meant nothing to me. To have a live-in client seemed very odd. There again, Tom and Mary were a very odd couple. Nothing they did surprised me anymore.

After breakfast, I prepared Angela's room. She was to have the large bedroom next to mine, leaving the spare room for my medical sex room. This was going to work out well, I was sure. Cooking, cleaning, and working for me as a prostitute, young Angela was going to be a valuable asset. And, if my lesbian desires got the better of me, she'd become a wonderful live-in lover. Business, not pleasure, I mused dreamily. I wasn't a lesbian. Besides, I didn't even know Angela. What sort of person was she? What was she like? Was she a moody teenager? She was beautiful, that was for sure. Answering the doorbell, I felt my stomach somersault. A beautiful teenage girl with a curvaceous young body and . . .

'Hi, Derek,' I breathed, hoping that he didn't want sex. 'Er . . . I'm expecting someone any minute now, so . . .'

'I just wanted a quick word,' he said, eyeing my miniskirt and naked legs. 'It won't take a minute.'

Leading him into the lounge, I frowned. 'I hope you're not going to tell me that you're going back to Tom and Mary's?' I said, fearing the worst.

'No, not at all. I – I'm not quite sure how to say this,' he began hesitantly. 'You see . . . The thing is . . .'

'Just spit it out, Derek,' I cut in.

'You and me, Helen. How about us living together?'

'What?' I gasped, holding my hand to my mouth. 'Are you serious? I'm sorry, I don't mean to sound rude. It's just that . . .'

'Yes, I'm serious. I know that I'm a lot older than you and you're probably looking for a man of your own age. But I have money.'

'Derek, I'm not looking for a man of any age. I'm not looking for a relationship. After ten years of marriage, I want some time to myself.'

'You haven't heard my proposition yet.'

'Derek, this is very sweet of you, and I'm extremely flattered. But I don't want to be with anyone. I'm discovering myself, enjoying my freedom after years of suffocation. It's nothing personal, and age certainly doesn't come into it. I just don't want to be tied down again.'

'I wouldn't tie you down, and I certainly wouldn't suffocate you. You could sell your house and come and live with me or I could move in with you.'

'I don't own this house, Derek. It belongs to my grandmother, I'm renting it.'

'There you are, then. Move in with me and –'

'Derek, this is so much out of the blue that I don't know what to say.'

'Just say yes.'

'I can't. I've just started my own business, and I have a girl moving in with me today.'

'A girl?'

'Her name's Angela. She's going to work for me and . . . Derek, I have plans. You wouldn't want to live with a prostitute, would you?'

'You wouldn't need to work, Helen. I have more than enough money.'

'But I *want* to work. I want to be my own boss, and I want to run my own life. I don't want to have to answer to anyone.'

'OK,' he sighed, hanging his head. 'Just promise me that you'll think about it.'

'There's nothing to think about. I know what I want.'

'I'll talk to you later, when you have more time.'

'Derek, I . . . All right, come over later and we'll talk about it.'

'That's great. And you can introduce me to your new employee.'

'Yes, yes I will.'

Seeing him out, I could hardly believe his proposition. That was the last thing I'd expected, and the last thing I wanted. To be tied down again, to become a housewife again . . . No way was I going to do that. As much as I was beginning to like Derek, I couldn't become his partner. Besides, I had Angela moving in with me. I had to stick to my original plan, I reflected. Set up in business, and earn a small fortune.

Angela arrived by taxi and lugged her things up to her room. She was wearing jeans, which disappointed me as I'd been looking forward to admiring her long legs, her naked thighs. I'd have to lay down some rules, I decided as she bounded down the stairs and joined me in the lounge. Short skirts, no knickers . . . Did she have a sweet little shaved pussy? Was her teenage sex crack tight and wet? My clitoris stirring at the thought of having sex with a beautiful teenage girl, I reckoned that the time had come to get to know young Angela.

'So, tell me about yourself,' I said, joining her on the sofa.

'Well, I'm eighteen,' she began, hooking her long blonde hair behind her ear and smiling sweetly at me. 'I'm not really a prostitute. Well, I suppose I am, but . . .'

'It's all right, I know what you mean,' I cut in. 'I don't consider myself to be a prostitute. We're working girls, Angela.'

'I was very short of money and couldn't find a decent job so it seemed like a good option.'

'That was my situation, too. Do you do lesbian stuff as well as entertain male clients?' I asked her hopefully.

'Yes, I do anything,' she replied with a giggle. 'I've always loved sex, but I've never been in a proper relationship. Not long-term, anyway. Getting paid for having sex is a real bonus. No strings, no ties . . . But, as I said, I don't think of myself as a prostitute.'

I didn't think of myself as a prostitute or a lesbian, and yet . . . There was no denying the fact that I was a bisexual whore. Had Alan stayed with me, things would have been very different. Was this meant to be? I mused, eyeing Angela's tight T-shirt clinging to the mounds of her petite breasts. Was Alan's timely leaving part of a great plan? I'd never been a philosophical person, but I was beginning to wonder whether my destiny had been planned. If that was the case, where was I to go from here? Again focusing on Angela's mammary spheres, the buds of her nipples pressing through her T-shirt, I felt my stomach somersault. I needed her, I wanted her . . . Where the hell would this path take me?

'Why don't you show me your body?' I finally asked her. I could feel my clitoris swelling, my juices of lesbian desire seeping into the tight crotch of my panties. 'I mean, I need to see what it is you have to offer the clients.'

'Yes, of course,' she agreed readily, rising to her feet and unzipping her jeans.

'I have one client who is rather partial to school-girls,' I said, imagining her dressed in a school uniform. Frank would be pleased with her, I was sure. 'Would you mind dressing in a uniform and allowing an elderly gentleman to live out his fantasies?'

'I have a school uniform,' she trilled enthusiastically. 'I know that some older men like the idea of a schoolgirl, and I have no problem with that.'

'Good, I breathed, becoming increasingly impatient to cast my eyes over her young body.

Watching closely as she slipped her jeans off, I gazed longingly at the swell of her white cotton knickers. Had she shaved? I wondered for the umpteenth time as she tugged her T-shirt over her head and revealed her small bra. Her long blonde hair framing her fresh face, cascading over her naked shoulders, she had a beautifully curvaceous body. My libido soaring out of control, it was all I could do to stop myself from leaving the sofa and holding her close. The time would come, I mused as she unhooked her bra. The time would come when she'd be mine for the loving.

Her neat little breasts fully exposed, her ripe nipples rising proud from the dark discs of her areolae, I quivered and licked my lips. She was so young and fresh, reminding me of my teenage years. I used to be full of life, I reflected. Happy-go-lucky, vivacious, sensual, sexual, free . . . Then I'd met Alan. Slowly, but surely, he'd suffocated me. He'd tried to mould me into something he'd wanted. A loyal and faithful wife, a good cook, a housemaid . . . And he'd succeeded. He'd turned me into the sort of person he'd wanted. But, then, he'd thrown me away.

Finally placing her thumbs between the tight elastic of her white knickers and her beautiful hips, Angela pulled the flimsy garment down slowly. I waited in anticipation as the top of her teenage crack came into view. No hairs, I observed happily. Was she teasing me? I wondered as she eased the tight material down a little further. She was driving me wild with passion, sending my arousal sky-high . . . Did she know what she was doing to me?

'Very nice,' I breathed as she finally slipped her knickers down her slender thighs and exposed the hairless cushions of her outer sex lips. 'God, you're beautiful.'

'Thanks,' she murmured, kicking her knickers aside and standing before me.

'Angela, I . . .'

'Yes?'

'No, it's nothing. I – I think you're amazing. You're so attractive and . . . You have a perfect body. Your shaved pussy looks so sweet.'

'I've always shaved,' she confessed. 'Actually, I use cream, not a razor. I remember when my pubes first sprouted above my crack. I thought they looked so ugly that I got rid of them. Do you shave?'

'Well . . . Yes, I've just started shaving.'

'Men like to see my pussy lips rather than a thick growth of blonde hair.'

'And women? Do you think that they like to see your hairless pussy?'

'Well, yes.'

'What have you done with women? Sexually, I mean.'

'Not a lot,' she replied, running her hands over the small mounds of her breasts. Was she again teasing me? 'They like my body, feeling me and kissing me all over, and I usually let them get on with it. I've only had a few lesbian clients.'

'Have you reciprocated? I mean, have you licked them or . . .'

'Oh, yes. I'll do whatever they ask.'

'Really?' I breathed shakily, again staring at her full sex lips rising alluringly either side of her tight vulval crack. 'Angela, I . . .'

'Yes?'

'Although we're going to have a working relationship, and become friends . . . What I mean is . . .'

'You want more than that?' she asked me knowingly.

'Well . . .'

'I'm yours, if you want me. I'm used to giving people what they want. That's how I've been brought up. Now that I'm eighteen, I'm used to giving people my body.'

'Come and stand here,' I said, moving forward and perching on the edge of the sofa. 'I want to take a closer look at you.'

Following my instruction obediently, she stood before me with her feet slightly parted. The fullness and symmetry of her hairless outer lips amazed me. She was perfect in every way. Her long blonde hair flowing over the firmness of her pointed breasts, her pretty face looking down at me, expectation reflected in the blue pools of her wide eyes ... I knew that we were going to enjoy a long-term relationship and indulge in lesbian sex daily. Would I find love? I mused. Was it possible to fall in love with a teenage girl? Her tightly closed crack inviting my wet tongue, I could resist temptation no longer. Leaning forward, I kissed the smooth plateau of her stomach and breathed in the scent of her young body.

She let out a sigh of pleasure as I moved down and pressed my lips against the gentle rise of her mons. The perfume of her sex crack filling my nostrils, I moved further down and slipped my tongue into her valley of desire. She tasted sweet, bitter, tangy ... Losing control of my inner desires, I parted her succulent lips with my fingers and repeatedly ran my tongue up the length of her open girl-slit. She moaned softly, her naked body beginning to tremble as her clitoris stiffened in response to my sweeping tongue. Clutching tufts of my long black hair, she pulled me close and pressed her gaping sex valley hard against my open mouth.

'Make me come,' she murmured softly.

'I will,' I replied through a mouthful of girl-flesh. Moving back and looking up at her sweet face, I smiled. 'Sit on the sofa, and I'll make you come like you've never come before,' I breathed huskily.

Reclining on the sofa with her naked buttocks over the edge of the cushion, she opened her legs wide. She was so innocent-looking and beautifully angelic, and yet she was offering the sexual centre of her young body to me. Not wasting a second, I settled between her feet and moved in and tasted the globules of milky fluid clinging to her protruding inner labia. Letting out another sigh of pleasure, she parted her fleshy sex lips to the extreme as I ran my wet tongue up and down her crack and lapped up her teenage sex juices.

Wondering where Alan was, what he'd think if he saw me enjoying oral sex with a stunningly attractive teenage girl, I felt a quiver run through my womb. I loved the notion of my husband watching me commit sexual acts with men and women. What was it about his voyeurism that turned him on? I mused, lapping up Angela's flowing sex milk. Did he enjoy watching other people having sex? Or was it the thought of other men fucking his wife that excited him? Where was he finding sexual gratification? Was he a client of Tom and Mary's?

Reaching up and squeezing the hard mounds of Angela's petite breasts, I slipped my tongue into the open entrance to her teenage vagina and explored her tight sex sheath. She was hot and very wet, and I knew that she would soon be writhing in orgasm as she whimpered and trembled. Did she masturbate? I mused, locking my lips to the pink cone of wet flesh surrounding her vaginal opening. Did she lie in her bed at night and take herself to massive orgasms? How many cocks had shafted her tight little pussy and filled her with spunk? Did she enjoy swallowing fresh spunk?

I knew nothing about Angela. Apart from her name and her age, I knew nothing of her past, her background. Had she told her parents where she was moving to? Would they come round to check up on their little girl? Was she spying for Tom and Mary? Drinking the hot milk spewing from her teenage love hole, I knew that she wasn't a spy. My mind was going off on tangents, I thought. Angela was simply looking for a home and an income. Hoping that I wasn't treading dangerous ground, I was sure that things would work out. Was she looking for love?

'Helen,' she murmured. 'Helen, I . . .'

'What is it?' I asked, gazing into her blue eyes. 'Don't you like what I'm doing?'

'Yes, I like it very much. It's just that I have a problem. I mean, I don't think it's a problem. But you might think . . .'

'Don't talk in riddles, Angela,' I sighed, licking my pussy-wet lips. 'Just tell me what it is.'

'I wet when I come.'

'You wet? Oh, I see what you mean.'

'I thought I'd better warn you.'

'Well, I must admit that I've never been pissed on,' I said with a giggle. 'But, I'll try anything once.'

Again licking her yawning vaginal crack, I couldn't believe how much I'd changed since Alan had walked out on me. Prostitution, group sex, lesbian sex, bondage and whipping, anal sex . . . And now, a teenage girl was about to come and squirt her golden liquid over my face. Had someone told me a month previously that I'd become a prostitute and enjoy lesbian sex with a teenage girl, I'd have said that they were mad. Had someone said that the old man over the road . . . God, I was going to have to deal with

208

Derek. He was the type who wouldn't take no for an answer. I didn't want to hurt him, but there was no way we could live together as man and wife.

'I'm nearly there,' Angela gasped as I licked and sucked on her ripening clitoris. The perfume of her beautiful pussy filling my nostrils, the taste of her secret valley driving me wild, I thrust two fingers into the very hot and tight sheath of her teenage cunt. I could feel her vaginal muscles spasming, tightening around my pistoning fingers as she writhed and gasped and teetered on the verge of her coming. Mouthing and sucking in my sexual frenzy, I waited for her hot gush to flood my hand. How much deeper would I plunge into the pit of depraved sex?

Angela came with a shudder and a scream. Her hot liquid jetting from her urethral hole, spraying my hand and flooding the sofa cushion, she lifted her legs and pressed her knees against the firm mounds of her breasts to give me better access to the sexual centre of her young body. Slipping my fingers out of her contracting vagina and massaging her pulsating clitoris, I pressed my lips to her open hole and drank her golden liquid. She was an amazing girl, I mused in my sexual delirium. Repeatedly swallowing hard, drinking from her trembling body as she rode the crest of her orgasm, I knew that this was only the beginning of our sex-crazed lesbian relationship.

My face dripping with a blend of teenage sex cream and hot liquid, I followed the girl's gasped instructions and thrust a finger deep into her rectal canal. Her secret duct was so hot and tight, gripping my finger like a velvet-jawed vice, and I knew that I'd plunged even deeper into the pit of depravity as she let out another scream of orgasmic pleasure. Was there no sexual act that I wouldn't commit? I wondered, managing to force a second finger into her spasming anal sheath. Was there nothing I wouldn't do in the name of lust?

'Slow down,' Angela managed to gasp. 'Finger me slowly now.' Obviously coming down from her climax, she shuddered and then began to relax. Her breathing was fast and shallow, her lower stomach rising and falling jerkily, her flow of hot liquid stemming, and I knew that she was recovering from a multiple orgasm. Would she reciprocate? I wondered, my knickers soaked with my juices of lesbian desire. Would she suck my clitoris and finger my sex holes until I shuddered in the grip of a multiple orgasm?

Easing my fingers out of her rectal sheath, I massaged the last ripples of sex from her deflating clitoris. Trembling, panting for breath, she finally opened her blue eyes and smiled at me. Her pretty face was flushed, her blonde hair matted with the perspiration of sex, and I knew that she'd enjoyed her lesbian-induced orgasm. She was incredibly sensual, I mused, eyeing the small mounds of her firm breasts, her ripe milk teats. Sensual, sexual . . .

'Thank you,' she breathed softly. 'That was amazing.'

'Thank *you*,' I returned with a giggle. 'I really enjoyed that. I can see that we're going to get on well together.'

'We will,' she said, sitting upright and pressing her wet thighs together. 'Living with you, working for you . . . It's going to be just perfect, Helen.'

'I think it's my turn to come now,' I said. My clitoris aching with desire, the taste of the girl's sex juices lingering on my tongue, I smiled at her. 'Would you like to lick me now and . . .' My words tailed off as the doorbell rang. I leaped to my feet. 'Damn,' I breathed. 'Take your clothes up to your room and I'll see who it is.'

'I'll have a shower, if that's all right?' she asked, gathering up her clothes.

'Yes, yes of course.'

Looking through the lounge window as Angela ran up the stairs, I sighed and my shoulders sagged. It was Alan. What the hell was it this time? I wondered angrily, heading for the front door. The time had come to sort this out once and for all, I decided. The time had come to confront him. Opening the door, I ordered him into the lounge. He looked somewhat bemused as I stood with my clenched fists on my hips and glared at him.

'Your blouse is soaking wet,' he said, frowning at me.

'A girl pissed on me,' I returned unashamedly.

'Is everything all right, Helen? You seem angry.'

'No, it's bloody not,' I returned. 'And yes, I am angry. What the hell do you want this time?'

'I was just passing and –'

'You're always just passing. Where are you living? And don't say that you're staying with your mother.'

'I'm lodging with friends at the moment.'

'Where?'

'That's my business, Helen. I don't pry into your business, so –'

'You don't pry into my business?' I quipped. 'That's a laugh. You're continually spying on me, you let yourself into my house and go through my post, you steal my panties and –'

'Steal your panties?' he echoed with a snigger. 'What the hell are you on about?'

'You stole my front door key from the hall table, didn't you? And you let yourself in and stole my panties from the linen basket. There's no point in denying it.'

'Yes, I have been through the post,' he finally admitted. 'I can't rely on you to let me know when

211

post arrives for me. I could never rely on you for anything, Helen.'

'And my panties? You stole them, didn't you?'

'I have no idea what you're talking about. Why on earth would I want to steal your panties?'

'For the same reason you spy at me through the lounge window, I would imagine.'

'Have you gone mad?'

'No, but I believe you have.'

'The only time I've looked through the window is when you've not answered the doorbell. I've had a quick look to see whether you're –'

'There's no point in discussing this further,' I cut in. 'You're obviously going to deny everything, so there's no point. Anyway, what is it you want?'

'I came here to show you these,' he said, pulling an envelope from his jacket pocket. Taking several photographs from the envelope, he passed them to me.

'Where – where did you get these from?' I stammered, gazing at several photographs of my naked body in Tom and Mary's sex room.

'The envelope was addressed to me and delivered by hand to my mother's house. They're disgusting, Helen. What sort of woman are you to –'

'It's – it's not me,' I murmured. 'You can't see the girl's face. It could be anyone.'

'Helen, any fool could see that it's you. That blindfold doesn't hide you. And the ones of you in that box clearly show –'

'You took these, didn't you?' I cut in.

'Me?' he gasped. 'Of course I didn't.'

'You were there, in that room.'

'Helen, I have no idea where this place is. I can see that it's not our house. Sorry, your house.'

'Have you been talking to Tom and Mary?'

212

'What? Tom and Mary? What the hell have they got to do with this? Look, I don't know what this is all about, but I don't want this sort of filth sent to my mother's house. You've obviously turned into some kind of vulgar whore.'

'Are you living at Tom's place?'

'Next door? No, I'm not. Why do you ask?'

'Do they call you Suds?'

'Helen, I really do think that you've gone mad. Suds? I have no idea what –'

'Go now,' I snapped. 'Get out of my house.'

Shaking his head, he stormed out of the room and slammed the front door shut behind him. At least he'd left the incriminating photographs, I thought, hiding them behind the bookcase. He must have been to Tom and Mary's sex room and taken the photographs. Sure that he was a client of theirs, I imagined him standing behind my tethered body and fucking my tight rectum. He was a bastard, I thought angrily. But, why show me the photographs? Was this another of his crazy mind games? Grabbing the ringing phone, I felt my heart race as Mary said that she'd just seen Alan leave my house.

'So what?' I snapped.

'Did he have some photographs with him?' she asked me.

'Er . . . Photographs?' I echoed. 'No, no he didn't.'

'Maybe he hasn't got them yet. We sent them to his mother's house and –'

'Mary, what the hell are you talking about?'

'Photographs of you in our sex room. We thought that Alan might want to see what sort of slut you really are.'

'I shouldn't think he's interested,' I returned. 'Besides, my life has nothing to do with Alan. What I do is none of his business.'

213

'We've got some more photos here, ready to post to your mother. She'll be interested, Helen. She'll be very interested in the things you get up to.'

'Mary, what the hell are you trying to achieve?'

'I don't take kindly to having my clients stolen. I've built up my business over several years, and you're trying to ruin it for me.'

'Had you not caned me, whipped me and –'

'You wanted the job, Helen.'

'Yes, but I had no idea that you were selling me to old men for sex. To use me like that was despicable, and I'll never forgive you for it. Alan was there, wasn't he? He was one of the men who fucked me, wasn't he?'

'No, he wasn't. Alan has never been to our sex room.'

'Mary, I know that Alan is lodging with you. There's no point in lying about it.'

'I'm not lying, Helen. You can believe whatever you like, it doesn't affect me. But what does affect me is you stealing my clients and trying to ruin my business. Unless you stop, I'll send the photographs to your mother. And if I discover that you've lured any of my girls away, then I'll –'

'What girls?' I asked her.

'I have girls working for me, Helen. If I lose any of them to you, I'll send copies of the photographs to the neighbours, your friends and family and . . .'

Hanging up, I bit my lip and paced the lounge floor. If my mother saw the photographs of me in the sex room . . . Shit, I thought, wondering what the hell to do. If Mary found out that Angela was working for me, and living with me . . . This was a mess, I concluded. There was no way I could allow my mother to see the photographs. And, if my grandmother saw the evidence of my debauchery, she'd

214

throw me out of the house. I had to do as Mary said and put an end to my business. Angela could live with me, and work for Mary, if she wished. But she wouldn't be working for me.

I'd thought that the future was looking good, I reflected, wandering into the kitchen and filling the kettle. But, now? Spooning coffee into a cup, I pondered on Derek's proposition. He had money, I mused, more thàn enough money. Maybe I should take him up on his offer. But, with Angela living with me . . . This was more than a mess. It was a bloody nightmare.

'Hi,' Angela said, joining me in the kitchen.

'Oh, hi,' I breathed, eyeing her school uniform. 'God, you look beautiful.'

'I'm glad you like it.'

'Angela, there's been a change of plan.'

'Oh?'

'I – I won't be running the business anymore.'

'But . . . Why not?'

'Things have happened. I'll tell you about it later.'

'You mean, I can't live here?'

'You can live here, but there'll be no work. It would be best if you carried on working for Tom and Mary.'

'No,' she stated firmly. 'I'm not going back there. I'm not going back to Mary and her whip.'

'Well, that's up to you. But I think you'd better let Mary know rather than just not turn up. Don't tell her that you're living here, though.'

'All right, I'll go and tell her now. I'll get changed and go round there.'

'By the way, do you know Derek? He's one of Mary's clients.'

'No, I don't. I've not met all the clients. I worked certain days, so I only saw certain clients.'

'That's a relief. He's a friend of mine and he'll be here later. He wants to meet you, so . . . Tell him that you're my cousin, OK?'

'OK, I will. What about money? I won't be earning any money, so . . .'

'I don't know,' I sighed. 'Look, we'll talk about it later. You go and get changed and then tell Mary that you won't be working for her. Tell her that you're moving away or something.'

'All right.' She sighed, and left the room.

As she bounded up the stairs, I felt despondent. Maybe the whole idea of working as a prostitute had been crazy, I reflected as I poured my coffee. Entertaining clients, taking money in return for sex . . . Wishing I'd never got involved with Tom and Mary, I sat on a patio chair beneath the summer sun and tried to relax. Should I take Derek up on his offer? I wondered. If he believed that Angela was my cousin . . . Living with Derek, I could hardly have sex with her, I thought dolefully. No, it simply wouldn't work out.

Sipping my coffee, I turned my thoughts to Alan. Now that I'd confronted him, I hoped that he'd not bother me again. Even though he'd denied everything, I reckoned that he'd leave me alone. The situation was crazy, I mused, gazing at the long grass and wondering where my gardeners had got to. I'd been working as a prostitute, Tom and Mary were running a brothel, Alan had been watching me have sex, a teenage girl had moved in with me . . . My life had gone completely out of control.

I finished my coffee and wandered across the lawn to the shed. I'd do the garden myself, I decided, opening the door. If young Dave and his friend couldn't be bothered, I'd do the work instead. I was about to haul the lawn mower out when I noticed a quilt in the corner of the shed. Had Alan been sleeping there? I wondered, eyeing a bottle of lemonade and a packet of biscuits. Alan, living in my garden shed? 'Surely not,' I breathed, leaving the shed and closing the door. That would explain why he was always around, I mused, wondering whether he slept there every night.

Wandering into the bushes, I peered into the garden next door. I wanted to find out why Dave hadn't been round to see me. Had he not enjoyed sex with an older woman? Maybe he'd found a teenage girl to fuck? Noticing Dave in the kitchen, I was about to call him but realised that his parents might be around. As he glanced my way, I waved at him. He must have thought me crazy, I mused as he returned my wave and headed towards me. He was wearing his shorts, and I felt my stomach somersault as I eyed his bulge. I wanted his cock, his spunk ... No, I decided. No more sex.

'Hi,' he said, grinning at me. 'How are you?'

'I'm fine,' I replied, not leaving the bushes. 'I was just wondering when you were going to do my garden.'

'Didn't your husband tell you?'

'Tell me what?'

'He said that he'd moved back in and you didn't need me anymore.'

'What? When was this?'

'A few days ago. I went to get the tools from your shed, and he was there. I said that I'd come to do the garden and –'

'He's not my bloody husband,' I breathed through gritted teeth.

'But, he said –'

'I don't care what he said, Dave. Technically, he is my husband. But we're getting divorced. And he's certainly not moved back in with me.'

217

'Oh, er . . . I see.'

'My lawn needs cutting. Are you free now?'

'Well . . . I think I'd better keep out of the way. Just until your're divorced and –'

'You don't want sex with me, then?' I cut in.

'Yes, of course I do. But –'

'Come round this evening.'

'Well, if you're sure it's all right?'

'Of course I'm sure. Come round at seven. OK?'

'OK, I will.'

Returning to my patio as Dave headed back to his house, I flopped into the chair and made my plans. Should I wait until Alan was in the shed, and then jam something against the door to imprison him? I mused. There again, I doubted that he'd be back after my confrontation. How dare he tell my gardener that he was no longer needed, I mused angrily. Hopefully, I'd seen the last of Alan, I thought as the sun warmed me. I didn't want to see Alan, Paul, Tom and Mary . . . Would young Dave like to fuck Angela? I wondered, imagining his solid cock driving deep into her teenage cunt. Would I ever stop thinking about crude sex? Feeling tired, I reclined in the chair and closed my eyes.

'Helen?' Angela said, shaking my shoulder. 'Helen, wake up.'

'Oh, I must have dozed off,' I said, looking up and focusing on her pretty face. 'What did Mary say?'

'She was fine about it. I said that I was moving away and she was fine.'

'That's good,' I breathed.

'I think Tom was talking about you.'

'Talking about me? What do you mean?'

'Well, it might not have been you. While I was in the hall with Mary, I heard Tom talking to someone in the lounge.'

'And?'

'He was talking to another man. He was saying something about photographs.'

'Go on.'

'I only heard bits and pieces as Mary was talking to me. The other man said that the photographs had worked, and Tom said that she'd been frightened off and wouldn't be a problem.'

'What made you think that they were talking about me?'

'Well, Tom said that he'd seen Derek going next door. You'd mentioned your friend, Derek, and I assumed that . . .'

'Who was Tom talking to, do you know?'

'No, sorry. Oh, he also said that Mary was coming here later.'

'Shit. OK, you go up to your room. If she's coming here, I don't want her to see you.'

'Will I have to keep hiding like this?' she asked me as she stepped into the kitchen.

'I hope not,' I breathed. 'I certainly hope not.'

Twelve

Angela had kept herself busy by spending the afternoon cleaning the house. I'd seen nothing of Mary, and Derek hadn't come back to persist with his proposition. Pondering on young Dave calling round in the evening, I was beginning to have a change of mind about closing my business. I needed to survive, and there was only one way to earn decent money. With Angela's beautiful body, her sweet pussy crack and beautifully firm tits, I knew that I could earn myself a small fortune. Dave the gardener would love to fuck her, I mused in my rising wickedness. Not that he was a paying customer.

'What are you looking at?' Angela asked, joining me in the dining room. 'Are you daydreaming?'

'I'm always dreaming,' I replied pensively. 'Actually, I'm looking at the shed. My husband – my soon to be ex-husband – has been sleeping in the shed.'

'Sleeping in the shed?' she echoed with a giggle. 'Why?'

'Because he's mad. It's a long story, Angela. And one I won't bore you with.'

'He's safe, is he? I mean, he won't come into the house and . . .'

'Yes, he's safe enough. You needn't worry yourself about him.'

'What I am beginning to worry about is money,' she sighed. 'What are we going to do?'

'I don't know,' I murmured, shaking my head despondently. 'The problem is that Mary has threatened me. She has photographs of me in her sex room and ... Basically, if I steal her clients and run my business, she'll send the incriminating pictures to my mother.'

'God.'

'God, indeed. So, you can see the predicament I'm in. You can see why I can't continue with the business.'

'Why not take the photographs from her?' she asked me, cocking her head to one side.

'Take them? What do you mean?'

'She has photos of everyone. She says that they're her insurance. If a client gets funny, starts to demand sex for nothing or whatever, she'll use the photographs to ...'

'How can I get hold of them?'

'I know where she keeps them.'

'Really?'

'They're in her lounge, behind a row of books on the shelf.'

'What about the negatives? Taking the printed copies won't help.'

'She keeps all the negatives with the photos in the same place. Look, just in case someone discovers them. I saw her go out with Tom earlier. Do you want me to go and get them?'

'What, you'll break into her house?'

'She keeps a key hidden in the back garden.'

'Well ... If you think you can do it. Why didn't you mention this before when we were talking about photographs?'

'When I overheard Tom talking, I didn't realise

that Mary was going to threaten you. I wasn't even sure that Tom was talking about you.'

'Angela, if Mary catches you in her house –'

'She won't catch me. I'll go there now.'

'All right. Get everything. I want to see who her clients are, so take the whole lot.'

'OK, I'll be back in a minute.'

This was amazing, I thought as Angela left the house. If she returned with the incriminating evidence of my debauchery, I'd have nothing to worry about. Mary might have copies, I reflected anxiously. Alan had left his copies with me, which was a relief. Did he have more copies? I mused anxiously. Twisting my long hair nervously around my fingers, I knew that I had to stop worrying. Maybe, at long last, things were going my way. If Angela managed to pull this off, if she grabbed all the photographs and negatives, I'd be able to see exactly who Tom and Mary's clients were. Would Alan be among the sordid pictures? I wondered. If I discovered that he'd been in the sex room, fucking my tethered body from behind ... Alan was out of my life, I reflected. There was no point in even thinking about him.

'Here you are,' Angela trilled as she came bouncing into the dining room. 'I took all of them.'

'Angela, you're amazing,' I said with a sigh of relief as she passed me a large envelope. 'Look, that's Derek,' I breathed, flicking through the obscene pictures. 'That's you, in the wooden box getting done from behind. These are all of me in the sex room and ... I don't recognise any of the male clients, so they're not my neighbours. And there aren't any of my husband, which is a relief.'

'What will you do with them? Burn them?'

'No, I'll hang on to these,' I replied, stuffing

everything back into the envelope. 'Mary will go mental when she discovers that they've been stolen.'

'So, are we back in business?'

'I think we are, Angela. I think we are. OK, my gardener will be here later so . . .'

'Is he also a client?'

'No, unfortunately he's not. Actually, I think we have time for something before he arrives. You did well to get the photos for me. Why don't you slip your knickers off and lie on the table? I think you deserve a reward.'

Pulling a chair up as she lay on her back on the table, I sat between her slender thighs and pulled her closer until her buttocks were just over the edge of the surface. Her hairless lips rising invitingly either side of her sweet girl-crack, I parted the fleshy cushions and exposed the inner folds of her teenage pussy. She was dripping wet, her sex milk streaming from her tight hole and running down to the brown ring of her anus. I began by licking her inner thighs, working my tongue slowly up to the creases at the tops of her legs. She writhed and whimpered as I held her lips wide apart and moved dangerously close to her erect clitoris.

'I need to come,' she breathed shakily. 'Helen, I need to come.'

'You will, my angel,' I replied, kissing the wet flesh within her pink valley of teenage desire. 'You will.'

'You know that I'll wet you, don't you?'

'I'm looking forward to it,' I said huskily. 'You know that I'm always thirsty for you.'

Sitting on the chair with the girl's sex crack gaping in front of me on the dining-room table, I knew that I'd be enjoying many a fleshy vaginal meal. This was a perfect position, I mused as I lapped up her flowing cream. Lifting her legs up and placing her feet either side of her hips, she parted her knees wide. This was even better, I thought happily, repeatedly running my tongue up and down her open love slit. She tasted heavenly, and I lapped and sucked fervently at her vaginal hole as she pumped out another deluge of hot sex milk.

Deliberately neglecting the swollen nub of her pink clitoris, I licked around her vaginal hole and nibbled on her inner lips. Teasing her, tantalising her, I wanted her to beg me for the relief of orgasm before allowing her the pleasure. She writhed, trying to swivel her hips and align her clitoris with my mouth as her arousal heightened. Working on her inner flesh with my tongue, tasting the creamy walls of her teenage vagina, I breathed in the heady scent of her pussy as my own juices of desire seeped into the tight crotch of my panties.

'Please,' she murmured. 'Please, I need to come.'

'Not yet,' I breathed, easing my fingertip into the tight hole of her anus.

'God, that's heavenly,' she gasped.

'I'm going to take you to heaven,' I said huskily, driving my finger deep into her rectal sheath. 'You're my angel, and I'm going to take you to heaven.'

Easing a second finger into her hot anal canal, I slipped another two fingers deep into her contracting vaginal duct and sucked her solid clitoris into my wet mouth. Her moans of lesbian pleasure growing louder, I teased her clitoris to the verge of orgasm and then moved back. Again, she begged me to make her come, but I only fingered her tight hole. I could see her clitoris protruding from beneath its pink hood. Long, hard and erect in arousal, her pleasure spot was in dire need of my tongue. Not yet, I decided as she pleaded for her orgasm.

Her pussy milk flowing in torrents, bathing my hand as I repeatedly thrust my fingers deep into her tight sex holes, I wondered how long she could endure my teasing. Her anal muscles contracting, her vaginal duct gripping my pistoning fingers, she shuddered and cried out. She'd waited long enough, I decided, moving in and sucking the solid bulb of her clitoris into my wet mouth. Gasping, shaking violently, she brought her knees up to her petite breasts and released a gush of golden liquid as her clitoris finally erupted in orgasm. The blend of girl-juice and urine splattering my face, raining over my head as I licked and sucked on her pulsating clitoris, I wished that Alan could witness my lesbian decadence. Maybe he was hiding somewhere, I mused.

The taste of Angela's gush driving me into a sexual frenzy, I felt my clitoris swell. She'd not yet returned the pleasure, I reflected. She'd not fingered my yearning vagina, licked and sucked my clitoris to orgasm or fingered my tight rectum. Soon, I thought as she let out another cry of ecstasy. Soon, she'd be licking and sucking between my legs, drinking my hot pussy milk and taking me to a massive climax. Was she into spanking? I mused as she finally began to drift down from her pleasure. She'd said that she'd not liked Mary's whip, but she might enjoy a little spanking.

Finally slipping my fingers out of her spasming sex sheaths, I ran my tongue from her wet bottom hole up to her clitoris. She writhed again, and I knew that she'd soon be begging me for another orgasm. Again running my tongue around her tight anus and working up to her vaginal entrance and her ripening clitoris, I gasped as she let out a gush of hot golden liquid. She was an amazing girl, I thought dreamily, locking my lips to the wet flesh surrounding her love hole and drinking her flowing urine. Never had I been so lost in decadence, never had I felt so sex crazed as I drank from her young body.

Make me come again,' she breathed shakily as her flow of hot liquid finally stemmed. 'God, Helen. I need to come off again.'

'And what about me, my feminine needs?' I asked her, sliding two fingers into her tight anal duct. 'Don't you think that I need to come?'

'Yes, yes, all right,' she conceded. 'Get onto the table and kneel over my face.'

Yanking my fingers out of her bottom-hole and almost tearing my knickers off, I took my position with my hairless vaginal crack yawning above her pretty face. Lowering my body, settling my fleshy outer lips over her open mouth, I threw my head back and gasped as her wet tongue entered my love sheath. She knew exactly what to do to pleasure a girl. *Only a girl knows how to pleasure another girl*, I thought, recalling Mary's words. Tonguing my sex hole, Angela moved to the solid protrusion of my sensitive clitoris and sucked hard. Again, I let out a rush of breath, my head lolling forward as the amazing sensations permeated my contracting womb.

'Now I need to come,' I gasped, my hot milk flooding her face as she sucked on my pleasure bud. 'Angela, make me come now.'

'Lick me,' she murmured. 'Do sixty-nine, and we'll both come together.'

'Yes, sixty-nine,' I murmured, eyeing the swollen pads of her outer sex lips.

Leaning over, I buried my face between her thighs and sucked hard on her inner flesh as she continued to work on my swollen clitoris. Slipping my tongue into her very wet vaginal hole, I quivered uncontrollably as I neared my desperately needed orgasm. She tasted heavenly. The cocktail of cream and golden liquid sending my arousal through the roof, I listened to the slurping and gasping sounds of mutual sex as we writhed in our lesbian loving.

This was another first, I thought happily as we each sucked on the other's solid clitoris. Sixty-nine with another girl? Never in a million years would I have believed that I'd be entwined in lesbian lust on the dining-room table. This was real sex, I mused as she drove a finger deep into the tight tube of my rectum. Reciprocating, I slipped my finger into her anus and massaged her inner flesh. We were going to come together, I was sure as our bodies quivered in the heat of our lesbian lust. Again following her cue as she slipped a second finger deep into my bum, I forced another finger into her rectum and sucked hard on her beautifully hard clitoris.

I so much wanted Alan to witness our lesbian loving. Where was he now? I mused as the birth of my orgasm stirred deep within my contracting womb. Was he lurking, spying, wanking? Angela cried out through a mouthful of vaginal flesh as she reached her earth-shuddering climax. I, too, cried out as my orgasm erupted within the pulsating nub of my clitoris and sent shockwaves of lesbian-induced pleasure throughout my trembling body. Clinging to each other, Angela and I shook uncontrollably as our orgasms peaked. Was Alan listening to the sounds of lesbian sex? Was he wanking and shooting his spunk into his hand?

Again and again, waves of lesbian lust coursed through my young body as I mouthed and sucked on my girl-lover's pulsating clitoris. She finally released her liquid of gold, filling my mouth and soaking my face as she rode the crest of her lesbian pleasure. Losing control, I allowed my waters to rain over her face as she tongued my spasming vagina. I could hear her gasping, obviously delighting in my golden offering. Slurping, swallowing, she sustained my orgasm with her tongue and her fingers until I could take no more.

Our orgasms receding, we teased each other's clitorises, and massaged deep inside each other's rectal ducts as we drifted down from our lesbian loving. Finally falling limp, I lay on top of Angela's quivering body in the aftermath of the best sex I'd ever experienced. Sliding my fingers out of her rectal canal as she slipped her fingers out of mine, I finally managed to clamber off the table. Swaying on my sagging legs, I helped Angela off the table and smiled at her. We were both soaking wet, our hair dripping with golden rain, our faces glistening with girl-cum. We climbed the stairs together, showered and changed into clean clothes. We were true lesbian lovers.

'Put the kettle on and I'll get that,' I said as the phone rang. I bounded down the stairs, into the lounge, and grabbed the phone. I wasn't at all surprised to hear Derek's voice. He wanted to come over to the house, but not to talk about us living together. He had a couple of young men, prospective clients, and wanted to know whether I was free to entertain them. Dave the gardener wasn't due for an hour, so I had plenty of time to earn some money. Things really were beginning to look up, I mused. I invited Derek over, replaced the receiver and joined Angela in the dining room. This was to be her first session, I thought, eyeing her curvaceous young body. This was to be her first paying job as my employee.

'That was Derek,' I said. 'He's bringing a couple of clients over.'

'What, now?'

'Yes, if that's all right with you?'

'Of course it is. We're in business, then?'

'Indeed we are. Now that you've got the photos back, we're definitely in business. OK, go and change into your school uniform. I take it that you're ready to start work? I mean, after our loving and . . .'

'Yes, yes I am,' she trilled, leaving the room and bounding up the stairs.

I'd not prepared my sex room, but had decided that it would be better to entertain my clients in the dining room for Alan's benefit. Should he decide to come round on one of his voyeur trips, should he go to the shed, he was bound to spy through the window. Shaking my head and sighing as I pictured him sleeping in the shed like a tramp, I had a feeling that I wouldn't be seeing him again. After my confrontation, I was sure that he'd give up. And I couldn't see him daring to come sneaking into my house. There again, Alan was a peculiar man.

Slipping into the lounge and spying through the net curtains as the doorbell rang, I gazed at Derek hovering on the step with two younger men. Derek was wearing dark trousers and a white shirt, but his friends were in long overcoats. This was going to be interesting, I mused. And profitable. Wondering whether he'd had a change of mind about us living together, I walked through the hall and opened the front door. Living together just wouldn't work out, and I hoped that he'd realised that as he grinned at me.

'I have two naughty schoolboys with me,' he said. 'I'm their headmaster, and I've brought them here to be punished.'

'You'd better show them into the dining room, Headmaster,' I instructed him. Closing the door as they filed through the hall, I held Derek's arm. 'You've changed your mind about us?' I whispered as the others went into the dining room.

'You don't want to live with me, Helen,' he sighed. 'And I can understand that. So, I thought I'd bring you some new clients to help build up your new business. And, I hope that we can remain friends.'

'Of course we can,' I said, kissing his cheek as Angela came down the stairs dressed in her school uniform. 'Intimate friends.'

Joining the young men in the dining room, I introduced Angela to Derek and the schoolboys. I knew that I could never give up my business, and I was sure that there was nothing that Tom and Mary could do to stop me now that I had the photographs. Taking money from the men, I turned and smiled at Angela. We were in business. Returning my smile, she stifled a giggle as the men removed their overcoats. They were wearing grey shorts and blazers, and it was as much as I could do to stop myself from laughing aloud. They were paying clients, I reminded myself. I shouldn't laugh at them.

'I will not tolerate disobedience,' I said, scowling at the young men. They were in their twenties, and not bad looking. 'What have they done, Headmaster?'

'They were caught wanking,' Derek said. 'That's not only against the school rules, but absolutely despicable.'

'It certainly is, Headmaster. Actually, your arrival is most timely. This girl has also been sent to me to be punished. She was caught with her knickers down in the cloakrooms, allowing another girl to play with her crack.'

'What punishment do you suggest?'

Turning to Angela, I winked. 'Lift your skirt up, girl,' I hissed. 'And bend over the table.'

'Yes, Miss,' she breathed, lifting her skirt and taking her position over the dining-room table.

Eyeing her white cotton knickers, I turned to one of the boys. 'Kneel behind her,' I instructed him.

'You're to be severely punished for your wicked behaviour.'

My womb contracting as I pulled Angela's knickers down just enough to expose her firm buttocks, I ordered the boy to open her bum crack and lick her anal hole. He complied eagerly, parting the rounded cheeks of her young bottom and running his tongue over the brown eye of her anus as his friend watched. Angela gasped, her young body trembling as she parted her feet further and allowed the boy better access to her private hole.

I felt a little jealous as the boy tongued Angela's anus. She was a beautiful girl, and I was beginning to think that I shouldn't be sharing her with clients. Her young body was perfect in every way. Her skin was unblemished in youth, her buttocks firm and well rounded, her legs long and slender . . . To watch men using her like this was hurting my mind. But she didn't belong to me, I mused dolefully. She was working for me, earning me money. Was I falling in love?

Ordering the second boy to lick Angela's anus, I glanced out of the window and noticed Alan peering out of the bushes. So much for getting rid of him, I thought as Derek instructed the boy to give Angela a good anal tongue fucking. The marital home, I reflected, watching Alan out of the corner of my eye. This was the dining room where we'd enjoyed Christmas dinners, birthday meals . . . And now it was just another room of crude sex and debauchery.

'Fuck her arse,' I ordered the boy. 'Ram your cock right up her arse and fuck her senseless.'

'Yes, Miss,' he breathed, leaping to his feet and hauling out his erect cock.

'You'll all fuck her arse. And that includes you, Headmaster.'

Slipping my wet panties off and clambering onto the table, I positioned the open crack of my vulva close to Angela's face and ordered her to lick me. She gazed at me, her blue eyes rolling, her mouth gasping as the boy drove his solid cock deep into her rectum. This was for Alan's benefit, I mused, again watching him out of the corner of my eye as Angela lowered her head and ran her wet tongue up and down my hairless vulval crack. This time, I'd really give him something to look at.

My clitoris responding to the girl's sweeping tongue, my pussy milk streaming from my gaping vaginal hole, I ordered the other boy to kneel astride my head and fuck my mouth. Clambering onto the table, he unzipped his shorts and pulled out his erect cock. He was big, I observed as he retracted his fleshy foreskin and exposed the purple crown of his magnificent organ. Opening my mouth wide, I glanced at Alan before taking the swollen knob to the back of my throat.

Gobbling on the young man's glans, sinking my teeth gently into his veined shaft, I could see Alan staring at me from the bushes. Angela's young body rocking with the crude anal fucking, my solid clitoris beginning to pulsate within her mouth, I sucked hard on the beautiful knob bloating my mouth. What was Alan thinking now? I wondered. Watching his wife sucking on a solid cock, having her pussy tongued by a young lesbian ... Was he wanking in the bushes?

As the man screwing Angela's tight rectum announced his imminent coming, and with the cock bloating my mouth pumping out fresh spunk, I reached my mind-blowing orgasm. The sounds of crude sex echoing around the dining room, I repeatedly swallowed the creamy spunk jetting from the man's orgasming knob as Angela sustained my climax with her wet tongue. I was in my sexual heaven, I thought dreamily. Sex for the sake of sex, pleasures of the flesh ... Prostitution. I'd found my niche in life.

My mouth was overflowing; I'd never known a man come so much. On and on his sperm gushed, bathing my tongue, filling my mouth, as I did my best not to waste one drop of his creamy offering. His swinging balls battering my chin as he throat-fucked me, he reached down and squeezed the firm mounds of my breasts through my flimsy blouse. Angela sucked the last ripples of orgasm out of my pulsating clitoris as the man's balls finally drained and his cock began to deflate within my cream-flooded mouth. The shuddering and gasps of sex finally receding, the man slipped his cock out of my mouth and left the table. The cock fucking Angela's rectum leaving her anus with a sucking sound, the first session of sex was over.

'Are you all right?' I asked Angela.

'God, yes,' she breathed, her pussy-wet face smiling at me. 'That was amazing.'

'Right,' I said, slipping off the table and unbuttoning my blouse. 'I want everyone naked.

Hoping that young Dave from next door would soon join us in our debauchery, I tossed my blouse to the floor and slipped my skirt down. Watching the others remove their clothes, I decided to give Alan a real show as I gazed at the three erect cocks. I opened the patio doors, stepped out into the garden and ordered the others to follow me. It was a beautiful summer evening, ideal for a session of group sex on the lawn. Ordering one of the young men to lie on the grass by the bush where Alan was hiding, I knelt astride him and slipped his cock deep into my tight vagina.

'You, boy,' I said, looking up at the second young man. 'Kneel behind me and fuck my arse.'

'And what would you like me to do?' Derek asked me.

'There's only one hole left,' I said with a giggle. 'So you'd better fuck it.'

Angela settled on the grass beside me as Derek knelt before me and slipped his purple knob into my sperm-thirsty mouth. Three cocks fucking my holes, I mused on my wickedness. Alan had a perfect view of the huge organs thrusting deep into the tight holes between my legs, and I again wondered what he was thinking. This was the ultimate in sexual deviancy, I knew as Angela reached beneath my naked body and massaged the firm mounds of my breasts. Alive with sex, my mind blown away on the wind of lust, I rocked back and forth as the men found their rhythm.

Kneeling beside me and pressing her cheek against mine, Angela licked Derek's shaft as he mouth-fucked me. She certainly knew how to please the clients, I mused, slipping his knob out of my mouth and allowing her to gobble on his purple plum. Derek gasped, obviously delighting in having two girls share his cock, and I knew that I was going to provide a far better service than Tom and Mary could ever dream of.

My tight rectal duct flooding with sperm, my vagina swallowing its share of spunk, I watched as Derek's orgasmic milk spurted from his swollen knob and splattered Angela's pretty face. Locking our lips together with his knob between our mouths, we both sucked and swallowed his male offering as he gasped and trembled. Sharing his cock with Angela was an amazing experience, and one that I reckoned would become our speciality. An orgasmic knob pressed between two lesbians' mouths locked in a passionate kiss . . . We were good, I thought happily as we drank from Derek's cock. Tom and Mary's business didn't stand a chance.

The three cocks fucking my holes finally deflating, Angela and I sucked the remnants of Derek's spunk from his knob and swallowed hard. As he sat back on his heels, we locked our sperm-glossed lips in a lesbian kiss. Was this love? I again wondered as our tongues entwined. Was it possible to fall in love with a teenage girl? After years of marriage, my life had taken so many twists and turns that I wasn't sure what my feelings were. I loved sharing a cock with Angela, but I didn't want men sharing her. Was I selfish? Was I jealous?

The spent organs leaving my sex holes, I clambered off the man below me and lay on my back on the grass. I was exhausted, fucked and spunked, and needed to relax before enduring another three-cock fucking. My eyes closed, I listened to Angela talking to the men. Through the mist of my dizzy mind, I heard her tell them that they could come back the following day for another session of sex. Derek called goodbye to me as they all went back to the house, but I didn't even have the energy to answer him.

Quivering on the lawn beneath the evening sun, I wondered where Dave had got to as I recovered from my incredible experience. Had Alan frightened him off? I mused. It was just as well that he'd not come round as I knew that I could never have taken four massive cocks into my wrung-out body. Two hard rods ramming deep into my tight cunt? Could I fit two penises into my hot rectum? This was only the beginning of my new business, and I knew that I'd be taking many more cocks into my hot holes. How many clients did I need each week? I wondered. Ten, eleven, twelve . . .

'You're a whore,' Alan said, emerging from the bushes and standing over my naked body. 'A filthy whore.'

'I couldn't agree more,' I replied, propping myself up on my elbows. 'And what are you, Alan?'

'Me? I was a good husband. Now, I'm a betrayed husband.'

'A good husband?' I echoed, giggling and shaking my head. 'Walking out on me time and time again? That's not what I call a good husband. And look at you now. Sneaking around my house, sleeping in the shed . . .'

'Sleeping in the shed? What the hell are you talking about?'

'There's a quilt in there, Alan. There's a bottle of lemonade, a packet of biscuits . . .'

'I've never slept in the shed. It must be a tramp.'

'So, what are you up to now? Hiding in the bushes, spying on me . . .'

'Tom and Mary have asked me to give them a hand. They were out and I was waiting for them in their garden when I heard noises. I looked through the bushes and saw you . . .'

'You love making up stories, don't you?'

'I don't care whether you believe me or not. You should never have thrown me out, Helen. We could have worked things out and we'd have been all right.'

'Firstly, I didn't throw you out. Secondly, we could never have worked things out.' I rose to my feet and stood before him. 'You walked out on me. You played your juvenile games and walked out on me. You thought that I'd beg you to come back to me, as I've always done in the past. But I didn't, did I? You lost the game, Alan. You played your pathetic game once too often, and lost. You can't live in my shed.'

'I'm not living in the bloody shed,' he persisted. 'Don't you think that you should get dressed?'

'No, I don't. Where are you living, Alan?'

'I've been staying with friends. But I now have somewhere permanent to rent.'

'Where?'

'You'll find out where I'm living soon enough.'

'I don't know why, but I feel sorry for you. Why did you ruin our marriage?'

'I didn't ruin anything. All this was your doing, Helen.'

'It's always the same with you, isn't it? Nothing is ever your fault, you're never to blame. I have things to do.'

'OK, you win,' he breathed.

'I never wanted to play games. And I was never out to win. Do you not understand that?'

'I don't understand you, Helen,' he returned.

'You played the games, and I didn't win because there was nothing to win. But there was a hell of a lot to lose. And you lost it. Goodbye, Alan.'

As he slipped through the bushes into Tom and Mary's garden, I was sure that I'd not see him again. On the other hand, he might try to spy on me, watch me getting fucked in the lounge or the dining room. Returning to the house, I found Angela sitting in the lounge. She was still naked. Her inner thighs sticky with sperm, her face wet with male cream, she looked up and smiled at me.

'Who was that?' she asked me.

'My husband,' I replied. 'My husband of ten years. Hopefully, we won't be seeing him again.'

'And I don't think we'll be seeing Mary again,' she said mysteriously. 'Take a look out of the window.'

'A removal lorry,' I breathed, brushing the curtain to one side and watching two men loading furniture. 'God, they really are moving. You know what this means, don't you?'

'We're in business?'

'Yes, we're in business – for good.'

'I wonder who will rent the place now?' Angela said, joining me by the window.

'Rent what place?'

'Tom and Mary's house, they rented it.'

'Shit,' I breathed, noticing Alan talking to the removal men. 'I think I know who the next tenant is.'

'Your husband?'

'It certainly looks that way,' I sighed.

Keeping an eye on Alan, I knew that this wouldn't affect me. He was always hanging around and spying on me, so his moving in next door wasn't going to make a great deal of difference. Watching Mary as she joined Alan by the lorry, I wondered whether she'd realised that her photographs had been stolen. There was nothing she could do now, I mused. Her sex business was over, and mine was just beginning.

As Angela stood beside me and slipped her finger into my sperm-drenched anal crease, I let out a sigh of pleasure. Easing her finger deep into my rectal tube, she kissed my cheek and smiled at me. She was a beautiful girl, I thought for the umpteenth time that day. Yanking the net curtain back, I knew that Alan was watching us as I sucked her ripe nipple into my hot mouth. I could see him out of the corner of my eye. He was standing next to Mary, and they were both gazing at us. He'd lost the game, I mused dreamily as Angela slipped her finger out of my bottom-hole. He'd played his pathetic game once too often, and lost. Did he realise that I was in love? I pondered as he stared at me. Was I in love?

'Shall we go to bed?' Angela asked me.

Her nipple leaving my mouth, I gazed into her blue eyes. 'Yes,' I breathed. 'We'll go to bed, far away from the prying eyes of our new neighbour.'

nexus

The leading publisher of fetish and adult fiction

TELL US WHAT YOU THINK!

Readers' ideas and opinions matter to us so please take a few minutes to fill in the questionnaire below.

1. Sex: Are you male ☐ female ☐ a couple ☐?

2. Age: Under 21 ☐ 21–30 ☐ 31–40 ☐ 41–50 ☐ 51–60 ☐ over 60 ☐

3. Where do you buy your Nexus books from?
☐ A chain book shop. If so, which one(s)?

_____

☐ An independent book shop. If so, which one(s)?

_____

☐ A used book shop/charity shop
☐ Online book store. If so, which one(s)?

_____

4. How did you find out about Nexus books?
☐ Browsing in a book shop
☐ A review in a magazine
☐ Online
☐ Recommendation
☐ Other _____

5. In terms of settings, which do you prefer? (Tick as many as you like.)
☐ Down to earth and as realistic as possible
☐ Historical settings. If so, which period do you prefer?

_____

☐ Fantasy settings – barbarian worlds
☐ Completely escapist/surreal fantasy

- ☐ Institutional or secret academy
- ☐ Futuristic/sci fi
- ☐ Escapist but still believable
- ☐ Any settings you dislike?

_____

- ☐ Where would you like to see an adult novel set?

_____

6. In terms of storylines, would you prefer:

- ☐ Simple stories that concentrate on adult interests?
- ☐ More plot and character-driven stories with less explicit adult activity?
- ☐ We value your ideas, so give us your opinion of this book:

_____

_____

_____

7. In terms of your adult interests, what do you like to read about? (Tick as many as you like.)

- ☐ Traditional corporal punishment (CP)
- ☐ Modern corporal punishment
- ☐ Spanking
- ☐ Restraint/bondage
- ☐ Rope bondage
- ☐ Latex/rubber
- ☐ Leather
- ☐ Female domination and male submission
- ☐ Female domination and female submission
- ☐ Male domination and female submission
- ☐ Willing captivity
- ☐ Uniforms
- ☐ Lingerie/underwear/hosiery/footwear (boots and high heels)
- ☐ Sex rituals
- ☐ Vanilla sex
- ☐ Swinging
- ☐ Cross-dressing/TV

☐ Enforced feminisation

☐ Others – tell us what you don't see enough of in adult fiction:

_____

_____

_____

8. Would you prefer books with a more specialised approach to your interests, i.e. a novel specifically about uniforms? If so, which subject(s) would you like to read a Nexus novel about?

_____

_____

_____

9. Would you like to read true stories in Nexus books? For instance, the true story of a submissive woman, or a male slave? Tell us which true revelations you would most like to read about:

_____

_____

_____

10. What do you like best about Nexus books?

_____

_____

11. What do you like least about Nexus books?

_____

_____

12. Which are your favourite titles?

_____

_____

13. Who are your favourite authors?

_____

_____

14. **Which covers do you prefer? Those featuring:**
    (Tick as many as you like.)

☐ Fetish outfits
☐ More nudity
☐ Two models
☐ Unusual models or settings
☐ Classic erotic photography
☐ More contemporary images and poses
☐ A blank/non-erotic cover
☐ What would your ideal cover look like?

_____

15. **Describe your ideal Nexus novel in the space provided:**

_____
_____
_____
_____

16. **Which celebrity would feature in one of your Nexus-style fantasies?**
    We'll post the best suggestions on our website – anonymously!

_____

THANKS FOR YOUR TIME

Now simply write the title of this book in the space below and cut out the
questionnaire pages. Post to: Nexus, Marketing Dept., Thames Wharf Studios,
Rainville Rd, London W6 9HA

Book title: _____

NEXUS NEW BOOKS

To be published in March 2007

BEASTLY BEHAVIOUR
Aishling Morgan

Genevieve Stukely is working as an erotic dancer in the American west when she learns that her uncle is dead and that she is to inherit the family estate on the borders of Dartmoor. Only when she returns to the mother country does she discover that Sir Robert Stukely did not die simply of old age, but was found with an expression of utmost terror frozen on his features. Nearby were the footprints of a gigantic hound.

Now Mistress of Stukely Manor and known to have a colourful past, Genevieve quickly finds herself the centre of attention for half the rakes and ne'erdowells in Devon.

Beastly Behaviour follows the Truscott saga into its fifth generation with a tale of bizarre lust and Gothic horror drawn from several historical and literary sources to make it one of the most elaborate erotic novels ever published, to say nothing of being also irredeemably erotic.

£6.99   ISBN 978 0 352 34095 5

CITY MAID
Amelia Evangeline

City Maid recounts the erotic adventures of an innocent young woman in Victorian London. When Eleanor enters service in the Hampton household she has no idea that beneath the façade of respectability the house is a secret world of lust and depravity. Her mistress, Lady Hamilton, soon teaches Eleanor her position in the sternest and most shocking manner. Immediately, Eleanor realises to her horror that once you've felt the thrill of submission, life will never be the same again.

£6.99   ISBN 978 0 352 34096 2

RUBBER GIRL
William Doughty

The *Nexus Enthusiast* series brings us a definitive work of fiction about the hugely popular world of rubber fetishism. In *Rubber Girl,* Jill has an overwhelming fetish for rubber – the sight of it, the scent of it, the feeling of its texture around her skin, its aerodynamic and aesthetic qualities as a sensual fabric and second skin for her voluptuous body, as well as its flexible properties for restraint and bondage. And her neighbour Matt is drawn into her shiny latex orbit when she combines her love of rubber with his weakness for female domination. Kinky Sue, who has a crush on Jill, is the next to join in the perverse and rubbery games in an isolated country house in Dorset, equipped with stables. Together, they reach the very heights of rubber fetishism.

£6.99   ISBN 978 0 352 34087 0

If you would like more information about Nexus titles, please visit our website at www.nexus-books.co.uk, or send a large stamped addressed envelope to:
  Nexus, Thames Wharf Studios,
  Rainville Road, London W6 9HA

NEXUS BOOKLIST

Information is correct at time of printing. To avoid disappointment, check availability before ordering. Go to www.nexus-books.co.uk.

All books are priced at £6.99 unless another price is given.

NEXUS

☐ ABANDONED ALICE	Adriana Arden	ISBN 978 0 352 33969 0
☐ ALICE IN CHAINS	Adriana Arden	ISBN 978 0 352 33908 9
☐ AQUA DOMINATION	William Doughty	ISBN 978 0 352 34020 7
☐ THE ART OF CORRECTION	Tara Black	ISBN 978 0 352 33895 2
☐ THE ART OF SURRENDER	Madeline Bastinado	ISBN 978 0 352 34013 9
☐ BELINDA BARES UP	Yolanda Celbridge	ISBN 978 0 352 33926 3
☐ BENCH-MARKS	Tara Black	ISBN 978 0 352 33797 9
☐ BIDDING TO SIN	Rosita Varón	ISBN 978 0 352 34063 4
☐ BINDING PROMISES	G.C. Scott	ISBN 978 0 352 34014 6
☐ THE BOOK OF PUNISHMENT	Cat Scarlett	ISBN 978 0 352 33975 1
☐ BRUSH STROKES	Penny Birch	ISBN 978 0 352 34072 6
☐ CALLED TO THE WILD	Angel Blake	ISBN 978 0 352 34067 2
☐ CAPTIVES OF CHEYNER CLOSE	Adriana Arden	ISBN 978 0 352 34028 3
☐ CARNAL POSSESSION	Yvonne Strickland	ISBN 978 0 352 34062 7
☐ COLLEGE GIRLS	Cat Scarlett	ISBN 978 0 352 33942 3
☐ COMPANY OF SLAVES	Christina Shelly	ISBN 978 0 352 33887 7
☐ CONCEIT AND CONSEQUENCE	Aishling Morgan	ISBN 978 0 352 33965 2
☐ CORRECTIVE THERAPY	Jacqueline Masterson	ISBN 978 0 352 33917 1
☐ CORRUPTION	Virginia Crowley	ISBN 978 0 352 34073 3

☐ TORMENT INCORPORATED	Murilee Martin	ISBN 978 0 352 33943 0
☐ UNEARTHLY DESIRES	Ray Gordon	ISBN 978 0 352 34036 8
☐ UNIFORM DOLL	Penny Birch	ISBN 978 0 352 33698 9
☐ VELVET SKIN	Aishling Morgan	ISBN 978 0 352 33660 6 £5.99
☐ WENCHES, WITCHES AND STRUMPETS	Aishling Morgan	ISBN 978 0 352 33733 7
☐ WHALEBONE STRICT	Lady Alice McCloud	ISBN 978 0 352 34082 5
☐ WHAT HAPPENS TO BAD GIRLS	Penny Birch	ISBN 978 0 352 34031 3
☐ WHAT SUKI WANTS	Cat Scarlett	ISBN 978 0 352 34027 6
☐ WHEN SHE WAS BAD	Penny Birch	ISBN 978 0 352 33859 4
☐ WHIP HAND	G.C. Scott	ISBN 978 0 352 33694 1
☐ WHIPPING GIRL	Aishling Morgan	ISBN 978 0 352 33789 4
☐ WHIPPING TRIANGLE	G.C. Scott	ISBN 978 0 352 34086 3

NEXUS CLASSIC

☐ AMAZON SLAVE	Lisette Ashton	ISBN 978 0 352 33916 4
☐ ANGEL	Lindsay Gordon	ISBN 978 0 352 34009 2
☐ THE BLACK GARTER	Lisette Ashton	ISBN 978 0 352 33919 5
☐ THE BLACK MASQUE	Lisette Ashton	ISBN 978 0 352 33977 5
☐ THE BLACK ROOM	Lisette Ashton	ISBN 978 0 352 33914 0
☐ THE BLACK WIDOW	Lisette Ashton	ISBN 978 0 352 33973 7
☐ THE BOND	Lindsay Gordon	ISBN 978 0 352 33996 6
☐ DISCIPLINE OF THE PRIVATE HOUSE	Esme Ombreux	ISBN 978 0 352 33709 2
☐ THE DOMINO ENIGMA	Cyrian Amberlake	ISBN 978 0 352 34064 1
☐ THE DOMINO QUEEN	Cyrian Amberlake	ISBN 978 0 352 34074 0
☐ THE DOMINO TATTOO	Cyrian Amberlake	ISBN 978 0 352 34037 5
☐ EMMA ENSLAVED	Hilary James	ISBN 978 0 352 33883 9
☐ EMMA'S HUMILIATION	Hilary James	ISBN 978 0 352 33910 2
☐ EMMA'S SECRET DOMINATION	Hilary James	ISBN 978 0 352 34000 9
☐ EMMA'S SUBMISSION	Hilary James	ISBN 978 0 352 33906 5

---------- ✂ ------------------------------

Please send me the books I have ticked above.

Name ....

Address ....

....

....

.... Post code ....

Send to: Virgin Books Cash Sales, Thames Wharf Studios, Rainville Road, London W6 9HA

US customers: for prices and details of how to order books for delivery by mail, call 888-330-8477.

Please enclose a cheque or postal order, made payable to **Nexus Books Ltd**, to the value of the books you have ordered plus postage and packing costs as follows:

UK and BFPO – £1.00 for the first book, 50p for each subsequent book.

Overseas (including Republic of Ireland) – £2.00 for the first book, £1.00 for each subsequent book.

If you would prefer to pay by VISA, ACCESS/MASTERCARD, AMEX, DINERS CLUB or SWITCH, please write your card number and expiry date here:

....

Please allow up to 28 days for delivery.

Signature ....

Our privacy policy

We will not disclose information you supply us to any other parties. We will not disclose any information which identifies you personally to any person without your express consent.

From time to time we may send out information about Nexus books and special offers. Please tick here if you do *not* wish to receive Nexus information. ☐

---------- ✂ ------------------------------